BRODY

USA TODAY BESTSELLING AUTHOR

MANDY HARBIN

Just as the heroine in this story discovers—life never works out like we plan. Sometimes, this is a good thing, although it probably doesn't feel like it at the time. I want to express my gratitude to my closest friends for giving me strength and being there for me when I went through a major change in my life. Your support, compassion, and love will forever be cherished.

PROLOGUE

Alexandria Collins paced with her cell phone clutched tightly in her manicured hand. Why hadn't Cole called? She was supposed to be at the rendezvous point fifteen minutes ago to get Devon from his nanny. Her four-year-old son was too young to understand what was happening, but Alexandria was doing this for him as much as she was doing it for herself.

And what she was doing was making a run for it. She had no other choice. She'd married Marco after he knocked her up at sixteen when she'd been too young and too stupid to see past his flashy car and charming smile. She hadn't realized her mistake at first. After all, he'd showered her with expensive gifts, and considering she'd spent her youth being shuffled from one foster care home to the next, being pampered was nice. Hell, it'd rocked. When she'd found out she was pregnant, he'd been thrilled and insisted on getting married.

And he'd been the perfect husband.

Until she'd given birth to a girl.

If only he just spewed nonsense about needing a male

heir to carry on the family business rather than beat her nightly until they'd conceived again. If only the family business he prided himself on was a legitimate one she'd be proud of her son taking over one day. If only her daughter hadn't died of SIDS after her son was born.

If only, if only, if only.

For the past three years, she'd kept her eyes open for a way to get out of here, and three months ago, she'd found her ticket to freedom in the form of a flash drive containing account numbers and data on shell corporations Marco used to launder money. Being a ward of the state until she'd married Marco, Alexandria had no family to turn to for help, so she'd done the only thing she could think of, the only thing any other law-abiding citizen would do.

She went to the feds.

After spilling everything she knew, which didn't feel like much to her, she was too important to be assigned one FBI agent to work her case. Oh no, Marco Collins was apparently second-in-command to her father-in-law's crime family, so she'd been assigned a whole team of suits. They'd told her about the crimes her husband and his family were suspected of, and it went much deeper than the domestic abuse she'd endured. They were a part of a true crime family. One she'd obliviously married into and couldn't get out of with an easy dissolution of marriage through the courts.

Her phone buzzed, startling her. She checked the screen and breathed a sigh of relief when she saw it was one of the contact numbers the FBI had given to her.

"Hello?" she whispered as she sat on the imported Italian leather sofa in Marco's study.

"Mrs. Collins, this is Agent Dave Simmons. You have to get out now. You've been compromised. We have a team en route, but our informant notified us that we won't reach you in time."

"Where's Cole?" She was supposed to await Cole's contact with her instructions, but he'd ensured her he'd be in touch at least thirty minutes ago.

Not waiting on an answer, Alexandria jumped off the couch and grabbed her purse. If the feds said she had to leave now, they didn't have to tell her twice. Cole was just one member of a slew of agents she worked with, so if they changed the game plan, there must be a good reason. She was already late picking up her son anyway. She trusted Devon's nanny so much so that she'd told her to flee with him if Alexandria didn't show. If anything happened to her, she wanted to make sure Devon still got away. If she could get to them in time, it'd save her the trouble of hunting them down afterward.

"Cole's been shot. Meet up with Ms. Chambers to get your son. There's an agent with them now, so they're safe—"

An explosion rocked her, hurtling her across the floor, her phone sliding in the opposite direction, the agent's frantic voice drifting as the phone slid out of reach. She crawled in her custom silk outfit, getting behind the couch, frantically looking for her purse, which housed her gun. She needed the protection, since it looked as if the feds wouldn't be coming in to save her after all. She spotted her purse handle dangling off the other side of the couch. Easing her way in that direction, she stayed hidden behind the safety of the leather furniture. Before she could reach it, gunfire erupted as the door to the study crashed open, bouncing off the wall.

"I'm going to kill you, you fucking bitch!"

Marco. Alexandria trembled. She was screwed. There was no way she could get out of here now. That door was the only way in, and even though there were windows, they were on the second floor, a second floor of a big two-story mansion with high ceilings. She could play dumb and hope he believed she was innocent of whatever he suspected, maybe get a severe beating out of her insolence. Or she could continue to hide.

Yeah, she liked that idea better. No need to just give up.

"I know you're in here, Dria. If you show your face now, I'll make it quick."

Marco stormed around the room, pushing antique bureaus and marble-top tables like stick furniture. Alexandria crawled around the couch as he neared. She had to stay away. If she averted him long enough, maybe he'd leave the room and she'd be able to sneak out.

"You think you can avoid me? I think you want to die slow. Right after I fuck you with the barrel of this gun for old times' sake."

Alexandria suppressed a sob. Marco was using the memories of his abuse to draw her out. She might've been an idiot to marry him, but she wasn't one now. She would not let him bait her. She glanced around the room, what little she could see of it, for a weapon. Anything would work. The jackass loved art and had all kinds of marble statues. The key would be getting a hold of something without him noticing. She just had to wait for the right moment.

Whenever that was.

He started to walk away, so she maneuvered over to the lowest shelf to grab the miniature *Venus de Milo*. As she snatched it, thin, cold fingers wrapped around her wrist and yanked her from behind the couch.

"Dria, there you are, *tesoro*," Marco sneered.

"Let go!"

Alexandria instinctively pushed at his chest, but he

didn't move. She tried kicking him, but he deflected her knees. Remembering she still held the weapon, she swung at his head. He ducked, but she managed to clip the side before he got completely away from the blow.

"You crazy bitch!"

She recklessly swung her hands, kicked her feet, tried to get away, but as he fell, he brought her down with him. They scrambled on the floor and he gained the advantage, grabbing her hair in an angry fist and banging her head against the hand-scraped floor.

"I love all this long, beautiful hair, *cara*." He smashed her head into the floor again. "Too bad your beautiful locks of gold are a treasure to me no more." He hit her again and she saw stars.

Grunting, she struggled to free his hands from her hair. "I n-never was your treasure. You used me."

"And you turned me in. For shame, *tesoro*. Too bad your little plan backfired. I have friends in all the right places. That so-called evidence you turned over is gone. They have nothing, and you'll never leave this house alive."

He raised the gun and she pushed, shoved, kicked...all to no avail, but she wasn't giving up. She must've landed a blow in a good spot because he yelled and hit her in the head with the gun. Blinking back tears leaking from her eyes and blood flowing into them, she could barely see Marco, but she heard footsteps just outside the door. It sounded like a herd of elephants, which was music to her ears. Marco reared back, looking toward the door as he hovered over her.

"You?" he yelled incredulously. "I thought I'd killed you already."

Did that mean all that noise was just one person? What was all that gunfire earlier? Surely there were more people here to help her. But she'd take what she could get. One was better than none.

Marco pointed his gun away from her and more gunfire sounded. Marco wailed in agony as fresh blood splattered on her face. Marco was hit. But the sound of something crashing to the floor, her savior, dashed any hope of survival. Marco was wounded, the other man severely, if not mortally.

Panting, Marco looked at her with his evil brown eyes filled with victorious resolve, turning the gun on her. Her world tilted as hopelessness filled her. The sound of a single bullet and the instantaneous feel of burning pain in her right temple were the last things Alexandria Collins felt before darkness surrounded her.

CHAPTER ONE

TWELVE YEARS LATER

"Mom, you just passed our exit."

Xan Bradley braked in reflex as if she'd be able to do a U-ey right here on the interstate in her beat-up hatchback. Where was her head? Oh, right. She was moving to a new town with her son yet again. Her brain was focused on other things, like always staying one step ahead of the mafia they'd fled when Scott was a baby. Of course he wasn't Scott then, and she didn't go by Xan.

They'd moved every two years like clockwork, not that it was actually planned that way originally. After Agent Dave Simmons had set up Xan and Scott in a little Arkansas town north of Podunk and south of Nowhereville, he'd apparently retired a couple of years later. Her new agent, Jack Parsons, immediately moved them for security measures, and had done so every other year since.

The moves she could do. Hated it, but could do. She didn't have control over her life now and hadn't in over a decade. Her one demand when entering the Witness Protection Program, however, was that Scott's name wouldn't be changed once his new identity was established.

It was hard enough to get a four-year-old to understand why his daddy wasn't coming around anymore, much less why he had to have a new name. To get his cooperation, she'd given him the opportunity to pick out his very own name.

She should've thought about that before opening her big mouth.

Letting a preschooler decide his own name was like, well, letting a preschooler decide his own name. For two weeks, he was SpongeBob. Xan had tried to find ways of backpedaling out of that horrid deal, but her son was sharp even then. After ordering some official SpongeBob stuff online and writing a letter, posing as the most famous sponge on TV, informing her son he was honored that Scott wanted to be named after him and asking if he could pick out his new name instead, she'd finally succeeded in undoing that mess. "SpongeBob" wanted to pick out a name for him with the same initials, and so Scott Bradley was born.

Why would she want to go through the nightmare of changing his name again? Bathing cats with claws sounded better.

Though Xan was encouraged to change her name repeatedly, the fact that she'd went to nursing school after getting free from her deranged ex-husband caused her to put up a fight every time they were forced to move. Sure, the feds could get her new diplomas and licenses in whatever name she wanted. Even "SpongeBob", Jack had told her several years before, thinking she'd seriously find that shit funny. But she'd worked hard at putting herself through school, and fake certificates and degrees were just that—fake. Her compromise was she'd go by a different version of her first name. Marco called her Dria, so she'd never willingly choose that one. But she'd gone by Lexa, Xandie,

Alexa, Lexie and Andria over the years, and now Xan would do. To help appease the FBI gods, she also changed up her hair to help cover her identity, but getting to keep some derivative of her first name helped her keep a little bit of her soul.

The very soul Marco had tried to take from her. She might've married him with her blinders on, but she'd wised up and gotten out of there...with barely her life. Marco had shot her at pointblank range. The caliber of his handgun should've killed her instantly. It was nothing short of a miracle, and she'd been grateful—as soon as she'd gotten out of her coma and realized she was actually still alive. By the time she'd awoken, her divorce was already underway courtesy of prearranged paperwork with the attorney the feds had secured before the attempted raid and subsequent fuckup. Since the evidence against Marco had mysteriously disappeared, the only thing they had on him was an attempted murder charge. She and Scott had stayed on lockdown until Marco's trial and sentencing since she was the victim and star witness. She shivered at that thought—she'd never forget seeing his evil eyes in court that day. It was that same look he'd had when he shot her.

She hoped she'd never have to see his face again, but she knew she and her son were living on borrowed time. Marco was sentenced to twenty years with a mandatory ten served.

And by her calculations, he should be up for parole at any time.

"Take the next exit a few miles up. Looks like there's a highway that backtracks to Mayflower."

Xan nodded as she shook off her thoughts. She didn't like walking down memory lane, much less taking up a permanent residence there, which she felt she'd been doing lately. She knew it was because of Marco's potential release, but she couldn't let that get to her. She had a life and a sixteen-year-old boy to finish raising.

Okay, so that was only partly true. She didn't have a life —not a social one anyway. She couldn't afford to trust a man enough to get close to one. Oh, she'd love nothing more than to have sex with a penis made of skin rather than rubber, but that just wasn't a risk she was willing to take. She hadn't had real sex in over twelve years. Surely there was some statute of limitations somewhere that'd make her an honorary virgin again, not that she'd be able to convince anyone she was virtuous with a practically grown son. Or one who fancied himself grown.

Xan gasped. "Is this the exit you're talking about?"

"Yeah, chill. Seriously, Mom, you should've let me drive."

"Not on your life, buddy."

Tires didn't screech, really, as they dang near skidded off the road to make their exit. "Where do I go now?"

"You need GPS, Mom. Take Harkrider to 365."

"In this beat-up piece o' crap?" she asked, chuckling as she followed Scott's directions.

They were only about seven miles from Mayflower, another Arkansas town. She hadn't been back in this state since right after going into hiding. It took her almost the entire two years to get used to southern life when she and Scott were yanked out and placed out west. She was a northerner at heart who liked the laid-back atmosphere down here, but she refused to say things like y'all and fixin'. She had her pride.

A loud pop jolted Xan out of her reverie. The sudden profuse smoke barreling out of the hood of her hatchback threw her into a panic. She gasped a curse, struggling to steer the car onto the shoulder, which was difficult since the power steering decided to evaporate into nothingness as soon as the car died.

"Mom, watch out!"

Yeah, Xan saw it. A pothole. "I'm trying," she gritted.

The car hit the gnarly imperfection as her not-always-trusty hatchback came to a stop. At least they were completely off the highway. She slumped against her seat, feeling her heart race. It seemed to be pounding even harder now that they were stopped. She so didn't need this. Agent Parsons decided on this move right at the end of summer. Scott's school and her new job started in two days, so she only had the weekend to get settled. Granted, they lived light, never knowing when they'd have to move on a moment's notice, but two days wasn't long enough even for the minimalist of packers. And now their one means of transportation was toast. Ugh! She was sick of running.

She grabbed her cellphone, but she didn't have a signal out here in the middle of nowhere. Surprise, surprise. She got out of the car and covered her eyes to block the blazing sun as she looked down the road. "That sign says it's one mile to town." She sighed, shaking her head. "C'mon."

He got out of the car, walking over to her. "Do you want me to carry some of our bags?"

"Nope, lock it. We'll come back later to get everything."

As they started down the road, Xan sighed. This wasn't a good way to start their new life in this town. Nope, not good at all.

———

"OH THANK GOD. There's an auto shop," Scott groaned as they rounded the corner after walking about two miles. They'd entered town about a mile ago, as the sign had indicated, but had only encountered a ranch and a farm as of yet.

"Really? Why are you complaining? You're young and in shape." She, on the other hand, was a melting, miserable old mess.

"It's a million degrees out here, Mom."

Try a million and one. Yeah, it was hot as hell. "Quit your bellyaching."

They walked up to an opened fence and Xan silently thanked the heavens for small favors. The garage looked as if it was open. They walked through the gate and into the old building with several antique and late-model cars out front. Walking through the front door, she braced herself for the blast of cold air to hit her face, relishing the thrill of the artificial air she was about to gloriously encounter.

She was sorely disappointed. It was hotter in here than it was outside. How was that even possible? Her wet clothes clung to her sweaty body, leaving nothing to the imagination. Didn't matter. She was past humility at this point. She'd have a teenage moment and flash her boobs, sweat and all if necessary, to get someone to help them out.

"May I help you?" a man with a gravelly voice asked as he walked into the makeshift lobby next to the bays, wiping his hands on a grease rag. He looked to be middle-aged, though she wasn't sure since he was bald. No gray hair to help her out with that assessment.

She looked at his nametag sewn into his shirt. "Yes, Colonel, is it?" At his smile and nod, she said, "Our car broke down a couple miles down the road."

A metal crash and very masculine curses mixed with raucous taunting and laughter startled her. Scott snickered at the colorful words coming from the bays. He'd heard them plenty of times, though Xan tried not to talk like that.

Really, she did try to deny her sailor-mouth tendencies. She just wasn't very good at restraining herself all the time.

"Sorry," Colonel mumbled. "Those are my mechanics, trying to catch up on some work. I took over this garage after I realized being retired was boring, and we stay pretty busy. Seems like I'm constantly hiring more help, but we stay behind."

The ruckus from the bays was finding its way into the lobby. Several guys walked into the room, and Xan felt a slight panic attack coming on. She not only lacked a love life, but she tended to avoid large groups of men. She didn't have anything against the male population, but after marrying into the mafia at a young age, dodging copious amounts of testosterone seemed like a good self-preservation tactic to live by. So she did, and when she wasn't prepared to interact with schools of men, her stomach took a nosedive when thrust into that very situation.

Taking a covert calming breath so she wouldn't look like some skittish girl, she tried to pay closer attention to each of the men as they came near. If she identified them individually, she could pretend she wasn't dealing with a mob.

A mob of seemingly beautiful, large, masculine men, looking to be around her age.

Oh shit. She so did not need this. Her nerves and sense of self-preservation took on a whole new meaning. She'd rather deal with certain fear than possible attraction.

As she surveyed the crowd, she noticed their looks were as various as the candy selection at the last gas station she'd stopped at. Male sweetness was *not* better than chocolate. She just had to remind herself of that as she stared at the variety before her. One guy had black hair, another blond, spiked all crazy. The two next to the hot version of Billy Idol had long dark-brown hair and curly light-brown hair.

There was another bald guy bringing up the rear, but that one had a goatee with green eyes. Colonel had brown eyes and was definitely older than this group that'd just come in.

"Where's Brutus?" Colonel asked the guys.

The dude with the spiky blond hair chuckled. "He's cleaning up his mess."

"It wasn't his mess, asshole. You're the one who knocked the tray over," Mr. Black Hair said with a snarl. Xan instinctively took a step back.

"Easy, Roc," Colonel said, and looked at her. "This is Roc." He pointed to the cranky man with black hair. "Blade." He gestured toward the spiky blond guy. His name made sense. His hair looked sharp enough to hurt if he were to head-butt someone.

"I'm Hunter," the man with long brown hair said, and then he pointed to the guy with curly brown hair. "That's Gauge. He's not as mean as Roc, but don't get too close to him." He chuckled.

"Fuck off, Hunter," Gauge growled.

"See?" Hunter snickered. "And that guy over there—"

"I'm Bear, and Hunter's a dick." He ducked his head and glanced at Scott. "Oh sorry. He's, er, I mean he's a punk."

Scott laughed. "Don't worry. I've heard it all. You should hear my mom talk. She has the biggest potty mouth."

Xan gasped. "I do not."

"Wow, he's your kid?" Blade asked. "Did you have him at twelve?" He laughed, but with sincerity twinkling in his eyes.

"Just about," she murmured.

After a few of the guys laughed, she immediately relaxed. Sure, they were all very handsome. None looked to be shorter than six feet, and each had a body to die for, though each had a unique look all his own. But she didn't feel any sparks, so she felt relieved. Maybe her libido was broken. If so, she was fine by that. She didn't need any man drama in her life.

Why did that make her feel a little depressed? She shook off that thought. She couldn't get caught up with any man, so there really was no need dwelling on the things she couldn't have, like love, companionship, trust, and sex. God, she'd love to have sex again.

Maybe in another life.

Focusing her attention back on the problem at hand, she looked at the assembled group of men. "Look. We need our car towed and a ride to a car rental company. Can you help us?" Xan asked the guys in general so as not to single anyone out.

Blade's eyebrows shot up. "I'd love to give you a ride, doll." Even though his tone was clearly teasing, she stiffened. Flirting was definitely not her forte.

Hunter whistled while shaking his head in exasperation. "Back off, Blade." He looked at Xan. "Sorry about Rico Suave over here. One of us would be glad to help you out. But you'd have to drive up to Conway or back to the Little Rock area for a rental. Best to call around first before making the drive."

"I'll call Bill and see if he can drive one out here," Colonel said to Hunter, then looked at her. "He owns the rental company in Conway. If they have something, he'll bring it out here and save you a trip. You'll be limited on your options, though."

"Oh, whatever it is will be a step up from my old hatchback. I'm not choosy."

Colonel nodded and looked at the guys expectantly. "Which one of you is available to help her out?"

"Bear and I aren't finished with the tranny that's supposed to be ready tomorrow," Roc barked, and turned to leave. He obviously wasn't volunteering. Xan was okay with that. She didn't like the vibe coming off him anyway.

"Sorry." Bear smiled to her as he followed Roc.

"Gauge and I have to finish puttin' tires on Ms. Rogers' minivan, then do Joe's," Blade told Colonel before turning to Xan. "I'd be *happy* to help you if you stick around, doll. It shouldn't take us more than an hour."

"Get to work," Colonel snapped, and Blade winked at her as he and Gauge headed back to the bays.

"I have one more oil change to do, so I can do it in fifteen," Hunter said with a crooked smile, "but Brutus just finished up on Mr. Jackson's '56 Chevy. He's been pickin' up the tools that Blade knocked over after Blade called him a pussy."

Oh, right. She'd forgotten there was another one around here. *Brutus* it seemed. What was with these names? Must be a man thing, not that she'd know. Or could even begin to understand the inner workings of the male brain, ego, or whatever it was that fueled their behavior. Oh, once upon a time, she knew one part of the male anatomy that tended to lead in the decision-making process, but she'd long ago fell out of practice with that too.

Hunter glanced at Scott, remembering there was an impressionable young man in his midst, looking contrite and shaking his head. "Sorry, man."

"Go," Colonel told him. "Brutus!"

Hunter left, but his departure barely registered. Just as he was walking toward the bay area, a man with long blonde hair and built like a freaking bodybuilder walked her way. With each step, his muscles rippled and his hair—what wasn't sticking to his sweaty brow—flowed in waves behind him.

She should not find this man attractive. She didn't care for bulky men, and she definitely preferred short hair on the opposite sex. Long hair belonged on women, like she used to have, but she wasn't dredging that memory up now.

So why was her body doing things she hardly recognized. *Hardly recognized,* not *didn't recognize.* She knew what that tingling sensation in her body meant. She shouldn't find him attractive because he didn't fit any description of her ideal type. But there was no mistaking the fact that her body didn't get that memo.

So much for not being attracted to any of the mechanics here.

As Mister Hold-Me-Down-and-Fuck-Me-Good walked up, his pupils dilated, turning his dark-blue eyes black as his nostrils flared, his gaze zeroing in on her.

She shut her eyes to break the connection her body was trying to make with this man. She had to be smart and remember all the reasons men were not a part of her life. She wasn't going to break her abstinence streak for anyone, especially not a man who could quite possibly fight off every one of the other mechanics singlehandedly. She didn't know him from Adam, and the last—the only—relationship she'd ever had was abusive. Hell, Marco tried to kill her in the end. She had to find the strength to avoid any and all temptation this sex god presented.

And she would. She was just strong enough to resist a man built like he could break her face.

Because, if she didn't, she knew she was just weak enough to let him break her heart.

CHAPTER TWO

BRODY STARED AT THE SLENDER, dirty lady covered in sweat and eyeballing him with a mixture of weariness and arousal, and maybe even a little fear, and he couldn't shake the dual sensations rocking him at the sight of her.

This first one was primal, carnal. He wanted her like he'd never wanted another woman before. Oh, he'd had his share of women, so he wasn't delusional enough to think this was love at first sight or some stupid shit like that. It had to be because of his recent dry spell in the lady department. Even covered in a little grime, she was a babe. Her hair was a tangled mess with tendrils clinging to her neck, her blue eyes, lighter than his, shuttered. She had secrets she didn't want to reveal, which was fine by him. He didn't need to know about them anyway.

He had no problem fucking a woman without getting mixed up in her personal business, but the tall kid standing next to her screamed hands-off. Brody was a selfish bastard, but even he had his morals. Well, maybe not morals, but he had his limits. He didn't do married women or single moms, and she was obviously at least one of the two. There were plenty of willing, unattached women available, ripe for his choosing, so getting mixed up with some lady carting baggage was not in the cards for him.

But that wasn't the only reason he couldn't indulge with this woman. The other sensation rocking him, besides the immediate carnal attraction, was the feeling he knew her from somewhere. It was more than a feeling. He was sure of it. The flash of memory he had was of a younger, more polished version of this woman and was too quick to analyze, but it was definitely her.

And considering he'd suffered a brain injury, causing him to only remember the last decade or so of his life, he couldn't place how he knew her. There was no way he was getting involved with a woman he may or may not already know intimately. And if the reason he knew her wasn't along those lines, then he didn't want to know the extent of their previous association. Brody had lived a reckless, dark life before his accident. He didn't want any ghosts coming back to haunt him, no matter how beautiful the ghost incarnate was.

Colonel was the only one who had much luck finding any specifics about his life prior to his amnesia. He'd been the one to find Brody in the northern part of the state on the side of the road, sans car and any identification, and called an ambulance. Brody remembered coming to in the hospital, but had no recollection of any memory prior. He'd contacted the authorities to see if he could be identified through fingerprint matches. Hell, he knew the risk he was taking going that route. If he'd had a record, he could've had a warrant out for his arrest or something, but not knowing was killing him.

It'd been a dead end. And knowing what he now knew

about his past life, that in and of itself was a miracle. He must've been really good at being bad to avoid any arrests.

"Brutus, I need you to take the wrecker out to get Ms. Bradley's car."

Brody's eyes cut to Colonel. With a short nod, he turned his attention back to the lady. "You ready, Ms. Bradley?"

Her eyes widened slightly as she nodded, clutching her purse as if it was some kind of lifeline. He motioned for them to follow him out to the wrecker, then headed that way.

"Dude, you've got serious muscles," the kid said as he opened the door for his mom while Brody grunted in response and walked around to the driver's side. He probably should've opened her door for her instead. It would've been the polite thing to do, but chivalry wasn't really his thing. He didn't try to be an asshole. He was just a loner, kept to himself for many reasons, including his shady past and the unorthodox demands of his side job. Unless he needed to spend a little time between a woman's legs, and he never really had to go out of his way to impress a woman just to fuck her. Chicks seemed to flock to him, and he was A-okay with that. Still, irritation prickled that he should've opened her door for her. At least the kid was on the ball.

They packed into the bench seat, the mom sitting in the middle. Good thing he had jeans on because her delicate bare leg rested against his. Not that it mattered. He could feel the heat of her skin burning into his thigh. He figured she'd at least stink since she was sweating like a horse, but no, he couldn't be that lucky. She smelled like vanilla and woman. *Aroused* woman. His dick twitched and he shifted subtly. He really didn't need a hard-on with her kid in here.

She cleared her throat softly and he glanced at her. "Brutus, is it? I'm Xan and this is my son, Scott."

At the sound of her voice, that old vision of her flashed in his head. For some reason, he didn't remember her sounding like an angel. "Er, nice to meetcha. Brody's my name, but Brutus is my handle."

"Your handle?"

"Nickname. What I go by. We all have them." And the last thing he wanted to talk about was nicknames. In fact, he didn't want to talk at all. He just wanted to get their car and get back to the garage so he could get out of this tiny cab. It was getting smaller as his dick was getting harder. If he didn't find a distraction soon, he'd have a permanent zipper imprint on his cock.

"What are the other guy's real names?" she asked as she pointed to the green hatchback on the side of the road.

"Ask them. Not for me to tell." He pulled over and backed up to their car.

"Wow, it only took like a minute to get back out here after walking all the way to the garage," Scott said as he jumped out of the cab.

"You walked?" Why did that bother him? It was only a couple of miles. Hell, he ran five miles every day, and that was just the start of his exercise regimen.

"Uh-huh. That's why we look a mess." She chuckled as she scooted to the passenger door. He immediately regretted the loss of heat, which was fucking ridiculous since it was the hottest part of the day in the hottest part of the year.

Thinking it best not to encourage conversation, he got out and hooked up the car. Scott actually volunteered to help, and it surprised him that the boy wasn't just some lazy teenager. He figured that was good, at least, for her. Not that it mattered to him. But the kid still watched as if he was trying to learn something.

Xan stayed out of the way, which was a fucking blessing. Her short shorts were loose around her thighs, and at this angle, he'd be able to see clear up to her pussy. Well, if she wasn't wearing panties. If she was his woman, he'd have to forbid them 'cause they just got in the way. Why was he even thinking about that? She would never be his woman. She was totally off-limits.

He had to end his dry spell tonight. It was Friday, so the local bar would be packed. If he didn't want the headache of hooking up with local tail, he could always hit the city.

Yeah, that idea sounded better. It'd cure the erection he'd been tamping down the last fifteen minutes and help him focus the next time he had to see this woman.

Because living in a small town, it was bound to happen.

And being the only garage in this small town made that possibility a guarantee when the woman drove a car older than her kid.

"Got it. Let's go," he mumbled without looking at them as he climbed back into the truck.

The cab definitely shrank. He was panting from the effort it took to rig up the car, and the only air he was inhaling was filled with vanilla and the honey of female arousal. There was no stopping his dick now. He had a full-on raging erection, and her damn leg kept rubbing against his, making him even harder than he thought was possible. He had to get them the hell out of here.

He threw the truck in reverse, backed up, and barreled down the road, making it back in record time. He backed the car up to the empty bay and got out, unhooking it with single-minded determination. *Get it down, so she can get her shit.* That was all he thought as he worked methodically.

As soon as he freed the car, he hopped back into the wrecker and parked it across the lot and away from that woman, taking his time to lock it up. He noticed some of the other mechanics hovering around her, helping her move some luggage and other stuff into the rental that blessedly arrived while they were gone.

Blade and Hunter seemed a little too eager to help her, and he noticed they each brushed up against her more than once. He bit off a growl, which surprised him. So what if they found her attractive? She was a sexy woman. But Bear managed to help too, without molesting her in the process. Surely, Blade and Hunter could manage that too. Roc and Gauge kept working while Colonel talked to Bill. His son must've followed him out here because he sat in the car, waiting in the air-conditioning. Brody shook his head. Scott not only stood outside while Brody had hooked up the car, but also volunteered to help. Bill's boy was probably the same age, if not older, and a worthless piece of shit.

Whatever. It didn't matter to him. He grabbed his portable tool case and stalked up to the garage as Scott got in the rental car and Xan glanced over at him.

"Thanks for your help," she said as she opened the door, keeping her eyes on him, making him just a little uncomfortable in his chest and a lot uncomfortable in his pants.

He nodded once and turned away, focusing a little too much on putting his tools up. He couldn't talk to her. He didn't want to talk to her. That woman was off-limits. He didn't see a ring on her finger, but she had a kid. That was strike one.

And he knew her from somewhere. Strike two.

Those were reasons enough for him to avoid her like the plague. He didn't need a third.

Thankfully, he heard two cars pulling out, and when he turned, she was gone. He breathed a sigh of relief. It was fucking ridiculous that he'd be avoiding a woman as if he was scared of her, but he had no choice. He would avoid her. The attraction was strong enough that he could've possibly talked himself into dumping his no-baggage rule where her kid was concerned. But the fact he knew her was a deal-killer. She hadn't acted as if she knew him, so that was good, but he couldn't take the risk of her recognizing him before he could figure out why he knew her.

And he may never know.

Before he turned back to the tools, he saw Colonel watching him. Shit. He was caught staring after that woman. He didn't need his boss busting his balls.

Too late, he was headed this way.

"What do you think of our lovely new citizen?"

Brody shrugged as he wiped his hands.

"That much, huh?" Colonel chuckled, then sobered. "I have a job for you," he murmured.

A job. That only meant one thing, and it wouldn't involve vehicle repairs. He was referring to the side jobs he and the other mechanics did. The truth was, Colonel's handle was more than just a nickname for a supervisor. He was the leader of their secret mission group. They were mercenaries who took on vigilante-type jobs the feds either didn't want to do themselves or private citizens wanted done with no trace left behind. The government contracts they got were the less savory ones, and the law looked the other way on their private gigs because they didn't do anything they hadn't done for the government. The guys on his team were all just shady enough to do whatever was necessary to get them done and had no problem blurring that legal line...or erasing it completely.

The shop doubled as their headquarters, so they jokingly called themselves the Bang Shift. Besides the hotrod connection, it was also a nod to being the hired guns that they were. As far as Brody was concerned, it was the perfect arrangement for a man good with his hands who had no memory of his past, and no hope of a future.

"Whatcha need?" This job was the perfect distraction. It'd give him something to focus his attention on besides that maddening woman.

"Xan Bradley. That's your new assignment."

———

XAN SPENT Saturday morning unpacking their things and going through the stuff Agent Parsons had sent, making a list of what she still needed to get. The FBI always tried to do their best to make her comfortable when she and Scott had to move. It was the least they could do since she was the reason one of the men they'd sought was now behind bars. She'd only hope that Marco stayed that way.

As she looked over her old and new clothes, she sighed. The comfortable, casual clothes from discount stores were a far cry from the designer, one-of-a-kind outfits Marco had wrapped her in. She'd been a trophy wife, so she had to look the part. Long, silky hair perfectly styled. Long, manicured fingernails—the real kind. He wouldn't stand for fake nails, which was ridiculous since he'd been discussing her getting a breast enlargement at one point. But the clothes—the clothes would've made a movie star jealous. Only the finest threads to cover her bruises.

Had she liked all her designer duds? Hell yeah. She was a chick who'd grown up poor and was thrust into a horrible marriage. The clothes had been a perk. They'd been her the-glass-is-half-full moment to her marriage. When Marco would send her out for a new pair of Christian Louboutin shoes or a Louis Vuitton bag, she'd almost felt loved. It wasn't until after speaking with the feds that she'd realized all her shopping expeditions had been orchestrated to get her out of the house or away from her husband so he could conduct his business, and after she'd learned how he'd made his money, she didn't want to keep anything that was purchased with it.

Cheap clothes off the rack? Yeah, she'd take those any day and revel in them if they meant her freedom.

After she finished hanging up her clothes, Xan went into the living room where Scott was setting up his PlayStation. "In your bedroom," she said, shaking her head.

"Ah, c'mon, Mom. The TV's bigger in here."

"You heard me." She walked into the kitchen and grabbed a bottle of water from the fridge, uncapping it as she walked back into the living room. "Have you finished unpacking your stuff?"

"Yes, ma'am."

"Uh-oh. You're breaking out the 'yes ma'am'. You must want something bad." She chuckled, taking a swig.

"Mommy," he said too sweetly. "I could really use the latest edition of *Battle Warfare*."

"There are starving kids around the world and you want me to spend sixty bucks on a video game just because you could use it? I don't think so."

"Ahh, Mom, what if I mow the lawn all summer? Will you buy it for me then?"

"First of all, summer's almost over. Second, you have to

mow the lawn anyway." She started to walk to the front door to assess the yard situation when he jumped in front of her.

Scott looked a lot like his father. He had the same chiseled jaw, same brown hair. But he got his blue eyes and smile from her, and already at six feet, he was taller than Marco. There was just enough difference that he wasn't a constant reminder of the horrible father he had, but the similarities were startling at times, especially after Scott had gotten as big as he had, and she had to remind herself Scott wasn't like Marco.

She was leery of men, but she wasn't afraid of her son. Oh, he had his moments of teenage moodiness, and like other young men who liked to test the limits of their parents, he pushed her when he could. But she did everything possible to counter the bad Collins genes in his system with love, support, and understanding. Her boy really was a good kid.

"What if we go in half?" he asked with a hopeful smile, and she tried her best not to smile in return. So he wanted to play a war game. It was much better than living it.

"I'll consider it."

"Thanks, Mom." Grinning, he kissed her cheek before walking away.

She shook her head and walked outside. The yard was small and the flowerbeds were in shabby shape. She could weed them later and maybe plant some flowers before fall set in. It wouldn't take much to liven up the place.

"Yoohoo?" a female voice called from behind her.

Xan turned around as she stood back up, facing the approaching woman. She looked to be around her age with auburn hair pulled loosely in a ponytail and a voluptuous figure spilling out of her skimpy shorts and tight tank top. "Can I help you?"

"Oh no, girl. I was just coming over to introduce myself and welcome you to the neighborhood," she said as she walked up to Xan. She offered her hand to shake. "Hi, I'm Roxanne Willis, but you can call me Roxie."

Xan shook her hand briefly and smiled. "Xan Bradley. It's a pleasure to meet you."

"Same here. You gettin' settled?"

"Trying to. We still have to run to town and get a few things."

"Well, this is a small town and the neighborhood is quiet, so you'll like it if that's your thing. If you like partying and the night life, then not so much. There's not much to do out in these parts. So where're you from, anyway?"

Xan was used to all kinds of neighbors. She didn't even have to think about her answers when people probed her about where she'd been in life because her responses flowed without effort. "All over. I'm a traveling nurse, going where the needs are."

"Oh, you working at the hospital in Conway? Surely you ain't working in Little Rock? That commute's a bitch."

"No. I'm working here for Dr. Peters."

"Oh, that's right. Joann's quitin' after she has that baby. She's due any day now."

The front door opened, making Xan turn around to watch Scott walk out. Her son shamelessly stared at Roxie's breasts before looking at her eyes. The boy needed a father to teach him how to look at a rack without getting caught. Xan felt as if she'd be betraying her sisterhood if she coached him on that.

"Scott, this is our neighbor, Roxie Willis." She turned to look at Roxie. "This is my son, Scott."

Roxie smiled brightly. Xan felt her mother claws extending. She didn't know Roxie from a hole in the ground, but the last thing she wanted was some cougar prowling around her son.

"Oh, this is great," she said excitedly, then turned toward her house. "Chad!" She whipped her head back around. "I have a boy too. Looks about your age."

The boy in question came out of the house across the street and headed their way. Xan was relieved that Roxie's sudden interest in her son seemed more genuine now.

"Yeah, Mom?"

"C'mere and meet our new neighbors." She turned back to Xan. "It's just the two of us. His daddy left when he was seven."

Chad closed the distance between them and nodded to Scott, who returned the manly nod of recognition.

"Chad, this is Xan and Scott Bradley. Y'all, this is my son, Chad. He'll be a junior this year." Roxie wrapped her arm around Chad's shoulder and rubbed it affectionately, motherly pride shining in her eyes, and Xan's relief from her earlier assessment grew. Roxie wasn't interested in her son. She was just animated.

"Scott's starting his junior year too."

The boys looked each other up and down, and Scott's eyes narrowed briefly. "You got *Battle Warfare?*"

"Nah, but I got *Bloodbath Four*," Chad said, shoving his hands in his pockets and rocking back on his heels. "You wanna play?"

Scott shrugged his shoulders as if it didn't matter much to him, but Xan saw the excitement in his eyes. Her boy loved those damn video games, and if Chad was anything like him, then he just found his new best friend.

"I'll be back later, Mom," Scott said casually as he followed Chad.

She fought a smile as she nodded at him.

"I swear Chad is drawn to those games of his like a fly on a honeysuckle. If your boy's the same, they'll be fast friends."

Xan laughed. "I was thinking the same thing. It's nice to have someone his age around and someone to show him around school if they hit it off."

"Oh, Chad'll give 'em the dime tour." She paused as she looked around, her gaze landing on the car in her driveway. "Say, what're you doin' with one of Laverty's cars?"

"Who?"

"Bill Laverty. He owns Laverty Rentals in Conway. Rents cars and limos."

"Oh, I, er, had some car trouble just outside town. Had to have the car towed."

That piqued her interest. Her eyes gleamed and a wicked grin flashed on her face. It seemed like the smallest thing got this lady's attention. Xan wasn't used to expressive women. Hell, she wasn't really used to women period. She understood why she never got too close to men, but she never really got close to women either. Attachments were hard to break, and once a gal got a girlfriend, those bonds were solid. Men could be dumped. Friends couldn't.

"So, you met the hunks of Sheppard's Garage?" She laughed seductively. "Girl, those men have women coming for miles just for a dadburned oil change. If they made a mechanic's calendar with nekkid photos of those guys, every woman in the tri-county area would gobble them up."

Now that she believed. Those men were gorgeous, but it wasn't the lot of them that'd kept her up last night. It was one long-haired Viking who did. Every time she shut her eyes last night, she'd pictured his massive body towering over her, him ripping her clothes right off, buttons flying, lace disintegrating. She'd fantasized about him possessing her in every way. She'd spent the night in one fantasy after another, torturing herself with what that man could do to her, with what she could do to him.

"Yeah, I'll bet," Xan finally managed to say, forcing the erotic images from her brain.

"So, which one helped you? It wasn't Teddy, was it?" Her smile faltered a little.

"Teddy? I don't think I met—"

"Bear," she said suddenly. "The younger bald guy with a goatee and green eyes. You can't miss him."

From the sound of Roxie's voice, she never missed an opportunity to look at him, and since she singled him out from the group, Xan figured Roxie had a little thing for the big lug.

"Oh yeah, Bear. I met him. Just didn't know his real name. Brody, er, Brutus is the only one who introduced himself with his real name."

She seemed a little relieved by that, as if keeping his real name a secret from her somehow meant he wasn't interested in her. She was fine with that. Brody was the only mechanic who got her engine running.

"Brody, huh? I only know Teddy's real name. He doesn't like it. His family used to call him Teddy Bear, which fits because I think he's a big ol' softy, but now they just call him Ted, or so I'd heard. I figured he dropped the Teddy part when he moved here. The only one in that group that's from around here is Hunter, but he grew up being called that. Apparently, he has a horrible name, so we'll never know what his real name is." She giggled as she flung the red hair flowing out of her ponytail over her shoulder and propped her hand on her hip. She seemed giddy at the prospect of gossiping about the town hunks, and Xan was apparently a glutton for punishment. She could feel the question forming on her tongue. She didn't need to ask it. She needed to keep her head clear, needed to forget about—

"So, what do you know about Brody?"

CHAPTER THREE

When Monday morning finally rolled around, Brody was no closer to finding a way out of this torturous assignment than on Friday when he'd been given it.

He recalled Colonel's words. *Keep your eyes glued to her ass. Where she goes, you go. Report back Monday morning at our regular debriefing meeting. We'll go from there.* When he'd tried to get answers as to why he'd had to do that, his boss had given him the cold shoulder, as was his right. It was Brody's responsibility to follow orders, not question them.

So he'd scoped out her house, watched her talk to her neighbor and her neighbor's kid. The boys seemed to have hit it off because they stayed over at the Willis' house all afternoon, and then the Willis boy stayed the night with Scott.

Brody strapped on his leathers before getting on his Harley and revving the engine, thinking that he was happy Xan's boy had found a new friend. He wished he knew how hard it was making friends at that age, but seeing as how he didn't remember his youth, he could only guess. But it seemed pretty hard at that age. Hell, it was tough making friends as an adult.

He knew he had a tough time trusting the guys at work and eventually befriending them. Roc, Blade, and Bear were already there when he came on. He hit it off with Bear and Blade right away. Bear was Colonel's unspoken second-in-command, so he was like another boss. But Blade became his brother from another mother. They were tight. Sure Blade liked to get under his skin and pull stupid-ass pranks, but his carefree personality seemed to counter Brody's don't-fuck-with-me attitude.

Roc, on the other hand... Brody shook his head as he backed his bike out of his driveway and headed down the main drag to the shop. Roc was a mean son of a bitch. No ifs, ands, or buts about it. It took Brody years to get comfortable enough around him without always being on alert, ready to kick his ass. Roc was vocal about everything. If he didn't like something, he'd make sure everybody knew. Brody had never seen him snap at an innocent person before, but Lord help the perps they'd taken in. Some of them got a beating beyond necessary at the hands of Roc. He was a hard-ass and made no apologies about it.

Gauge and Hunter came along after Brody. Hunter had been from around here and moved back after something went down in another city. He didn't talk about it much, and Brody never pushed for answers. Gauge also had a haunted look about him, but he was still the newbie, and Brody didn't trust him fully. It took time to earn his trust. Granted, Gauge hadn't done anything to make Brody question him—he lived by the book, doing whatever he was told and never complaining, but it was to the point it seemed almost too practiced—he just hadn't earned his keep yet. Both of those guys had secrets they didn't share, and Brody respected their privacy. He had his own secrets.

What little Colonel had found out about Brody's life made him appreciate the need to keep his past in the past. He didn't want to go shouting from the rooftops that he'd been a hired killer.

Brody parked his bike and strode into the shop. He stripped off his leathers as soon as he could. In cooler months, he'd leave them on longer. In the middle of summer, he hated wearing them. He was already sweating, and the air conditioning was shoddy in this building. He entered their meeting room, seeing that everyone else had already made it in.

"It's about damn time you got here," Colonel growled.

Brody grunted as he took his seat. He was here with two minutes to spare. It wasn't as if he needed brownie points for showing up early. Colonel narrowed his eyes, glaring at him briefly before turning to the rest of the guys.

"Let's get started so we can open the shop. We have a new assignment, which I've tapped Brutus for. He's to get close to Xan Bradley and know every move she makes."

"You never said to get close to her," Brody growled. "You said to stay on her. I can tell you everything she did this weekend without once having talked to her."

"That might work for now, Brutus, but eventually, you'll have to get friendly with her. The FBI wants her watched, so you know the score. I'm not pissing off our client because you're too pigheaded. She's a private person, so the only way you'd be able to do your job is to get close. I'm not saying you have to marry the bitch, just be her friend."

Brody felt his hair standing on his neck at Colonel calling Xan a bitch. He knew nothing was meant by it, that

Colonel generally respected women. But now Xan wasn't a woman to Colonel. She was a mark. Brody tamped down the urge to forcibly remind his boss just how womanly the little minx was.

That'd get him nowhere in the argument he was trying to present. He didn't need to be around her any more than he absolutely had to. He'd spent his days following her, his nights dreaming about her. Her vanilla and womanly scent enveloped him to the point of madness. He couldn't get that scent out of his system. Everything he smelled, tasted, was her. He'd made his dick raw masturbating so much this weekend, envisioning her in every sexual position imaginable, and he still wasn't sated. No, there was no way he'd be getting close to that woman. His sanity and his cock couldn't take it.

"So what's the deal with that little doll anyway?" Blade asked.

Colonel straightened, his all-business mask forming on his weathered face. "Xan Bradley, AKA Alexandria Collins, is the ex-wife of Marco Collins, second-in-command in the Collins crime family." At the blank stares everyone gave him, he continued. "Also known as the Colleoni family before migrating here from Italy."

Fuck. Everyone had heard about that international mafia. They were a ruthless bunch who had their hands in everything from drugs and money laundering to human trafficking and arms deals.

"The feds've had a jones for taking down that family for years and had at least one agent working deep undercover within the organization, if not more, when evidence gathered had disappeared, which just so happened to be around the time Marco had tried to kill his wife. He was brought up on attempted murder charges. They knew it was probably their only shot to stick it to him, so they went at him with everything they'd had, showing the attempt on her life was premeditated, and she's been under federal protection ever since. And now Marco Collins has a parole hearing next week. He gets out, he'll kill her. He doesn't get out, he'll still want her dead."

Colonel sighed, rubbing his head. "We'll all do our part in keeping an eye on her, but she avoids men like we're all the devil's sons. When she's around a group of men, she clams up and is even harder to penetrate, so it'd make our job easier if only one of us gets close to her, which is where Brutus comes in. We watch her until we get orders otherwise. I'm sure the feds will swoop in and take her if the shit hits the fan. Right now, we're just eyes."

Brody's head was swimming. He didn't want anything happening to her. The thought of some sicko trying to kill her had his blood boiling, fists clenching. This was worse than he'd imagined. He knew he had to avoid actually getting close to Xan, but he didn't want anything happening to her. If the feds had them watching her, then Marco's men could be on to her, and she was in deep shit if that was the case. If he stayed close enough to watch over her but far enough like he'd done this weekend, then he could jump in if she needed help.

He recounted her activities over the weekend, which didn't amount to much, and Colonel dismissed everyone. Before his boss left the room, Brody grabbed his arm and pulled him aside.

"Listen, boss. I'll shadow her, stay on her tail, but I can't get to know her. It's best if I stay hidden in the background." He didn't want to tell him that he recognized her from his past. He knew the circumstances behind his accident were shady. Evidence showed it was more likely he'd been beaten with a baseball bat and left for dead rather than some car accident. Besides the fact there was no car, the markings on his body showed a violent attack. Until he could place why he knew her, he needed to keep that little tidbit to himself.

"I don't want you to stay hidden, but I don't expect you to do this all by yourself either. I know you can't watch her twenty-four-seven, so when you're not with her, one of us will always be tailing her. Maybe even when you *are* with her too. But this is your gig, man. You're point on this assignment, so don't fuck it up. I don't know what your problem is, but you'd better get your shit together."

"Colonel—"

"Fuck, Brutus. You never complained about orders before, and I'm getting damn tired of hearing you do it now. You don't have a fucking choice."

Colonel stalked out of the room and Brody growled under his breath. Oh, he had a choice, all right.

He'd just follow her like he'd been doing, and let the chips fall where they may.

Because no matter how attracted he was to her, he'd be damned if he inserted himself into her life when she had enough problems already.

———

XAN DIDN'T HAVE any trouble finding Dr. Peters' clinic this morning after seeing Scott off to school. She hadn't even needed Roxie's directions. With a town this size, everything was a stone's throw away, according to Roxie, and she'd been right.

What Roxie failed to prepare her for was the extent of the nosy people around here. Oh, small towns had their appeal, but everyone seemed to know about everybody else.

And being the new girl, every patient she'd encountered wanted to know her story. She figured she should've guessed this would happen. After all, Roxie didn't seem to mind gossiping about the locals.

Of course, when Xan had asked her about Brody, Roxie wasn't much help. All she knew was that he'd moved here about ten years ago and, with the exception of taking an occasional woman to bed, and never the same one twice, he kept to himself. Xan figured he hadn't grown up around here—he had a country accent, but it was mixed with something else and definitely lacked that twang she'd heard in the locals. But she didn't really care for the one-night-stand tidbit she'd learned.

She guessed since he was single it was his right to get a piece of ass wherever he could, but it still irked her for some reason she couldn't identify. She didn't like the fact she was attracted to him. He was too big for her comfort level, and now it seemed he was too impersonal to allow himself to get involved in a relationship. Big with commitment issues. Yeah, she didn't need a man like that. Hell, she didn't need a man at all. She'd been doing just fine without one for the last twelve years.

But even as she tried to be logical, her body was rejecting the idea. Her brain was even betraying her with thoughts like, if he had commitment issues, then he wouldn't hover around if she was to fuck him. *I could get laid, and he wouldn't call the next day.* That idea held both appeal and irritation for her. It was a moot point anyway. She wasn't going to act on her attraction.

She sighed as she gathered the charts from the busy morning and prepped the ones for this afternoon. Being in a small town, she wouldn't have thought Dr. Peters would be as busy as he was, but since he was the only doctor within twenty miles, he had a little racket going on. She chuckled as she finished prepping the charts, but before she could file the ones from this morning, her phone buzzed.

"Hello?" she answered right away, not wanting to get in trouble for taking a personal call on the clock. It *was* her first day and all.

"Xan, hi, it's me, Agent Jack Parsons."

"Oh hi, Agent Parsons."

"How many times do I have to tell you to call me Jack?" He laughed affectionately. "Did you get settled?"

"Sure did. Thanks. I'm at work now, so I can't talk long."

"Then I'll get right to it. I just wanted to let you know you're being watched. I can't tell you any of the specifics, but you've already encountered our backup. You still need to watch your back, but we had to take preventative measures." He sighed and Xan's stomach dropped. Jack Parson sighing was never a good thing. "Marco's up for parole next week."

"What?" Oh God, this wasn't happening.

"Listen, Xan, I don't want you worrying about this. We knew this was coming. I just wanted to let you know we're already taking precautions for the worst-case scenario."

"And that being my ex-husband gets out of prison, hunts me down, and kills me in my sleep?" she asked sarcastically.

"Xan, we are *not* going to let that happen. You have to stay vigilant, be wary of your surroundings, but don't put your life on hold."

She took a deep breath. She knew he was right, but it was really hard to think logically right now. Her palms started sweating and her head was pounding. "Okay. Keep me posted," she croaked.

"Xan," he murmured. "You'll be fine. I'll call you next week to let you know how it goes. In the meantime, call me if you need anything. We've got you covered. Trust us, kiddo. We know what we're doing."

Trust them? She didn't have a choice. She quickly ended the call and shoved the files on the shelf before walking into the hall to call the next patient, trying not to freak out, and not doing a very good job. Ten years went by way too fast for her liking. She wanted to cry, to scream, and she didn't know how to get her emotions under control long enough to get by the rest of the afternoon.

But walking into the lobby jolted her thoughts.

Her lungs locked, seeing Brody sitting in the waiting room with a bloody towel wrapped around his hand. She should be grateful for the needed distraction, but instead, she felt a sense of panic. She looked at the chart and numbly called out Ms. Roger's name, never taking her eyes off him. He was hurt, and she wanted to run right to him and see if he was okay.

She quickly got Ms. Rogers in room 4, taking her vitals and noting the reason for her visit, before rushing back out into the lobby.

"What happened?" she asked before she even reached him.

He stood slowly, towering over her, but she was too concerned with his well-being to feel uncomfortable with his size. "Sliced my hand working on your car."

"Oh shit. How bad?" She gingerly took his hand and unwrapped the towel. "Does Dr. Peters know you're here?"

"Yeah, Colonel called him as I got into his car. Couldn't take my bike like this."

She winced when she saw the cut. "You need stiches. Hold on, I'll be right back."

She rushed into Dr. Peters' office as he was finishing up recording his notes on his last patient for the transcriptionist. "Ms. Rogers is in room four and Bro—er, Brutus from Sheppard's Garage is here."

"Ah, put him in room three. I'll check him out first."

Xan walked back to the lobby to gather Brody and escort him to the exam room. He followed closely behind, his body heat radiating off him in waves that crashed over her back. She tried to ignore the electrical sparks tingling up her spine, but she wasn't doing a very good job. She felt weak in the knees, hoping she didn't fall on her face right here in front of him. How long was this hall, anyway? It hadn't seemed this long this morning.

"Here we are. Take a seat and the doctor—"

"Is right here," Dr. Peters said as he stepped around her and into the room. "Let's have a look."

Dr. Peters unwrapped the blood-soaked cloth and grabbed some cotton swabs to wipe away the excess. "You need some stitches." He looked at her. "Do you feel comfortable taking care of him, Xan?"

"Yes, sir."

He smiled and nodded in approval. "She'll stitch you right up, Brutus. I'll leave you a prescription for some pain meds. Keep an eye on it. If it swells or smells, give me a call."

"You got it."

God, that voice. So deep and sexy, just like the rest of him. *Get your shit together*, she chastised herself. Good grief, the man was bleeding and in pain, and all she could think about was how sexy he was now that she knew it was just a cut. She quickly grabbed the rubbing alcohol and some cotton swabs. She didn't look at the doctor as he left the room or at Brody as she started to work. She had to stay focused. If she thought about the male musk seeping out of his pores, she wasn't sure she could stop herself from licking his skin. Yeah, that'd be professional. She needed psychological help. She just had to keep her mind on her job and get him out of this office.

And she was doing a good job of staying in the zone until she heard him wince. Her head jerked up and she saw a hint of a blush tinge his cheeks. She couldn't remember the last time she'd seen a grown man blush, and she had to admit, it was a little adorable on him.

"I haven't even started," she said playfully.

He grunted and looked away, and she felt bad for her remark. This was her job. She needed to remain aloof.

"I'm sorry if I hurt you. I have to get it nice and clean before I begin. The shot will numb it up before I start, though."

He nodded, looking at her through his lashes, and her heart raced. Why did she have to be attracted to him? She gave him his shot, set about administering the stitches. Standing this close, she could feel his breath hitting the crook of her neck. She shuddered and saw her hands shaking. She did not need to botch this up. Besides the fact she needed this job, she didn't want to screw up his hand. She renewed her focus and got busy, blocking out the feel of his skin beneath her fingers, the way his knee bushed her outer thigh.

He cleared his throat. "How, er, do you like livin' here so far?"

She glanced up at him and smiled. "No complaints. How long do you think it'll take you to finish my car?"

He laughed and she smiled brighter. She got the feeling not too many people heard that out of him. "Not sure, but I'll let you know as soon as we have an estimate."

She finished her work on his hand and bandaged it before taking off her rubber gloves and discarding them. "Sounds good. And you're good to go. Pick up your prescription at the front and call the doctor if you see any signs of infection like he said."

She tried to step back so he wouldn't brush up against her when he stood, but she stumbled in her attempt. She would've been embarrassed if given the opportunity, but he reacted too quickly. He grabbed her with his good arm and yanked her up against him to keep her from falling. With him still sitting, they were at eye level.

Her breath picked up as she watched his pupils bleed into his irises, turning his blue eyes black. He'd had the same reaction the first time she saw him, and she wasn't sure what to make of it. Her experience with men was lacking, to say the least, but if she was a betting woman, she'd think that the attraction was mutual.

Just that thought made her lose all sense of self-preservation and self-control. She stepped close, and his hand flexed on her arm. She didn't know what to do, her inexperience confusing her, but she knew this level of contact wasn't enough. She had to do something, touch him, or—

Her lips hastily brushed against his, and for the briefest moment, he hesitated. It was just long enough for her to panic and start to draw away at his rejection, but he clutched her to him, stealing her breath and taking the kiss with a guttural groan. Her insides rioted in elation and nervousness, joy, and trepidation at the feel of him consuming her. His injured hand pressed against her back, forcing her flush against him. His hard body dug into her as he angled his head for deeper penetration. His tongue massaged hers as his good hand tangled in her hair, directing her movements.

She should feel scared at the sudden control he exerted, but fear was not the prevailing emotion right now.

She moaned as she threaded her own fingers through his soft hair. His fist tightened his hold on her hair, and he growled into the kiss, his tongue plundering her mouth, teeth nipping at her lips.

And it still wasn't enough.

She thrust her hips forward, rubbing herself against him. He grabbed her ass and forced her to do it again, groaning at the contact.

She knew she was at work and her boss could walk in at any minute, but she just couldn't muster up a reason to care right now. She had to touch Brody. Nothing else mattered. She let one hand slip out of his hair, caress his face, and he stilled.

He grabbed her arms and pushed her away. His eyes were blue-black fire, eating her up as he panted, his chest heaving with effort. He stood suddenly, staring down at her with a look of lust, then panic, then what she could only describe as resolve.

"Stay away from me," he rasped, before opening the door and stepping out, slamming it behind him.

She gasped, covering her kiss-swollen lips, staring at the closed door. Oh God, what had come over her? Had she just thrown herself at a man who'd done nothing but help her all because she couldn't separate her fantasies of him from reality? Surely, she wasn't so rusty in the man department to have forgotten how to read a guy's interest, though that really didn't matter now.

Stay away from him? Not a problem, because after what just happened, she wanted to crawl into a hole and die.

CHAPTER FOUR

Mortification was a strange emotion. Xan had never fully enjoyed the benefits of this glorious feeling in all her life. Until yesterday. Standing before Brody, her heart in her hand in offering, waiting for him to caress—or even crush—it, and he just rejected her. Yeah, she got to experience being truly mortified firsthand. She pondered reasons why poets didn't devote sonnets to the joy derived from such a sentiment.

Mortification may have been new for her, but sarcasm surely wasn't, Xan thought as she fixed breakfast. She and sarcasm went together better than one of Elvis' peanut butter and banana sandwiches. And was probably just as good for her. She needed to shake this uneasy feeling and forget about what happened yesterday. She had more important things to obsess about, like her ex-husband's parole hearing. Life or death things were more important than a little lust.

Tell that to my body.

She really needed professional help. The man was obviously not interested in her, and here she was still panting over the guy as if he was dipped in Hershey's chocolate.

Ugh. It wouldn't even matter if he was interested. She needed to keep her priorities straight. And she would, dammit.

"Scott, breakfast's ready!"

Her son came barreling into the kitchen as if he hadn't eaten in days. Growing boys never seemed to get enough food in their bodies. According to her grocery bill, that was the case with Scott.

"Uh-oh. What's wrong?" he asked as he grabbed his plate of fried eggs and bacon.

She furrowed her brow in confusion and shrugged her shoulders. "Nothing."

He arched an eyebrow, giving her a knowing look. "You cook for dinner or when you're upset. You obsess about food when you have something on your mind. And face it, Mom, this isn't Lucky Charms I'm eating."

"That's not true." Though she felt the lie in her response. Her son was too observant. She'd wanted to bake homemade biscuits this morning, and the only reason she hadn't was because she didn't have any flour. Her thoughts were all over the place, and she couldn't get a handle on any of them. Food was her distraction, and since she didn't want to have to grease doorways for her to walk through them, she tended to cook food instead of gorging on it. "I try to cook you breakfast at the beginning of every school year," she continued to defend herself. "I usually don't start slacking off until after your first week. Next week it's Lucky Charms for you, buddy." She laughed and he rolled his eyes, inhaling his eggs. "Did you talk to the coach?" she asked as she sat down to eat her breakfast, grasping for a subject change.

"Yeah, he wasn't going to let me on the team since tryouts were last school year and they've been practicing all summer, but he let me run some drills and decided to give me a shot. I can't miss any practices and I might be benched the first couple of games or so, but if I do good in practice, I'll get to play. Maybe even start before the end of the season."

"Good." This was great news, actually. Scott loved playing football, and as much as they'd moved around, it'd been one of the few constants in his life. Plus, it helped him make friends faster at new schools since teams fostered that brotherly connection. "Just get me your practice and game schedule, so I can make sure I'm off work."

"Already on the fridge," he said as he hopped up. He rinsed his plate before putting it in the dishwasher. "I'll see you tonight. I'm riding to school with Chad."

"Okay, honey. I love you."

"Love you too." He paused and looked back at her. "You sure you're okay, Mom?" He frowned.

"Yes," she said with mock exasperation.

He nodded with a crooked smile before leaving. She could tell he didn't quite believe her, but was smart enough not to press the issue.

Xan took a deep breath as she looked unseeingly at the kitchen. She was a grown-ass woman who wasn't even fooling her teenage son. She needed to get it together. And she would.

Starting right now.

She grabbed her purse and got into her rental. The fact she didn't have to be at work for almost an hour didn't register until she was almost at the clinic. She was thinking she could just drive around to help clear her head until it was time to be at work, but then she heard a loud rumbling in the distance over the hill, distracting her from her thoughts. As the noise got closer, she saw a broad man with long blond hair tied at his nape, wearing sunglasses and driving a Harley, and her heart stopped. *Brody.*

The man was sex on a stick, and she just wanted to eat him up. She'd be all too happy to gorge herself on him. Where was her mortification now? And where the hell was her resolve to get her shit together? One look at him and she was a puddle of horny goo.

As he passed her, his head followed her for those brief seconds, and she could feel his blue eyes burning into her, even though she couldn't see them. She shouldn't have every golden fleck in his sapphire eyes memorized. Her body shook in that suspended moment in time, and all she wanted to do was pull over, rip off her clothes, and jump his big, scary bones.

She watched him in her rearview mirror until he was over the next incline and out of sight.

Okay, starting *now*, she would get her shit together.

Yeah, she was hopeless. She needed chocolate.

———

BRODY WATCHED XAN PASS BY, feeling like the biggest prick in the county. Why the hell had he told her to stay away from him? As if it was all her fault they were kissing. Hell, he was two seconds shy of throwing her down on the exam table and taking her right there at her place of work. Her breathy moans and shy little hands damn near brought him to his knees. He'd never been that turned-on that fast before. And he'd screwed up royally. A night of getting drunk couldn't undo the fuckup at the doctor's office. He'd know. He had the hangover from hell to prove it.

She was getting to him on a personal level, and he didn't understand why. All he knew was that his control was slipping, and before long, he wouldn't be able to define the word, much less be able to exert it.

The one good thing about his visit with Jack Daniels last night was the realization he had to do his part to stay away from her, and that didn't mean by telling her to stay away from him. No, he had to tell his boss he'd recognized her from his past and hope the boss man would show some understanding and forget about Brody having to get close to her. He could do his job just as efficiently by shadowing her. Well, except for last night. Fuck, he hoped Colonel didn't have one of the other guys following him, making sure he was staying on her because the only thing he watched last night was the disappearing act of his liquor.

He parked his bike and grunted his greetings to the other guys. Roc had his nose inside the hood of a car. Bear was talking to Colonel. Gauge and Hunter were standing to the side, tinkering with tools, not really doing anything, and Blade was texting, laughing, and stuffing his face with the donuts Colonel usually brought in, procrastinating, the little shit.

"I need to talk to you," Brody said as he approached the Colonel and Bear. "Alone."

"I'll just, yeah," Bear mumbled, walking off, apparently not even attempting to come up with a parting excuse.

"What's up, Brutus?"

"It's about this plan of yours where Xan Bradley is concerned."

Colonel narrowed his eyes. "Look, you've made your feelings on this known—"

"No, I haven't. Not really. There's a reason why I want to stay in the shadows." He sighed, rubbing the back of his neck. This was harder than he thought it was going to be. He shifted his weight and took a deep breath before looking at his boss again. "I-I know her, man. I mean, I remember her from my past. I just can't place her. She hasn't acted like she knows me, but that could just mean it hasn't clicked for her *yet*. I don't want to take the chance of her recognizing me when I don't even know how I know her."

Colonel took a slow breath and hiked his leg over the corner of the table he was standing beside. "I see. Well, your stubbornness makes sense. But, Brutus, you didn't exactly have a stellar life before—"

"That's what I'm afraid of," he growled. "If I know her because of my previous line of work, then that can't be good."

"You're jumping to conclusions here, son. You might remember her from when you were kids. It's a known fact she was a foster care kid. And you... You lived a life of crime, so chances aren't great you were born with a silver spoon. You could have crossed paths in the system as kids."

"No." He shook his head jerkily. "I clearly remember her dressed nicely, long hair, very polished. Granted, she seemed pretty young, but no kid in foster care would dress like that."

"Okay," Colonel said slowly. "But she doesn't recognize you, and she's the one without a brain injury here. If you had some association with her, she would recognize you. With the exception of longer hair, you don't look much different than when I found you. Who's to say you don't remember her being connected to the mafia? You could've seen her and remembered her. She's a beautiful woman. Maybe you just liked what you saw," he said with a smirk.

Brody's muscles tensed, ready to attack the bastard for... what? Saying she was beautiful? Apparently, his boss saw the anger flaring in his eyes because he scowled at him.

"You need to take it down a notch, Brutus. I'm just trying to tell you there could be any number of reasons you recognize her. Do you have any memories of actually talking to her?"

His shoulders slumped. "No."

"Being in the same room with her?"

"No."

"Has she said anything to you about you looking familiar to her? Or anything else that might suggest a connection?"

"No, damn it." He rubbed his forehead, shaking his head. "I just don't like this."

"Tell you what." Colonel stood and patted him on the shoulder. "I'll see what I can find out. I'm not promising anything. You're already a ghost, but if the connection is out there, I'll find it. In the meantime, nothing changes. I still want you watching her and getting to know her. If Marco Collins gets out, she might run, and we don't want that. She's less likely to do that if she thinks she can turn to you for protection. But she won't do that if you stay in the shadows."

Even though this didn't go exactly like he'd wanted, the thought of Colonel finding out his connection to Xan brought Brody a sense of relief. If he could just answer that nagging question, maybe then he wouldn't feel the need to avoid her. Because it was a need, he realized, that couldn't easily be ignored. But he had to keep trying. He'd just have to find the strength to keep on resisting her in other ways. "Thanks, man."

"You bet. Now that we have that out of the way, I have a

job for you. Bear and I were just talkin' about some intel we got on a possible Collins spy. Just checked into a hotel in Conway last night. His name is Dale Adams." Colonel gave him a cold stare. "Find out what he wants."

Meaning through any means necessary. Normally, he'd feel bad about using his muscles to get what was needed. He figured it was his conscience working overtime after the life he'd led before his accident. But if the man was here on Collins' order, then he was here to hurt Xan and Scott, and Brody would kill the motherfucker for even thinking he could harm one hair on either of their heads. Just because he needed to avoid his siren didn't mean he couldn't protect her.

"Consider it done." It'd be his pleasure. "What about Xan?"

"She's at work, right? Roc and Bear will take turns watching her until you get back."

He started walking toward the exit when he spotted Blade, still texting and smiling, probably chatting with some pretty little thing. The boy was a serious flirt. Brody turned back to Colonel. "I'm taking Blade." He looked over at the man in question. "Get off your ass and make yourself useful. C'mon." He waved him over as he continued out the door.

Blade jogged after him, pocketing his phone, then hopped into the wrecker. "We pickin' up a car?"

"No. Doing a job."

Blade's eyes lit with understanding. "Ah, well, stop at the gas station so I can get some smokes."

"You need to quit that shit. I doubt all your girlfriends like kissing an ashtray," Brody mumbled as he backed the wrecker out and headed down the highway.

Blade smirked. "I ain't gotta girlfriend. But I've had no complaints from any of my lady friends. They've had their mouths all over me and never once said nothin' about an ashtray." He gave Brody that devil-may-care smile of his.

He stifled a groan. Blade was the closest thing to a brother he had, but the man had some serious growing up to do, which was ridiculous since he wasn't that much younger than Brody.

He pulled into the gas station, sliding out and walking into the store behind Blade, figuring he could use a cold drink since they were here anyway. He saw Blade eye the store while walking up to the cashier, but then detoured, following Brody. Probably going to grab a drink too.

Brody turned the corner and ran right into someone, smelling a womanly essence with a hint of vanilla, right before grabbing her arms reflexively to steady her. He stared down and had to stop himself from dragging her soft body up against his. Xan. Those panicked blue eyes turned sensual instantly and he bit off a moan as his dick twitched. He had more important things to worry about than his cock. Like her safety. What the fuck was she doing here? Her ass was supposed to be at work every morning, and he saw her heading that way thirty minutes ago. And now he was on his way to investigate someone who was here to hurt her while she was out dallying around the town as if she didn't have a care in the world.

"Why aren't you at work?" he barked before he could stop himself. He winced at the sound of his own hard voice, but that wasn't his only reaction. His balls damn near shriveled when that sensual look she'd had morphed into one of fiery anger. She yanked her arms and he let her go, shoving his hands into the pockets of his worn jeans to keep from touching her.

"I had some time to kill before I had to be at work. Not that it's any of *your* business," she snapped.

He sighed, rocking on his heels and feeling like a damn idiot all over again. He wasn't used to feeling like this. He was out of his fucking element when it came to her. "Look. I'm sorry. I just remember seeing you heading to work is all." He shrugged as if it wasn't a big deal. He didn't need her suspecting anything, especially not the fact that her safety was an issue for him. How much of an issue, he refused to analyze. If he focused on the work aspect, he didn't have to even think about the personal one.

She stepped back, narrowing her eyes. "Well, if you'll excuse me, I have to stay away from you," she said with false sweetness, and damn it if his dick didn't get hard at her sexy little attitude. Yeah, he knew he was an ass yesterday and he needed to avoid her, but he didn't want her thinking of him like that.

He grabbed her arm as she tried to step away. "And I'm sorry about yesterday too. I had no right to act like that. I just wasn't prepared to deal with kissing you," he murmured, but it didn't matter. The male choking smirk behind him was all the proof he needed to know Blade had heard him. "Fuck," he breathed, letting go of her arm. "I'm just sorry," he mumbled, and left the gas station without getting a drink. *Real smooth, jackass.* He just kept screwing up every encounter like some wet-behind-the-ears kid. He needed a drink all right. A hard one.

He waited in the wrecker for Blade, scoping out the parking lot and spotting her rental. Hell, the car he was driving was better on its worst day than her car would be on its best. It didn't give him any incentive to get her car fixed anytime soon.

But the sooner he got it fixed, the sooner it would be out of the garage and away from the temptation to make up some stupid shit as a reason to call her.

He watched her walk out and straight to that car without even once looking in his direction. Those scrubs she was wearing shouldn't be sexy. They had cartoon fish on them, for Christ's sake. But seeing her in them just reminded him of their heated exchange in that little exam room, not that he needed any help remembering.

He'd have jumped when Blade opened the door if he wasn't used to always being on alert.

"You wanna explain what that was about, brother?" Blade asked, doing a piss-poor job of containing his laughter.

Brody waited until Xan pulled out and was heading back in the direction of the doctor's office before merging onto the highway. "Nope. I don't ask you about the women in your life."

"Oh really? What was all that bullshit about my women kissing ashtrays?" Before Brody could respond, Blade's gaze cut to him. "So she's in your life then?"

"If you don't shut the fuck up, I'm gonna pull over and beat the ever-lovin' shit out of you."

He sighed. "Fine. I can see you've marked her. You might want to let the other guys know. She's a beautiful woman and new in town. Sorry, man, but she's considered fresh meat around these parts." Brody's head whipped around, seeing red, and Blade's hands shot up in placation. "I'm just saying." He shrugged his shoulders. "I'm not gonna poach, but, dude, why deny yourself? Maybe you should just fuck her and get it over with."

"I'm not talkin' about this with you," he gritted out.

"And I ain't no dummy either, man. Just remember you can talk to me if you need to. It's not like you to not go after something you want. You must have a reason."

"I hear ya. If I want to talk, you'll know. Now, shut it."

They pulled into the parking lot of a shitty motel, not hotel, on the outskirts of town, not in town.

"This the place?" Blade asked.

Brody grunted. He parked the wrecker and they got out, walking up to the room Colonel said the lowlife would be in. Brody knocked and the door edged open. The lights were off. He and Blade walked into the room and flipped the switch.

"Looks like the guy isn't here," Blade mumbled after a quick look around.

Brody turned and looked at him. "You take the bathroom, I'll—"

A blow to the back of his head sent him to his knees.

CHAPTER FIVE

Xan was beyond relieved to be home after the day she'd had. First, her son had called her out this morning on her cooking, then she'd run into the object of her obsession, then Dr. Peters had kept her late because a lady in town had a baby and couldn't make it to the hospital in time for the delivery. She loved assisting with deliveries, but being a small town office, Dr. Peters hadn't canceled the rest of his patients. Nope, he just backed them up and stayed until every one of them had been seen. It was a mark of a great doctor, damn it. Someone should tell her feet that.

At least it had kept her from thinking about yet another horrible encounter with that arrogant asshole of a mechanic. Thankfully, there was no tongue action this time. And that was a good thing, right? Hell, she didn't know. Her emotions were all over the place. She knew she was attracted to Brody in a major way, one she'd never experienced before, not even with her ex-husband before they were married. And that was why the situation baffled her. Being a nurse forced her to meet new people every day. She'd had her fair share of men hitting on her, but denials were so ingrained within her, she could let down any man and let him think it was his idea. With as unpredictable as her life was, she liked things as orderly as she could get them. Throwing a man into the mix just invited chaos. And heartache.

And danger.

She walked into her kitchen and smiled at the pizza boxes and Scott stuffing his face. No matter how bad life was, he always brought her joy.

"Couldn't wait until I got home, huh?"

"Nah. I figured I'd help out with dinner tonight." He smiled angelically.

"Thanks." She smiled back and sat down, groaning at the relief of being off her feet. She grabbed a plate and a piece of pizza. "How's school going?"

"Good." He blushed a little and her motherly radar sounded. There was definitely more to it than just that.

"Good how?"

"I, er, I met a girl." He shrugged as he inhaled half a piece of pizza in one bite.

"I'd hoped you'd have met more than one girl," she said coyly.

"Mom." He gave her an exasperated look. "That's not what I mean."

She kept her smile hidden. She knew exactly what he had meant. Sure, she wasn't in the love game anymore, but that didn't mean she couldn't read the signs when other people played it. "Who is she?"

He sat up straighter. "Her name is Malorie Kimber," he rushed the words out. "And she plays volleyball."

"And you like her." It wasn't a question. She knew her son better than anybody in the world.

"She is so pretty. And nice. Dang, Mom, you wouldn't believe how nice she is."

"That's good. I'm sure she's a wonderful girl if she's caught your eye. Are you going out with her?"

"I friended her on Facebook, and I—"

"Scott," Xan sighed. "You know how I feel about you putting personal information about yourself online. I know it sucks that all your friends are into that, but you have to be careful. We have to live a low profile, remember?"

"It's cool, Mom. I don't put my personal information out there. No real names or birthday or addresses. With as much as we move around, being online helps me make friends I don't have to leave." When he saw her frowning at him, he added, "But I'm always careful."

She nodded slowly. She didn't like this, but he was right. He had to sacrifice enough as it was. Unlike her, he was actually born with a silver spoon in his mouth. Unfortunately, that spoon had been tainted with blood, and Xan had sacrificed everything to get her son out of that hellhole. Life wasn't as easy for Scott as it could have been, but she wouldn't have it any other way. Now he had a chance at a real life. An honest one. "So tell me what you were going to say before I interrupted. Did you ask her out?"

"Yeah, we're going out Friday after the game with Chad and his girlfriend, Becca." He jumped up and threw away his paper plate. "In fact, I'm supposed to be at Chad's in five minutes to play *Bloodbath Four*." He paused and looked back at her. "Did you think any more about *Battle Warfare*?"

"No, Scott. I'll let you know." In fact, she hadn't thought about much other than one deliciously tall Viking on a motorcycle.

"'Kay. I'll be back by midnight," he said as he started out of the house.

"It's a school night. Be back by ten."

"How about eleven?" he called out from the living room.

"Fine."

Xan stood and put the pizza away. She couldn't wait to get her aching body into the shower, so she hightailed it to the bathroom to do just that.

The shower was just what she needed. It helped relax all her muscles. Well, almost all of them. She contemplated taking care of herself in another way to achieve the ultimate relaxation, but her heart wasn't in it. It made her feel a little too pathetic because she knew exactly who she'd be fantasizing about. Oh, she tried conjuring up images of Matthew McConaughey, but his blond hair was too short and his body too narrow. Damn, she knew she was in trouble when that sexy man wasn't cutting it for her.

Frustrated in more than one way, she got out of the shower and threw on some cute boy-short panties before dressing in shorts and a tank top, not bothering with a bra since she'd just be going to bed in a couple of hours anyway. Maybe then she could give ole Mr. McConaughey another go.

"Yoohoo?" The high-pitched feminine voice traveled down the hallway as a knock sounded on her door. It was Roxie.

Xan walked down the hall and unlocked the door. "Come on in," she said as she pulled on the knob. Good Lord, Roxie was dressed as casually as Xan was, but the girl looked a hundred times better while Xan looked like a wet cat. It was amazing to her that her neighbor didn't have at least a steady boyfriend. Men should be chomping at the bit, praying Roxie would notice them.

"Hey, girl. The boys got that game blarin' in the living room. Thought I'd swing by and see ya."

Xan didn't really feel like company, but that was probably because she wasn't used to having a girlfriend. Maybe if she talked to her neighbor about unimportant stuff, she could forget about one hot-ass mechanic. Well, she could hope. "You want a glass of wine?" she asked, walking into the kitchen.

Roxie followed her. "Oh yeah, hook me up." She giggled as she took a seat at the table. "How's your new job going?"

Xan groaned theatrically, tossing a look over her shoulder while she grabbed the corkscrew. "Today was hell."

"Oh, I heard Sara went into labor. Mac must've been beside himself. He's been plannin' routes to the hospital since she entered her second trimester. Like there are really that many ways to get there from here." She shook her head as Xan handed her a glass of wine. "Mmmm. Thanks."

"So yeah, Mr. Rogers was panicked, but the labor went just fine. The fact Dr. Peters kept all of his appointments anyway is what made the day a disaster."

"Hmm. Is that the only reason?" Roxie asked with a scandalous look in her eyes.

Uh-oh. She knew something. And that something had Xan wiping her hands nervously on her shorts before taking a big gulp of wine. "What do you mean?" she hedged.

"I mean, I heard from Anna Sue that you ran into one hot bod at the gas station." She paused, her eyes getting bigger. "Literally. Like, I mean you ran right—"

"Yeah, yeah, I got what you meant," Xan sighed. "Brody was there with one of the other guys."

"Blade," she said matter-of-factly with a shrug, clutching her wineglass. She seemed to be waiting for something, but trying to act casual about it. Xan was too good at reading people not to notice.

"Mmm-hmm. And that was about it."

"Ugh. You're no good at this, hon. Fine. Anna Sue overheard him apologize for locking lips with you the other day." Xan gasped in horror. She didn't want the town thinking she was seeing him, or any man for that matter. "Oh, now, none of that. Although, I should've gotten the gossip directly from the source. You could have told me yourself." She gave Xan a disappointed frown. "But you can make up for it by telling me when you are going to suck face with him again." She giggled.

Xan needed a subject change, like right now. She shouldn't be talking about this with anyone. Her life was supposed to be as private and uncomplicated as possible. The last thing she needed was the town gossiping about her, regardless if the talk was true. That whole *there's no such thing as bad press* didn't apply to her situation. She needed no attention. At. All.

Roxie put her glass down and leaned toward Xan. "I get the feeling you don't have many friends," she said softly. "If you want to talk about this, you have my word I'll keep it between just us. I know I like getting the goods on everybody, but I do right by my friends."

Her head was spinning. She had a strong urge to jump up and run to her bedroom, get away before this conversation got out of control. But she had another urge, one stronger than the need to flee.

One that insisted she embrace this friendship and enjoy it while she could. She wasn't getting any younger, and there were only so many things she could talk to her son about. If she kept the important details of her life a secret, why couldn't she talk to Roxie about her feelings, her confusion about Brody?

"I'm not sure what to do about him," she finally mumbled.

Roxie sat back and took a deep breath. "What happened?"

Xan recounted the kiss in the office, the order to stay away, and the encounter today while she downed the rest of her of wine.

"Whew, girl. It sounds like y'all have some serious chemistry goin' on, and neither of you knows what the hell to do about it."

"That's putting it mildly, though I can't be sure about his side. It's just been a long time since I've been attracted to a man. I'm not sure how to go about dealing with it."

"You need to march right over to his house and tell him to quit jerkin' you around. Damn, girl, he's a man, not an alien. They all squeal like piggies when you grab 'em by the balls."

"I don't even know where he lives," she said, defeated.

"Honey, you're new here, so I'll forgive you for that, but in small towns, everybody knows everything about everyone. Addresses are the first thing, right before marital status."

Either it was the wine or the surge of estrogen swarming in the atmosphere with the girl power talk that was making Xan see the rightness of Roxie's argument. Really, why didn't she just tell him off? She didn't need to mope around here and avoid masturbating because of that SOB. Just thinking about it made her eyes narrow, her blood heat, muscles tense.

"You're right." How stupid had she been?

"Oh, I know I am, honey. And judging by the look on your face, I'd hate to be one arrogant mechanic right now."

Xan jumped up, pacing the kitchen. "That jackass told

me to stay away from him. *Me* away from *him*. Who the fuck does he think he is?"

"Go on, girl!" Roxie raised her glass in salute, laughing.

"Okay, so I started that kiss." She leveled a stare at her friend. "Started. *He* jumped into it and took control of it like a man dehydrated, gulping water after being stuck in some godforsaken desert."

"Right on, sista!" She slapped her hand on the table, riling up Xan even more.

This was exhilarating. Liberating. Freeing. "What gives him the right to dethrone Matthew McConaughey?"

"Huh?" Roxie's brow creased, frowning at her.

Xan waved her off as she kept walking. "Nothing, nothing," she mumbled. She turned to face her friend. "You think he's at his house? His motorcycle was still at the garage when I drove by on my way home, but the shop was closed."

"Oh yeah. I heard that bike revving up and peeling away on my way over here."

"Good." Xan nodded, feeling the resolve settle into her bones. If she didn't do this right now, she might lose her nerve. "Give me that address. It's time that man learned just who he is playing with."

———

BRODY GRUNTED, stumbling into this house, tossing his motorcycle keys and gun onto the hall table before walking into the kitchen where he gave his face a quick wash and grabbed a beer.

He and Blade were jumped by more than just one man in that damn room, though Brody seriously got the worst of it. Blade had jumped out of the way as the other guy came for him, but if his attacker had been just a few seconds earlier, Blade would've been just as bad off as Brody was. Unfortunately, neither one of them could grab their weapons in time or had seen the guys who did it before they'd fled. And to top it off, Dale Adams was probably reporting back to his cronies right now. Shit. If they were here because of Xan and Scott, he'd just fucked up big time. The element of surprise was no more.

And his head hurt like a son of a bitch. He searched the kitchen for some Ibuprofen, taking four of them once he found the bottle, and wrapped some ice in a towel for the shiner over his left eye. He twisted the cap off his beer, tossed it into the trash, then stalked into the living room and fell onto the couch.

The motel wasn't the only fuckup today. Oh no, seeing that spritely little woman at the gas station brewed an even bigger mess than the one that'd gotten him a fist in the face and, he was pretty sure, a two-by-four to the back of the head. Nope, the wounds he'd gotten from running into Xan wouldn't leave *physical* scars.

God, he hated hurting her. She deserved so much better than the treatment he was giving her. Hell, any woman deserved better than the brushoffs he was dishing out. He took a pull of his beer, drinking half the bottle before setting it back down. He didn't have a choice. He could not risk her recognizing him. At least not until he got that information from Colonel. He needed to keep his head in the game, not fantasize about sinking his dick into her pussy. If he thought about it, he'd want to act on it.

Damn, but he wanted to act on it.

Growling, he picked up his cell , and hit Gauge's number.

"Yeah?"

"Hey, man. I need a favor." He needed to stay on track, and he knew just what to do. "I need you to dig up everything you can on Xan Bradley. See what you can find tonight, and I'll be at your house in the morning to go over it." Gauge was their computer guru. If anyone could find old skeletons or any information floating in cyberspace, he'd be able to do it.

There was hesitation on the line, so Brody had to rein in his anger. "Why not talk at the shop?"

"Too distracting. I need to be able to concentrate." Translation—he didn't need his ass handed to him by the guys. Brody asking about Xan would be like tossing fuel onto the heckling fire. *No thanks.* She might make his dick harder than steel, but he still had a job to do here. Drowning himself in research would help keep his mind on his responsibility, but he knew the assholes he worked with. They'd look at this as if he was taking a personal interest in her.

"Okay, sure. See you in the morning."

Brody ended the call and pulled out his laptop. It felt as if his head was in a vise, and he could feel the blood pumping in his bruises. He wasn't jumping for joy at the thought of digging up info on Xan right now, but he didn't have a choice. His ass was working and not thinking about her luscious body.

He got as far as typing her name in the search engine when a heavy pounding sounded on his door. He jerked up, grabbing his weapon before silently walking to the door. Had Adams and his gang found him? He wasn't taking a chance.

He clutched the doorknob, twisting it slowly as the angry banging continued. One of the things Colonel had taught the guys was to never allow vulnerability. If someone was here to kill him, the fucker would have a Glock on the peephole. His only mode of protection at this point was the element of surprise. Besides, he was ready to kill the motherfucker just for the noise his headache couldn't take. He jerked the door open, drawing his gun as dark-blonde hair whipped about a tiny head from the force of the door opening, stirring up an enticing scent of vanilla.

"Fuck," he breathed, dropping his gun, his heart pounding as he stared at the woman he couldn't seem to do anything right around.

Man, he just couldn't get through this day without one more fuckup.

CHAPTER SIX

Xan stared in shock at the barrel of a gun shoved in her face, her anger spiking. One would think she'd freak out, but she was already spitting mad at him that this stunt just added icing on her anger cake. Oh, there was a split second where she'd felt fear in her haze of shock—he'd shoved a gun in her face, for crying out loud—but that emotion was short-lived.

Very short-lived.

He dropped the arm with the gun, and as she drew in a breath, readying herself to let him have it, her eyes finally traveled to his face from his little metal toy he was clutching as if it was his only friend.

This time, when she gasped, there was no anger mingling in with myriad emotions attacking her. His normally golden skin was peppered with blue and black splotches, his back rigid, eyes shielded.

"What happened to you?"

"Don't ask," he barked at the same time as she asked her question. He obviously saw the worry building on her face before she expressed it. He sighed, shoulders relaxing a little. "I'm fine," he said without the edge. "What're you doin' here?"

What was she doing here? Oh, right. She was here to chew him a new asshole. Somehow, staring at him in this state was like sprinkling water on her flame. It wasn't a bucket dousing it out because she still felt mad at how he'd been treating her, but something bad had happened to him, and, no matter how angry she might be with him, she didn't want him physically hurt—unless she was the one dishing it out. "We need to talk."

He inclined his head and stepped aside to let her in, though she didn't get the feeling he was really acquiescing, just biding his time. He hadn't answered her question about what had happened to him; rather, he jumped right into why she was here, changing the subject. He was probably plotting excuses for his bruises or a new way to make her stay away from him.

As she stepped into his house with him following right behind her, her liquid courage seemed to disappear, and without the estrogen fest that was this evening, her resolve started to waver. Her anger was slowly evaporating, leaving behind her worry and, if she could be even more pathetic, arousal. Once she entered the minimally decorated, masculine living room, she turned, facing him.

"We do repos on the side. The guy didn't want to give up his car." He stepped around her to the couch, picking up an empty bottle. "You wanna beer or something?"

Couldn't hurt to revitalize that liquid courage she was just thinking about. She nodded as she processed his answer, then watched him walk into the kitchen. She could still see him since the only thing separating that room from this one was a small bar. If she didn't know any better, she might've believed that piece of bologna he'd tried to feed her about the repo. He said it so effortlessly that he might actually do those jobs on the side and he might've gotten into a tussle a time or two because of it. But the answer was a bit too forced and his stance a bit too nonchalant for her liking. He was trying too hard to distract her from the truth. Why? Was it because he was a private person?

Maybe it's because he's asked you to stay away from him and here you are inviting yourself over like you're BFFs.

She shook off that thought as he walked back into the living room, handing her a beer. Well, if he wanted to play it like this, then fine.

"Did you get the car?" she asked, taking a sip of her beer as she sat on the couch. He followed her lead, sitting beside her but not close enough to touch.

He grunted, shaking his head. "Got away. He had some friends."

Now *that* she believed. "Maybe you'll have better luck next time."

His gaze cut to her. "I'm countin' on that."

They sat and drank in silence for a couple of minutes. Not long, but long enough for her to get antsy. She came here for a reason, and she needed to get to it. She couldn't wait on the beer to renew her motivation. She'd just have to discuss this without the edge of anger from before.

She eased her beer onto the table and turned to face him. Because it was the polite thing to do, he did the same, turning to face her. Though why he bothered to be polite now, she didn't know. "What's your deal?"

He immediately stiffened, his eyes shielding again. "What do you mean?"

She sighed, rubbing her hand in her hair and realizing she probably should've taken some time to gussy up a bit. Too late now. "I mean, you act like you're interested in me, but then you avoid me. This isn't high school," she chastised lightly. "If you regress any more, you'll be pulling my hair and running behind the monkey bars." She laughed to try to ease the tension in the room.

It didn't work. His already stiff body seemed to grow, his chest expanding, his presence strengthening before her eyes. She couldn't help it. She looked, and yeah, it looked as if he was housing a damn Louisville Slugger in his worn jeans. He was getting bigger everywhere.

"If I was pulling your hair, you'd be too busy screaming my name, and I'd be too deep inside you for you to run anyway," he rasped.

Oh. My. God. Xan felt heat creep up her face, her nipples tighten, her pussy creaming. Any question she had about him being interested just flew out the window. She tried to latch on to her sanity before it followed that same path.

What in God's name was she doing here? She'd avoided men ever since she'd gotten away from that psycho ex of hers, and now it seemed she walked right into the lair of the very beast she'd tried shunning. She should've heeded Brody's request to stay away because she just realized it wasn't a request. It was a warning. She didn't know how to get out of this, but one thing was for certain. She was going to kill her nosy neighbor for fueling this craziness.

"I-I should go," she mumbled, attempting to get up. It was no use. He closed the distance between them, anchoring his hand around her tummy on her hip to keep her from moving.

"Not yet," he breathed right before his lips crushed hers.

And there went the sanity she'd tried desperately to keep. His lips were like fire, like a balm. Both hot and soothing, moving over hers. She moaned as his hand caressed her cheek and slid into her hair. She knew all logic escaped her, but she tried to minimize the damage he was doing to her body.

"Let me in," he growled against her lips as his hand tightened in her hair. She gasped at the erotically sharp tingle on her scalp, giving him the access he sought, breaking her last defense against his invasion.

His tongue dove into her mouth while his other hand tangled into her hair to control the kiss. He tugged at her hair, creating electrical currents that arced through her body and straight to her pussy. Then he massaged the pleasure-pain with a gentle caress. The sensation was so confusing to her mind, but pure ecstasy to her body. It was too much.

It was not enough.

Xan mimicked Brody's actions by running her fingers through his long hair, giving herself over to the kiss. Why hadn't she found long hair attractive on a man? She was nuts if she thought this wasn't sexy. She fisted her hands into his locks, loving the growl that rumbled up his chest.

He broke away, trailing kisses along her jaw to the sensitive skin where her shoulder met her neck, controlling the movements of her head with his demanding hands.

This was the most exciting experience of her life, and all he was doing was kissing her. That thought brought her up short. She was out of practice, and it was obvious that this sex god knew what he was doing, stealing her breath, overloading her senses with the most pleasurable of attacks.

If she was going to give in after all these years, she wasn't going to be timid about it. She'd worry about tomorrow when that day of regret got here, because she knew she'd regret this when her brain started working again.

But, for now, she'd enjoy this moment. After all, she could be a senior citizen before she let herself give in to something like this again.

As he traced his lips down to the swell of her breasts, he tugged at the straps of her tank top, exposing the right one. With an agonized sound, he sucked her nipple into the hot cavern of his mouth, drawing on it with a desperation she didn't fully understand, but somehow seemed to share. One hand slipped between her shoulder blades, positioning her as an offering to his ravenous mouth. The other was pushed up underneath her shirt, rubbing and squeezing her other breast. And all she could do was hold on to his head as her body shook with need and a little uncertainty.

He pulled back, gripping the hem of her shirt and yanking it from her body before descending to her newly exposed nipple, giving it the same treatment as the other, licking and sucking it so hard that it flattened to the roof of his mouth.

"Fuck, your nipples are like candy," he groaned, alternating his attention between her breasts.

She was lost in ecstasy, in a pleasure so intense she could do nothing but let him ravish her, but her own hands ached to explore his body, and her mouth demanded to taste him all over. She might never have another chance to taste a man, and she damn well was going to do everything she could to draw his essence into her body to remember in the cold nights ahead. She freed her hands from his hair and tugged on his shirt, pulling it from his jeans. He was a little dirty, but she didn't care. The hint of mechanical grease and male power was like an aphrodisiac she couldn't ignore.

He lifted his head and helped her remove his shirt, staring down at her once he was divested of it. His fingers grazed her wet, swollen nipples, and she thrust them up into his touch, her head falling back as she moaned. His mouth latched on to her throat, kissing and suckling the sensitive skin, and she finally rubbed her palms along his chest, feeling his muscles bunch and tighten under her caress. He kissed up to her ear, worrying her lobe with teeth as he panted. Chills raced over her body, making her want more right now. She didn't want to wait another minute to enjoy this man fully. She tweaked his flat nipples, squeezing and pinching them lightly as he grunted into her ear. He took her mouth again, kissing her forcefully while she clutched his jeans, finding the button and releasing it from its mooring. When the zipper rasped, his arms came around her, holding her to him tightly, one hand grabbing her hair while the other snaked around her back.

She freed his cock and couldn't seem to grab it fast enough. He growled into her mouth as she fisted it, stroking it without mercy.

"Damn you," he muttered when taking a breath, still kissing her. His hips jerked up, fucking her hand as she continued her assault.

He tried pushing her down onto the couch, but she wasn't having that. She broke away from his kiss, which took effort because of the hold he had on her head. He relaxed his grip, letting her kiss his jaw, his neck, trailing down to his chest, kissing and nipping him as she went. She rubbed the flat of her tongue against his nipple, then bit down on it while she continued to jerk him off. He winced, but his hands found her hair again, holding her to him. As she resumed her exploration of his body with her mouth, she drifted down, licking his bellybutton, feeling the rasp of his hair against her tongue. She was eagerly waiting to taste his cock, and she wasn't the only one. The hands in her hair began pushing her down, guiding her to the engorged erection. Her tongue eased out, lapping the wetness pooled at its tip. His cock jerked and he moaned, his hands tightening in her hair almost painfully. Even though feeling him guide her did kick up her excitement, she wanted to be the one in control, not him.

She ignored his cock and kissed to the side of it as she grabbed his pants and tugged. He lifted his hips enough for her to pull them down to his knees. He kicked off his shoes so she could remove his pants, but she already had enough room to work with. She kissed one thigh then the next, enjoying the rasp of his hair against her nipples. He tried tugging her head back to his cock, but she swatted at his arm. He growled in frustration, but eased up on his demand, letting her explore.

She kissed his balls before kissing and biting all over his thighs and belly, running her hands up his chest to pinch his nipples as she worked her way back up his body.

"You're fuckin' killing me, baby." His hips rocked, seeking contact with anything.

As she navigated back down his abdomen, she discovered a trail of pre-cum from his dick to just below his belly-button where it hovered.

"Mmmm." She licked the salty treat from his tummy, tasting the sweat beading on his skin before giving the tip of his cock a quick swipe.

He groaned, and she decided he'd had enough torture. Without any preliminaries, she took him into her mouth, to the back of her throat, sucking him hard, greedily.

"Fuck. *Fuck.*" His hips came off the couch, shoving his cock deeper. "Oh God, Xan. Like that, baby. Just like that."

As she relished the perfect treat, she squeezed his balls, letting her finger rub the sensitive area just behind his sac. She sucked him relentlessly, taking him deep and pulling back to suck the head while her tongue rubbed under the sensitive crest, and she repeated this over and over. She hadn't sucked a real cock in years. From the way his body was tightening and groans were escaping, she was doing everything right. But now it was time to blow his mind.

She relaxed her jaw and swallowed him, milking him with her throat, the hair at his groin tickling her nose when she took the whole thing. A low rumbling growl built deep within his chest as his hands fisted brutally in her hair. She didn't care. The pain just added to the erotic thrill she was getting just out of giving him this pleasure.

"Fuck, Xan. I'm gonna come if you don't stop."

His words were a plea she ignored. She eased back a bit to breathe before renewing her efforts.

He shouted a litany of curses, trying to hold back, but his attempt was futile. Within seconds, his whole body stiffened, his cock growing impossibly hard. "I'm coming," he groaned. "Swallow me, baby. Take it all. Fuck!"

The first splash down her throat startled her, but she worked her throat, milking him and taking everything he had to give. She continued sucking until he softened and relaxed his hold on her hair, but his dick was still harder than she figured it'd be.

He grabbed her sides and pulled her up to his lap. He kissed her with such intensity that she wondered where he found the energy. He'd come, so their sexual escapade was over. She should be relieved by this, but she couldn't help but feel a little regret that it was ending with this sensual kiss. She figured her subconscious utilized the blowjob as a self-preservation mechanism to keep from fucking him. But, right now, she didn't want logical.

The kiss built, intensifying, as she heard a soft rustling, her world tilting, swaying.

"Hold on, baby," he whispered into her mouth, and she opened her eyes as she clutched his shoulders, realizing they were moving, already in a hallway when Brody shouldered his way into a room.

He deposited her on a bed, and she saw he was nude, a gloriously naked body before her. The rustling she'd heard must've been him shucking his jeans. He reached down to pull her shorts off her, and she stiffened. Lying here in only her lacy boy-short panties, she felt too exposed, too vulnerable. It was one thing to suck him off, keeping the control. It was a completely different thing to let him have his fill of her. Sensing her sudden discomfort, he caressed her legs, easing her as he pressed gentle kisses above her knees.

"God, you're so beautiful," he murmured against her skin as he worked his way up her body. He kissed right in the center of her lacey panties, and instead of relaxing and enjoying the attention, she trembled. The idea of sex was so far removed from her understanding that having a man touch her like this was too foreign to her. In theory, she didn't have a problem with the mechanics of the act.

In reality, she was petrified.

"Easy, baby," he mumbled when her tummy jumped. He gently clutched the lace and tugged, pulling her panties off.

"It's, um, been a while for me." Shit, her voice was shaking too. How embarrassing.

He hummed his acknowledgement against her thigh as he kissed his way back to her core, his long hair tickling her overly sensitive skin.

At least she'd waxed recently, she thought. It being summer and all, she did that for swimsuit season. The last two summers, she'd waxed it all off, not worrying about any man seeing her. Now she wondered if that was a mistake.

She had no idea what men liked, but she found herself wanting to please him, which made no sense since she was also freaking out about him touching her like this. God, her emotions were all over the place.

Then his tongue sneaked out of his full lips and licked her from her ass to her clit. Her moan of surrender was mixed with his groan, their sounds rending the air.

And her resistance was gone. Her legs fell numbly open, giving him greater access. She shut her eyes and lost herself in the pleasure his mouth provided. He licked and sucked her lips, and as he tongued her, she creamed profusely, drowning him in her honey. Her hips shot up when he sucked her clit into his mouth. She moaned and clutched his head, begging him not to stop, and he grabbed her, pushing her back down, holding her still as he circled her clit, teasing her.

She was dying. This was so good she knew she wouldn't survive him eating her. Then he shoved one finger into her pussy, and she had to redefine the definition of dying. Her pussy latched on to that lone finger, hoping it'd take up residence and never leave.

"God, you're fucking tight."

She couldn't hold out. She felt fire lick her spine as her pussy fluttered around his finger in anticipation of the orgasm that was imminent.

"Oh God." She didn't want this to end, but she couldn't take any more. "I'm coming," she yelled as he fucked her with his finger and sucked her clit into his mouth again.

She rode out her climax until she was utterly spent. Then he eased his finger from her and placed a chaste kiss atop her mound. Her eyes were shut, her arm thrown over her face. She was panting when he shifted, so she peeked to see him fumbling with his nightstand drawer. He pulled a foil packet and donned the condom in what had to be some kind of record. He hovered over her, lifting her leg, his cock poised at her entrance. He eased in, but she didn't want easy. She grabbed his ass and pulled him to her, forcing him to thrust harder.

"No, baby. Let me take you slowly. At least until I get in."

She thrashed her head on the pillow, enduring the agony of his slow possession.

"Ahh, you're so tight," he breathed. "You're like a vise, squeezing the life out of me."

"Hurry, please. Please!" she begged. She didn't care if she sounded desperate. She just wanted him in already. She pulled him to her on his next thrust, forcing him in halfway.

"Fuck, Xan." His hips bucked, seemingly involuntarily as he buried himself to the hilt.

She screamed and clutched his shoulders, her nails biting into his skin. His lips sought hers in a powerful kiss as he fucked her hard. She was beyond understanding sensations. He was so big and hard that the pleasure bordered on pain, but she met him thrust for thrust, seeking the deepest contact possible.

Out of nowhere, she climaxed again, screaming into his mouth. He grabbed her ass and angled her differently, pounding into her almost recklessly. His lips ripped from hers as his head fell back and he roared his release.

They held each other, bodies sweating, hers shaking. She tingled everywhere, so much so that her lips felt numb. She didn't think she could speak even if she wanted to, which she didn't right at this moment. He eased back, staring down at her. His eyes were soft as he caressed her face, and she realized she could get used to having him around.

If only she could tell him her secrets and trust him with her life, but she knew that would never happen. Still, she reached up and traced the bruises on his face, feeling him lean into her touch. But then he sighed and pulled free, groaning at the drag of flesh against latex-covered flesh. He left the room to dispose of the condom, and Xan wondered what she was supposed to do now. It wasn't as if she did this. Ever. She didn't know the protocol once the deed was done. *Thanks for the fuck? See you around?* Neither option sounded good. At least she had a reason to go. It wasn't as if she could leave her son at home overnight. Well, technically, she could if they were a normal family, and she was comfortable with the idea of spending the night with a man, but neither scenario applied, so she wasn't going to stay.

He strolled back in, the softness of his eyes gone, and she got a sickening feeling. She didn't resist the urge to pull the sheet over her, covering her nakedness, her vulnerability.

"This shouldn't have happened. You should leave," he said with no emotion, staring right into her eyes.

Humiliation washed over her. She had wanted to leave, but not like this. Oh God, not like this. It was all she could do to leave his house without crying in front of him.

She wasn't as lucky hiding her shame.

CHAPTER SEVEN

Brody revved up his motorcycle as he pulled out of his driveway to go to Gauge's house the following morning. He hadn't slept worth a shit last night. After tossing Xan out, his fucking conscience ate away at him until all he could do was replay the entire encounter.

He didn't know what it was about her, but she got to him, dug deep, and touched him in places no other person—let alone, woman—had ever before. After getting the hottest blowjob he'd ever received, he'd tasted and sank into the sweetest pussy he'd ever experienced. She'd been timid at first, as if she wasn't sure she wanted to fuck him, but her body had responded with intense want that his body refused to ignore. And she'd been tight, so fucking tight, that he believed her about her apparent sexual dry spell. How long she'd gone without taking a man, he didn't even want to guess. On the one hand, he felt elated that she'd let him be the one to end it for her. On the other hand, he felt paranoid. That paranoia drove him to be the biggest asshole he could be and kick her out.

He felt connected to her and so fiercely protective that

it shamed him to push her away like he had. It'd gone against his basic instinct to do it, but he knew he had no other choice. He knew her from somewhere, and they both had questionable pasts they wanted left buried. He needed to stay on the ball and not get distracted again. Having her hate him hurt like hell, but it was better than making either of them face something that should stay buried.

He pulled into Gauge's driveway and killed the engine. He stalked up the stairs and banged on the door. It didn't take long for Gauge to answer.

"Dude, what the fuck? It's not even seven yet." His curly brown hair was mussed and hazel eyes narrowed as he stepped aside to let Brody in.

"Didn't take you long to get the door. You must've been up already." He could smell the coffee from where he was standing, which was a good sign Gauge had either already been up or had set the coffee, expecting Brody to show up early.

"I'm a light sleeper, though I wouldn't have to be by the way you were beatin' down my door," he growled, stomping off to the kitchen. "You should drive your truck more. It's a hell of a lot quieter too."

"Don't knock the hog," Brody said, grabbing a cup and pouring some coffee. "Did you have any luck finding anything out last night?"

Gauge elbowed him away from the coffeepot to fix his own cup, then sat at the table. Brody sat across from him, toying with his cup as he watched the other man, waiting for his answer.

"Yeah." He shook his head as he sipped. "You're not gonna like it either."

"Well, don't beat around the fuckin' bush. Spit it out."

"I called in some favors with some of our FBI contacts.

Seems our little Miss Bradley got herself into some trouble with her ex-husband."

Brody suppressed a growl. "Tell me somethin' I don't already know."

"He had a friend. On the inside. Someone either with the FBI or someone close enough to an agent to tip him off. I'm bettin' a dirty agent myself."

"Shit," Brody breathed. "That could explain why her husband attacked her. It's amazing she got out alive."

Gauge shook his head. "He shot her pointblank in the head. He had no intention of her gettin' away."

Brody couldn't stop the panic building in him. She could've already been killed, and she wasn't safe now. "We need to find that dirty agent. He could still be with the bureau."

"Agreed. I'm looking into it. I do know her handler is Jack Parsons. He took over after Dave Simmons retired."

"How long has Parsons been her agent?"

"About ten years from what I've gathered. Simmons handled her around the time of the trial and got her settled with her first identity. He retired about two years later."

Brody finished his coffee and leaned back in his chair, rubbing his hands on his face. This wasn't much to go on, but it was a start. "If Parsons wanted her dead, he could've done it by now. He's had ten years to make it happen."

"True, but if he's working for Collins, his assignment could be to keep tabs on her, so Marco could do the deed himself."

"But why? Why not ice her and be done with it? She's the reason he's in jail."

"I don't know, man. The kid maybe?"

Shit. That was possible. "Okay, but why did Simmons

retire? Maybe he was the one on the take and got out when Collins got sent away."

Gauge leaned into the table, pointing his finger. "That's a good theory, but I also found out that when she went to the FBI, they were salivating so much at the idea of taking down Collins that they put a mess of agents on her case. It could've been any of them."

That still wasn't a lot to go on, but it was more than what he had. "Okay. You find out what you can about the agents assigned to her case before he attacked her. I think we're dealing with an agent who had earlier contact with her. But Parsons and Simmons ain't in the clear. One of 'em could've been assigned to her case before or close enough to the case to push for reassignment after her attack. I'll check them out."

Gauge eyed him, and Brody didn't like that look. "Why are you doin' this, man? You're supposed to tail her, befriend her. You don't have to go diggin' in her past to do that."

What could Brody tell him? That he was concerned about her safety? *Not gonna happen.* That he needed the distraction? *No way.* "We're supposed to protect her. Knowledge is power and all that." He shrugged as he stood and headed for the door.

"I get that, but, umm, I think we should keep this little research to ourselves."

Brody turned, facing him. "Why?"

"Because I think you have a thing for her, and Colonel will go ape-shit crazy if he discovers you're packin' wood for her."

"I don't have a fuckin' *thing* for her." Uh-oh, he said that just a little too quickly to be believable. And Gauge smiled. Fuck.

"I know all about denying feelings." Something dark, haunted crossed his eyes, but was gone just as quickly. "You can't bullshit me, Brutus. I won't rat you out. But I think we need to keep quiet about this. At least until we find somethin' concrete that Colonel could use or go to his contacts with."

He had a point. Besides, he really didn't want the other guys knowing...*thinking* he had a thing for Xan. If they found something useful, they'd pull in the other guys. "Fine. Er, thanks." He stuck his hand out and Gauge shook it.

"Just doin' my job, man. Just doin' my job."

XAN BUSTLED around the doctor's office all day, trying to keep her mind on work and off one sorry-ass mechanic. Oh no, he wasn't a Viking to her anymore. He was a jackass. Or an asshole. Or, or...ugh! He didn't even deserve the brain power she was exerting to come up with terms, that sorry son of ass-cheese.

What the hell had happened yesterday? She'd gone to his house to tell him off, and she'd ended up getting him off instead. Yeah, real smooth, idiot. And what did she get for her trouble? A swift kick in the rear. He practically tossed her out of his warm bed and into the cold. Okay, so it was ninety degrees last night, but it was the principle, damn it. She had never felt more mortified in all her life. He'd treated her like a paid whore, but at least hookers understood the score—and actually got something for their troubles. Plus, there was no love lost once the deed was done and they parted their bodies. No, she wasn't even treated as nicely as that. No date beforehand and no cuddling after. She got shafted all around.

But wasn't that what she wanted? Once she realized it was going to happen, she knew she couldn't allow a repeat. But she hadn't expected him to treat her so shitty right after. Her pussy was still practically fluttering with after-spasms when he ordered her out. No matter what she thought she wanted, having him treat her the way he had hurt her more than she could've imagined.

Thankfully, she hadn't cried in front of him, but that'd been a monumental feat. The floodgates opened before she'd even pulled out of his driveway. She was so upset she couldn't drive straight home and face her son, so she'd driven around town until the waterworks had dried enough for her to make a hasty entrance and dart into her room.

Twelve years, three months, four days. Last night, she'd counted the time since her last sexual encounter. She would've counted the hours and minutes too, if she'd looked at the clock.

And for what? A wham-bam-thank-you-ma'am encounter. Only she hadn't gotten a thank you. Or a compliment of any kind. She didn't need him to stroke her ego—she knew it'd been a long time since she'd had sex and would be rusty—but demanding she leave? That was low. Lower than low. And she felt like scum, dirty.

She stormed out of the office and was still brewing on her drive home after work. She pulled into her driveway and tried to make her way in her house when she heard Roxie call out her name. She turned and saw her neighbor practically running across the street over to her.

"Hey, girl. How'd it go last night?"

Xan took a deep breath to keep from throttling her. She knew it wasn't Roxie's fault, that she only encouraged Xan to embrace her inner feminine power, but it was really hard to remember that.

"Like shit," she sighed.

"Oh no. What happened?" Roxie asked, grabbing her arm, her eyes growing.

"He...we...I...ugh." Xan shook her head. "We had sex, and he threw me out."

Roxie gasped, but her shocked expression didn't stay that way for long. "How did it happen?"

Xan explained all the gory details because she knew she wouldn't be getting away from Roxie without spilling everything. And, as she spoke, her partner-in-feminine-power's eyes got narrower and narrower.

"That punk! Don't you worry, girl. We'll find you a different man. A better man." She looked genuinely pissed, and Xan couldn't help but feel a little vindicated, but she was already shaking her head before Roxie could finish. The last thing she wanted to do was invite more humiliation like last night. Nope, her vibrator never kicked her out. She'd stick with what she knew.

"No thanks. Last night was enough to do me in for another decade or so."

"Why? C'mon. I'm not sayin' you have to screw a new guy, but you could let a man take you out. Show you a good time. Or we could just go to the bar and hang. Let guys buy us drinks all night." She wagged her eyebrows, smiling at Xan.

"I don't think so." Before she could say more, her phone rang. Xan cursed under her breath as she pulled it out, hoping it wasn't that ass-wipe with the stringy blond hair. Okay, so his hair wasn't stringy, but she'd call it that if it made her feel better. When she saw it was from Agent Parsons, she sighed in relief, accepted the call, and looked at Roxie. "I have to take this. I'll talk to you later." She turned to walk into the house.

"Think about what I said. Nothin' wrong with getting drunk on a hunk's dime."

Xan waved her off as she went into the house. A bar meant men hitting on her. She'd pass on that. She'd have to embrace her inner bitch before she could even think of doing something that dangerous.

Once she was safely away, she put the phone up to her ear and said, "Hello?"

"Hi, Miss Bradley. It's Agent Parsons"

"Hi, Jack. I've told you to call me Xan." It was their little game. One would be formal and the other would insist on casual references. She couldn't remember when it'd started, but it was one of the few constants in her life. She chuckled, but he didn't jump in and join in their usual bantering, causing a sense of dread to creep down her spine.

"I've got bad news. Marco Collins just got paroled."

———

BRODY WORKED DILIGENTLY on Xan's late 70s model Ford Pinto, replacing the radiator. This thing was on its last leg, and fixing it cost more than the damn thing was worth. As crazy as her life was, she needed a more reliable vehicle. She sure as hell wouldn't be using this piece of shit as a getaway car if she found herself in trouble and had to get away from Collins' men. She'd have better luck running barefoot across hot asphalt.

"How's it coming?" Colonel asked, walking up to him.

"Slow. But I should have her ready in a day or two."

"Good." Colonel turned toward the other bays, eyeing the rest of the crew. "Gather around. We need to have a quick meeting."

Brody cleaned his hands on the rag that was draped on

the side of the car, then followed the guys into the meeting room, sitting down while Blade turned on the fan, trying to circulate the stifling air in this sauna.

"I'll get right to it since we're still open and it's hot as hell in this room," Colonel said, squatting on the corner of his desk. "Marco Collins got paroled."

Brody schooled his expression, but inside, he was raging. This was the last thing they needed, the last thing Xan and Scott needed. With Marco out, he'd surely be on the hunt for his former family.

"Sources tell us that he'll head to Michigan, but once he touches base with his pop, there's no telling where he'll go."

"We know where he'll try to end up," Bear mumbled, shaking his head. "You know he's comin' for the lady and her kid. It's only a matter of time before he finds them."

"Agreed." Colonel nodded. "But we haven't gotten any new orders. We're still the eyes on this."

"Shouldn't the feds just pull them out?" Blade asked.

"And do what?" Roc sounded disgusted at Blade's question. "He doesn't know where they are now. They should sit still. If they start running, they'll raise red flags all over the fucking place."

"He's right," Hunter agreed. "And you know I don't like agreeing with that asshole." He chuckled as he shoved his thumb in Roc's direction.

"Fuck you, hotshot," Roc spat.

"Not even if you grew tits, lover boy."

"Knock it off, you two," Colonel sighed. "Gauge? Brutus? What are y'all's thoughts on this?"

Brody eyed Gauge, hoping he wouldn't spill that they'd been doing their own little research into this mess.

Gauge's eyes cut to Brody in silent understanding before speaking to the group. "There's nothing to say." He shrugged. "Until we hear otherwise, we keep doing what we're doing. If Brutus needs help, he'll let us know."

It was an unspoken acknowledgment that Brody had already exercised his right to seek help, and he was relieved his coworker had kept his mouth shut about it. Gauge was still new around here, but if he pulled through on this assignment, he just might earn his keep for good in Brody's eyes.

But now, Colonel was waiting for him to put his two cents in. Xan definitely needed the protection, but after having sex with her, he needed to revitalize his efforts to alter Colonel's plan. Brody couldn't afford to protect her from the inside because he knew he wouldn't be able to resist her for long. He couldn't afford to be longing for more. No, he needed to stay in the shadows.

But he couldn't discuss that in front of everyone.

He crossed his arms and leaned back in his chair. "I agree with Gauge. It doesn't matter what we think she should do. As long as we've been hired to watch, we keep doing that."

Colonel stood, nodding. "Good. Then I'll keep everyone posted on any changes."

The guys stood up to leave, but Brody held back, waiting for the room to clear. His muscles tensed and his head pounded. He didn't want to have another confrontation with his boss, but as hardheaded as Colonel was, it was the only outcome.

"I want your permission to stay in the shadows on this."

"Damn it, Brutus! What in God's name is your fucking problem?"

He took a deep breath and tried relaxing. If he punched his boss, it wouldn't do any good. "I feel I'm more effective working that way. The goal here is her protection, and I want to make sure I do my job right."

"And you think you can't do that being her friend? Or do you just want to fuck her so bad you're worried I wouldn't approve? If that's the case, don't worry. Fuck her ears off. Just stay on her ass when you're not staying in her bed."

He was seeing red. The urge to grab his boss by the throat and throw him against the wall almost consumed him to the point of immediate action. "That is irrelevant," he finally gritted out.

Colonel stepped closer, stabbing his finger in Brody's chest. "That little bitch has you by the balls. I can see it. Don't fucking play me, Brutus. Use it to your advantage. Now that Collins is on parole, she's a flight risk. If she had somebody close to her, she might either confide in her desire to leave or decide to stay because she trusts that person enough to watch out for her. If you're not willing to fucking do it, then fine," he yelled, throwing his arms up. "I'll get Blade to do it. I'm sure he'd *love* to stick to her through any means necessary. Fucking her would be a bonus for him."

Brody's control was hanging on by a thin thread. He stepped up to Colonel, nose to nose. "You will *not* put anyone else on her."

Colonel smiled mockingly. "I figured you'd see it my way. Bring this shit up again, and you're out. You got that?"

Brody gritted his teeth so hard he'd be surprised if he had any molars left after today. "Got it."

Colonel took a step back, his shoulders relaxing before taking a deep breath. "I do have a little bit of news regarding your previous connection to Xan Bradley."

Brody's eyes widened, body tensing all over again, but for a very different reason.

"Turns out you were one of Marco Collins' hired guns. I'd hoped to be able to tell you more, but I still have people working on it."

It wasn't great news, but if he was honest with himself, this wasn't a surprise. Colonel had already discovered he'd been a killer, and Collins was as ruthless as they'd come. "You think that's why I know her? If I was a member of his gang, she should recognize me."

He shook his head. "No, you were an independent contractor. I know it's not a lot, but it's a start. Don't worry. You'll get your answers. I'll see to it."

"Thanks, man." Brody nodded before stepping back out into the bay to continue working on her car.

He had to figure out a way to become her friend without getting attached to her and keeping her from ever discovering who he was. And after the way he'd been treating her, he had no idea how he was going to accomplish that. Besides, even if they'd never officially met in their other lives, he still didn't want her to know the truth about him.

This had disaster written all over it.

CHAPTER EIGHT

THIS HAD disaster written all over it, Xan thought as she stood in front of the video games at Walmart. Scott's first football game was tomorrow night, and she wanted to surprise him with that game he'd asked her for, so she'd rushed here right after work. She'd told him the news about his sperm donor the night Jack had called, and he'd taken it really well. He'd even helped talk her off the proverbial ledge when she was ready to flee to some tiny island country. Her boy was turning into a responsible young man, and he deserved a surprise for the effort he'd always exerted.

She just couldn't quite remember the name of that dang game, and she had to elbow her way around kids playing the latest systems on display. Where were these kids' parents anyway? She was about ready to break a wrestling move and start checking them out of her way.

"Can I help you, ma'am?" a young employee asked her.

"Er, yeah. I'm looking for a game for my son, but I don't remember the name of it."

"Hmmm. Okay, let's see." He pointed toward the

display. "We have a new SpongeBob game that just came out."

She suppressed a laugh, but she did smile. "He's grown out of that." *Thank you, Jesus.* "I think it was Blood War something."

"*Bloodbath Four?* Great game. It's right over here." He started to open the case, but the name didn't sound right.

"No, no. I think he has that one. Or his friend does."

"Well, if his friend has it, he may want it too, so he can play online. If he already has the game, he can return it for another as long as he doesn't open the case."

Shit. She didn't want to get him the wrong game. "What other games are popular right now? You know, at that level?"

"*Zombie Alive* came out a few weeks ago, but we're sold out right now."

That wasn't right either. She thought for a few seconds, trying to remember her conversation with Scott, gasping as it finally came to her. "*Battle Warzone.* That's it." She sighed, smiling, tickled she actually remembered it.

"*Battle War*fare. Yeah, we got it."

Hallelujah, same difference. "I'll take it."

She paid for the ridiculously priced game and headed out to the car, humming to herself, lost in her immediate joy. She had to take pleasure in these small things because she'd learned the hard way that life was too short not to. She'd had another child who she didn't get to spoil—Tess' life was over before it started. But Xan knew Scott would be thrilled with this game, and that put a smile on her face. It was much needed after the news of Marco's release, and she needed to try to not let that get her down. Oh, she'd be more careful, but she wouldn't let him ruin the rest of her life if she had any say in the matter.

As she crossed the parking lot heading to the rental she was still driving, a late-model Mustang roared, coming straight for her. She froze for a brief second and tried to process why it was heading her way. Oh shit! She screamed as she tried jumping out of its path.

Only she wasn't alone.

As soon as she jumped, strong arms caged her and sheltered her as she was tossed out of the way.

And then he was up and running after the car.

As she stood, she stared in shock at her savior while he chased the vehicle squealing out of the lot and flying down the road. Brody pulled out his cell phone and was mumbling into it as he jogged back over to her, ending the call and pocketing the phone before he reached her.

"You okay, baby?" he asked so softly that she barely heard him over the blood roaring in her ears, but as he asked, he was running his hands down her arms, body, looking for any sign of injury.

She was trembling from fear, but her body was too aware of the hands caressing her to ignore that wonderful sensation.

"I-I think so. Where did you come from?"

He sighed, resting his forehead against hers, squeezing her shoulders. "C'mon. Let me get you home."

She pulled slowly away from him, remembering his hateful words after they'd had sex. She wasn't going anywhere with him. But he tightened his hold, refusing to let go.

"I can get myself home."

His eyes narrowed, head lowering. "Don't fight me on this, Xan. You could've been killed."

He didn't let her answer. He dragged her toward his truck as if he was some modern-day Neanderthal, grunting at her when she tried to protest. He opened the door, lifted her in effortlessly, buckled her up, and stalked to the other side before getting in and driving off.

They were in Conway, so they had at least fifteen minutes until they made it to her house. She figured she'd ask Roxie to drive her back up here to get the car. In the meantime, she folded her arms and flattened her lips. She could sit in silence for another fourteen minutes and fifteen seconds.

Two more minutes passed and her shoulders sagged as she stared out the window. She didn't know what to think about this man. He wanted to avoid her, but he wanted to help her. He wanted to avoid her, but he wanted to fuck her. He wanted to avoid her but he...ugh, it was no use. She glanced at the clock. Was the damn thing even moving?

He fiddled with the radio, turning it on and lowering the music a little. She had to admit she was a little surprised at the music selection, so much so that she broke her silence.

"Not country? I'm shocked." She widened her eyes mockingly. "That must be sacrilege 'round these here parts," she drawled, butchering a Southern accent.

He chuckled. "Nothing wrong with country music. I just prefer rock." He shrugged.

She did too. In fact, she loved rock music, but she didn't recognize the band. "Who is this?"

"Mayday by Midnight, an Arkansas band. I also have some We Are The Fallen, which also has Arkansas ties." He picked up his iPod that was connected to his radio and thumbed through his selection.

"Really? I didn't know that." She was a fan of We Are The Fallen, but Mayday by Midnight sounded really cool too.

"Yeah, there are several places in Little Rock where you

can see local and big-name acts. Juanita's, The Rev Room, Fox and Hound. It's a great way to hear good music."

She nodded at that, not really knowing what else to say. She'd lived in some really big cities, but she couldn't remember the last time she'd gone to a concert. She couldn't imagine how much fun it'd be to just relax and listen to some tunes without wondering if anyone would recognize her. The only major thing she did to disguise herself was alter her hairstyle and color, but some women did that every few weeks.

By the time the second song finished, they were pulling into his driveway. She paused, then looked around.

"Why are we here? I thought you were taking me home."

"Blade and Bear are on their way over to get your keys. They're gonna get your rental and find the fucker who almost hit you. C'mon." He tilted his head, motioning her to get out as he slid out the driver side. She followed suit, getting out and following him into his house.

She did her best not to think about what happened the last time she was here. She needed to go into protection mode, call her agent and let him know what had happened to her. But she wasn't doing a very good job staying focused on what she should be doing. Just staring at the couch where she'd taken Brody into her mouth made her salivate.

"Have a seat," he said hoarsely, making her think he was reminiscing too. "I'll get us a couple of beers."

She sat, taking a deep breath, inhaling his very masculine scent. She needed a clear head right now. The last time she was here, she did some very naughty things, and he'd tossed her out like yesterday's garbage. She'd be damned if he made her feel like that again.

He walked back out, handed her a cold bottle, and

started to sit, but the doorbell rang before he was seated. "Give me your keys," he murmured, putting his beer on the table and standing upright. She fished them out of her purse and handed them over before watching him walk to the front door.

She heard masculine mumbles but didn't see anyone else, only Brody's very fine backside. He shut and locked the door before walking back over to her. He sat, picking up his beer and taking a sip. Then he turned toward her. The carnal fire in his eyes made her whimper. She had no defenses against him. She watched helplessly as he slowly put his beer down, then lowered his head, keeping his eyes locked on her.

"I thought you said this was a mistake," she breathed.

"I'm good at mistakes. Let's make a big one."

———

BRODY GRABBED Xan's hair and forcefully kissed her, not giving her the opportunity to remind him of the way he'd treated her the first time he'd had her.

Because he was going to have her again.

God, she tasted sweet, not like the vanilla coming off her skin, but like honey, rich and delectable. She moaned as he fed from her, and his already rock-hard cock throbbed, demanding he take her with no preliminaries. The rest of his body was seconding that motion. With one hand fisting tighter in her hair, he wrapped the other around her back, pressing her up against him.

She squirmed, her timid little hands clutching his shirt. Then she pushed, forcing him to lose contact with her warm body.

"You told me to leave last time," she panted. "You threw

me out right after." And damn if her voice didn't quiver. "And you've been standoffish other times too."

He sighed, dropping his hands, but landing them on her thighs, caressing them. "I know I've been a dick, but I have my reasons." He tilted his head, kissing her neck where it met her shoulder, needing the intimate contact. "I can't promise that'll change," he murmured. "It's how I'm wired, baby. I don't know why you affect me so much, but what I do know is that I can't stay away from you for very long." If the little voice inside his head reminded him that he had to get close to her for his job, he ignored it.

He kissed his way up to her ear, feeling the shudder that rocked through her body. She leaned her head to the side, giving him better access. Taking her move as a sweet surrender, he slid his hand to her cheek, holding her while he nuzzled, kissed, and nipped at her.

"So you want something casual then?" she breathed.

He stilled briefly before nudging his lips against her ear. "I don't want to plan anything," he whispered. "I just want to live in the moment. I can't give you anything more than that."

She sighed, and he felt like cringing. He basically told her she was just a fuck for him. While his brain was congratulating him on being reasonable with her while his dick was running the show, he felt a suspicious heavy feeling in his chest at the thought of using her just for physical pleasure. That little inner voice shouted he was doing his job, but that just made him feel like an even bigger asshole, especially since he couldn't deny the need to have her. A part of him prayed she'd push him away, tell him to go to hell.

A very small part.

The much larger, demanding part was fucking hoping

she'd take what he offered because he couldn't imagine never having her again. That just wasn't an option he could accept.

God, when did he turn into such a pussy? He'd fucked many women without giving them much thought after. Sure, he knew how to please a woman, and he loved wringing every last bit of pleasure out of one because it just heightened his own. But he actually cared what Xan thought, how she felt.

"I think I can handle that," she purred, kissing his own neck and trailing her hand down his abdomen.

He didn't have time to relish in this victory because fireworks exploded when she squeezed his cock through his jeans. He moaned, threading his fingers through her soft hair, pulling her head up so he could kiss her. His lips found hers, and he tried to temper the raging beast that lurked beneath. Kicking her out the last time wasn't his only regret. He'd taken her too hard for as tight as she was and too fast for what she deserved. She needed to be cherished, coddled, worshipped. This time, he wanted to enjoy the feel of her writhing beneath him.

The kiss deepened, shooting ecstasy straight to his balls. Kissing and touching her was like the darkest sin because he knew he couldn't have more than a few stolen moments with her, yet he wouldn't stop himself from having her. It was wrong, but it felt too right to ignore. He could have this.

He *would* have this.

Her hands tugged at his t-shirt, and he leaned back so she could pull it from his body. But before he could pull her back to him, her hands grazed over his chest, circling his nipples. He watched in rapt fascination as her head lowered, licking one flat disk. He gritted his teeth at the sensation, loving the feel of her tongue against his skin, and when she bit down, he let out a low groan.

He warred with the need to go slow and let her explore with the need to ravish her again. Unable to resist touching her any longer, his hand dove into her pants, secretly rejoicing in the easy access her scrubs provided. He traced his finger along the silk before sliding it beneath to the warm heaven he longed for. She whimpered against his chest, and damn if he didn't feel weak just hearing her make that sound.

He buried his nose in her hair. "You like that, baby?"

"Mmmm," she murmured around the hard nipple she was torturing.

His finger burrowed in the folds of her pussy as he felt her unbuttoning his jeans. He pushed into her and she gasped, her head falling back on her shoulders. He seized the opportunity her free lips provided by taking her mouth again, his tongue darting in and out, teasing her as he teased himself, swallowing her moans.

She released his cock from the confines of his jeans, grabbing it tightly and stroking him, and he soon found himself delivering those moans right back to her. She was attacking his senses with every stroke, tug of his dick, with every spasm around the finger buried inside her. She flooded his hand with her cream, and he ached to have his cock where his finger was right now.

She shifted, coming over him, and he leaned back to accommodate her. Straddling his hips, she was able to work his cock harder, faster, and all he could do was growl into her mouth at the sweet pleasure she was giving him and fuck her with his finger faster. He moved his hand so that his thumb could swipe her clit, hoping she'd go off because he was not that far from it himself. He should feel silly that they were masturbating each other like a couple of teenagers in the backseat of some car, but he couldn't seem to make himself stop.

Her pussy squeezed his finger, and his hips jerked up, his cock desperate to feel what his finger was enjoying. She whimpered, rocking against him, and he grabbed her hair, holding her while he fucked her with his finger and rubbed her clit with his thumb with greater intensity. She was close, and that only made her pump him harder.

He broke his lips away from her. "C'mon, baby," he enticed, hoping to throw her over the precipice she dangled on.

She gasped, then yelled, and he covered her mouth with his, swallowing her screams as her pussy convulsed around his finger. Her coming only made her stroke him harder, and he couldn't hold back. She felt too damn good. His cum boiled, his balls tightened. He shot off with a painful frenzy as he roared into her mouth.

She kept stroking him and he kept fingering her until they both came down from the peak of pleasure. Hazy passion clouded his vision, but he could smell the vanilla of her skin and the sex between, and he was wrapped in lust all over again. He wasn't rock hard yet, but the tingling in his spine warned him it was only a matter of time and would be sooner than he thought.

Slowly, they both stopped their ministrations, but he was loath to move his hand from her pants. He caressed her gently as he watched her lift her hand. She sucked a finger into her mouth and he hissed, watching her take his cum into her body.

"Mmm. Yummy."

His cock stirred and his gentle caress of her mound turned naughty when he slipped his middle finger through her folds. "You don't want to start this again so soon. I might not let you leave before dawn."

She looked up at him through her lashes, and for the first time, he felt as if he was in trouble. Serious kinda shit trouble with this woman. Because that look would probably make him crawl around the floor and lick her toes in front of a room full of people if she wanted.

"I'm not done playing," she purred.

Oh hell. Neither was he.

He scooped her up and stalked to his bedroom, needing the space to lay her out and devour her. He set her down by the bed, frantically removing her clothes while she giggled at his single-minded determination. Once she was naked, he shoved off his shoes and socks, pants, and underwear. He zeroed in on her waxed pussy and didn't even bother stifling his sound of appreciation. She was wet, swollen, ready for him. He sat on the bed and turned her to face him. He dipped his head and swiped his tongue along the seam of her sex. She gasped and he moaned at the taste of her.

Her hands trailed through his long hair as she rocked up on her toes to get closer to him. He clutched her buttocks, dragging her flush against his face. He licked, nipped, and sucked at her as if she was the sweetest addiction. And she was. He'd never tasted anything more potent than her. She was a drug, a fix he'd never be able to satisfy, especially when her little sounds of entreaty only fueled him more, drove him higher.

"I love that you're bare for me," he groaned. No hair in the way of his delectable treat. But then a sour thought crossed his mind. Maybe she had done this in the past for another man. That thought had him growling like a damn dog with a bone. Maybe she had before, but never again. She was his treat, and he'd be damned if another man even thought about partaking in it. He knew he had no right thinking like that. It only made him an even bigger prick. But at least he could admit that he was a selfish prick.

"I-I wasn't sure if you'd like it. I don't know what men find attractive."

He eased back, kissing her mound before looking up at her. What had she meant by that? From the look on her face, she seemed unsure, maybe even a little scared, and he hated seeing that in her eyes. He caressed her thighs as he gathered his thoughts. She'd said it had been a while for her, but it was his experience that women said things like that to stroke a man's ego. But he was learning Xan wasn't other women. She'd been tight when they'd had sex, so her inexperience could be genuine. She wasn't a virgin, though. She had the kid to prove it.

A big kid she had to parent on her own. And she'd been on the run for over ten years. She probably was selective with men for those reasons alone. He felt thrilled knowing he'd made it into that exclusive club, and he wanted to ease her worry.

"I can't say what other guys like, but I think it's sexy as hell, and if you hadn't already waxed, I probably would've coerced you into it."

He gave her a crooked smile and her shoulders relaxed. She threaded her hand through his hair, looking down at him with relief, and he got the sudden urge to wrap her in his arms and do nothing but hold her.

He had a better idea.

He stood, gathering her in his arms and laying her on the bed. He grabbed a condom, ripping it open and putting it on before joining her. This time when he took her, he was gentle. He slowly worked himself in, loving the feel of her clasping around his dick. When he was fully seated, he kissed her deeply as he angled her ass for deeper penetration. He pulled back to look into her eyes as he thrust into her, feeling her breath wash across his face with every plunge.

He fucked her with long, slow strokes as she wrapped her legs around his hips, taking him deeper and throwing him into a mindless pleasure like none other.

They continued fucking, caressing, kissing, groping, panting for what seemed like hours. She came several times, but he couldn't hold back on that last one. He squeezed her against him as he exploded, groaning into the crook of her neck as he lost himself to the condom, and part of his soul to her.

He'd never felt like this before, and that realization had him facing reality like the bitch that it was.

He could fuck her over and over again, but he couldn't lose his heart to her, which was exactly what would happen if he continued down this path.

Sex was fine. Sex would be mandatory. But his emotions were off-limits.

CHAPTER NINE

AFTER BRODY and Xan had had the most emotionally connecting sex of her life, she had watched helplessly as he literally closed himself off from her again. It hadn't been as bad as the first time—at least he hadn't thrown her out—but it had been a tangible reaction, even if he'd escorted her outside to the car and kissed her goodbye before she'd left his house last night. She didn't even want to think about his friends hearing them having sex when they'd dropped off the car she'd been driving.

And, thankfully, that incident had turned out to be nothing. Living a life in hiding, she never assumed anything was just a coincidence, but Bear had called Brody and informed him the Mustang had been stolen by a kid who'd taken it out for a joyride. She hadn't been the target, just an obstacle.

Since she didn't have to worry about that event as impending danger, she'd spent the night wondering if she'd made the right decision to become involved with him, knowing he didn't want anything more than some dancing between the sheets. But ultimately, she'd decided she was a grown-ass woman who was tired of denying herself the pleasure of a man. Besides, it'd do her some good to gain the experience. She hadn't been as timid as the first time, but she was still nervous around him last night. Spending time with Brody would help her body and soul. Plus, her vibrator needed a little time off anyway.

Before she'd left for work this morning, Xan had given Scott his video game. He'd been beyond thrilled, throwing words around like, "You're the best mom ever," and, "This is so tight." The first, she'd reveled in. The second, she'd needed remedial help understanding. But he'd been excited and showered her with hugs and kisses. She'd done her good deed with him.

Now she was back home, grateful that it was finally officially the weekend. She only had about fifteen minutes to change out of her scrubs and into something comfortable if she wanted to get a good seat at the game. Well, at least that was what she'd thought. This was a small town. Maybe there wouldn't be a big crowd. She hustled to her bedroom, stripping as she went down the hall since Scott stayed after-school in preparation for tonight's game. She threw on some shorts and a t-shirt with the school's mascot on it that she'd picked up on her lunch break. She was rushing back into the living room, holding her tennis shoes, when the doorbell rang.

She tossed her shoes over by the couch and walked to the door, smoothing her hair as she checked the peephole to see who it was.

Her eyes widened at the gorgeous hunk of man standing in her doorway. She unlocked her door and opened it. Her big, strong Viking was already smiling before she managed to greet him.

"Hi," she breathed, and he smiled wider.

"Hey, baby," he whispered, glancing around her. "Scott home?"

"Nope, he's at school. He's got a game tonight."

"Oh." But his face glowed, showing he wasn't as indifferent as he was trying to be. "Can I come in?"

"Er, sure. Only for a minute, though. I've got to get to the game."

He stepped past her, his hand sliding down the length of her arm and grabbing her hand as he did so. He pulled her behind him, dragging her into the living room. He turned and crushed his mouth down on hers, kissing her passionately, but Xan got the feeling he was holding back. She didn't think that for long because he ripped his mouth from hers, spun her around, and shoved her shorts and panties down her legs. His actions disintegrated any thoughts she had.

He pushed her over the back of the couch, lifting her so her feet dangled just above the floor. She gasped as he grabbed a handful of her hair and yanked her head back, his mouth finding her ear.

"Then we don't have long," he growled, and she felt his hand move between them right before she heard the rasp of a zipper. He bent and surged forward, taking her in one powerful thrust, shoving her harder against the couch. "Fuck, yeah," he said as he pounded into her.

She was stuck, literally. He had her pinned right where he wanted her and all she could do was submit to his demand. She should be scared to feel a man control her like this, but all she could think was *don't stop*.

She tried clutching the cushions to stabilize herself, but with Brody grinding her against the back of the couch as he ruthlessly plowed in and out of her and his hand pulling her head back, she wasn't going anywhere anyway.

"Brody!" She was already coming, hard.

"Fuck, Xan. Like that, baby. Take it!" He grabbed her hip so hard she'd be bruised, and she didn't care. She wanted him to hold her harder, fuck her harder.

He growled then shouted, lifting her off the couch, but keeping her pinned, as he squeezed her breast and flooded her with his cum.

He was panting, easing her back down as she felt his wetness slide down her inner thigh.

"Shit," he breathed, but she didn't need him to explain that. He hadn't worn a condom. "Xan, baby, I'm sorry, I—"

"I know." She extricated herself and went to the bathroom to clean up.

When she returned, he was sitting on the couch, elbows resting on his knees, and his head in his hands. "I don't do that," he mumbled, not looking up at her as she sat down. "Ever."

"Well, as long as you're clean, we're okay. I'm a nurse, so I'm kinda anal about getting tested for everything under the sun. Plus, I got pregnant at a really young age, so I'm on birth control." Technically, she was on birth control to regulate her periods, but that was neither here nor there. As long as she was on it, he probably didn't give a rat's ass why.

He nodded, finally looking at her. "I'm good. *Clean*, I mean." He took a deep breath and picked up her hand, drawing circles on it while he watched. "I actually came here for a reason."

"You mean you didn't come here to maul me?" She chuckled. "I'm hurt."

He laughed and looked at her then. "I have some good news that I wanted to deliver in person."

"Oh yeah?"

"Uh-huh. Your car's ready. Finished it today."

"Yea!" She clapped her hands like a giddy schoolgirl, which probably wasn't attractive, but she didn't care.

He shook his head. "I don't know why you're excited about getting back that piece of shit. It'll probably end up back at the shop next week. You should really think about getting a new car."

"Hey, I resent that. That car has seen me through a lot of years."

"And it's in its golden years now. Time for it to retire."

What could she say? Honestly, she'd love to get a new car. She wasn't picky. She didn't dream about a brand new Lexus or BMW. A nice, shiny Honda would be a dream come true for her. Problem was she didn't like to leave a paper trail, so financing one was out of the question. And she didn't have that kind of money stashed to pay cash.

"I'll be driving that thing 'til the wheels fall off." The truth sucked, but it was what it was. She couldn't spend her time dreaming of a better car. If she was going to dream, it'd be about not having to run again. "When can I pick it up?"

"Tomorrow. You can leave your rental at the shop. Colonel will contact Bill Laverty and tell him to come get it."

"Thanks." She smiled and leaned in to kiss him. She barely touched his lips and he barely caressed her cheek when his phone rang. He moaned as he pulled away and fished it out.

"Brutus," he barked. His displeasure at being interrupted gave her those warm, tingling feelings. His eyes slid to her as he listened to the caller. "Got it." He hung up and looked back at her.

She wasn't sure what to make of that, but she figured it was rude to ask. Though hearing him use his nickname got her to thinking...

"Why Brutus? Why not another name?"

"Umm." His brow shot up as he considered his answer. "I don't know for sure. Colonel picks them out." He shrugged a shoulder as he looked at her.

"You know Brutus was also who the Romans called Marcus Junius Brutus the Younger, the man who led the attack on Julius Caesar. In Shakespeare's play dramatizing the event, he quoted Caesar as saying '*Et tu, Brute?*' upon his death. That phrase basically represents the biggest betrayal."

He laughed, shaking his head. "Nah, Colonel had a dog named Brutus once. Told me it was fiercely loyal."

"Ah, well, I guess that's good then."

"Unless he just liked the idea of naming me after a dog. That could be bad."

She smiled and thought about how to respond, enjoying this little banter between them. But then she jumped when someone pounded on her door, propelling her out of her whimsical musings.

Brody jerked up, grabbing her and pushing her behind him so that he was blocking the door. He stalked over to it and yanked it open before she could even protest. It was her house, damn it.

She heard a female squeak and rushed up beside him.

"Hi, Roxie."

"Hi, Xan," she said, her eyes still wide from the shock of Brody glaring down at her. But she visibly relaxed and even smiled a little. "Brutus," she said with a quirk of her eyebrow. Then she turned back to Xan. "I was headed to the game. Came to see if you wanted a ride. Doesn't make sense for us to take two cars when we're goin' to the same place." She paused. "That is if you're not takin' someone else up on a *ride*."

Xan shut her eyes, faintly shaking her head at her neighbor's innuendo.

"I'll see you tomorrow," Brody said, walking past Roxie and to his truck.

"Well, well, well, from the way your cheeks are turnin' all red, I'd say you already got a ride," Roxie said as Brody pulled out of the driveway and out of sight. "A more thrilling one."

"Gawd, Roxie, can you be any more obvious?"

"Can *you* be any less obvious?" Roxie laughed. "Seriously, if you don't wanna get the town a talkin' you'll tone it down a notch."

Xan sighed. She didn't want to be the latest topic at the corner café. She could just see it now. All the retired folk gathered around shooting the shit, gossiping about Brody and the new single mom. Even though her voice hadn't picked up that little annoying accent yet, apparently, her thoughts had. She almost chuckled at that, then remembered she'd been thinking about what her friend had said about Brody. She probably needed to hide her feelings for him better if she didn't want everyone talking.

Feelings? Where'd that come from? Surely it was just that connection virgins got with the men who'd deflowered them. Granted, she hadn't been a virgin, but she was smart enough to know a bond could be forged because he'd broken her dry spell. Her very long dry spell. Shrugging off that train of thought, she turned to her nosy neighbor. "Yeah, I'll take that ride."

She grabbed her purse and hopped in the car with Roxie. The ride didn't take very long since everything was within a couple of miles of everything else in this town, but parking had been a nightmare. The lot was small and it seemed everyone and their dogs—yes, actual dogs—were here to see the game. She'd credited it to the lack of entertainment within a fifteen-mile radius.

They paid for their tickets, but she couldn't figure out why they were actually selling tickets. Seemed like a waste of a tree to her since the man who took the money and gave the ticket took it right back. They stopped at the concession stand to get some sodas and popcorn and made it to their seats right at kickoff.

"What number's Chad?" Xan asked, munching on her snack.

"Thirty. Scott?"

"Seventeen. What position does your boy play?"

Roxie laughed. "What position *doesn't* he play? This is a little bitty school, girl. Our boys will be on the field all night, playin' offense and defense. Even their pride and joy quarterback is also the kicker. It's funny to watch him switch shoes on the field."

"I'm not sure if the coach will put Scott in. He said something about Scott having to prove himself first."

"Oh, he'll get to play. He might even regret it."

She'd been right, Xan thought by halftime. After the opening kickoff, Scott was thrown in, and by now those kids looked exhausted and still had half a game left to play. It'd go easier on them if it wasn't so freaking hot out here. It should be a sin to be over ninety degrees during football season. At least they were up by ten, and the game had been exciting to watch.

Not that she got to watch much of it. Roxie talked her ear off and introduced her to everyone in town that was in yelling range of her. It'd been embarrassing at first, but after the first seven or eight times it happened, Xan had started to get used to the attention.

In fact, there were a lot of men sitting around her,

groups of them, and she hadn't freaked out. Interesting. She couldn't remember the last time she'd been around a bunch of men she hadn't met before and didn't feel anxious, or even downright sick.

With the exception of her skin about to melt right off her bones sitting on metal bleachers under the blazing sun, she felt almost fine. She was aware of all the men and felt the need to keep her guard up, but she didn't feel a panic attack building. Major progress.

"Ooooh, look. There's Blade and Hunter," Roxie said. "Yoohoo!" She stood and wiggled her fingers at them. They were sitting at the top of the bleachers. She sat back down, looking around. "Wonder where Teddy is?" she mumbled, but didn't sound as excited about the prospect of seeing Bear.

"Not sure. Maybe he's off with the other guys." Xan considered Roxie for a moment, thinking even more that something was either up between her new friend and the bald mechanic or Roxie wished it.

"So I was thinking," Roxie said, pulling her out of her reverie. "I know I mentioned something to you about going to a bar. I wanna have a girls' night tomorrow night. We can go to Hank's Honkytonk. It'd be a blast!" Roxie's eyes were bright and Xan wanted to cringe. She was almost patting herself on her back for not running and screaming from all the men around them and these men weren't focusing on her. If she went to some meat market, it'd be a totally different story.

"I-I don't think so." She shook her head, picking up her soda and drinking thirstily.

"Why?" Roxie's lower lip actually fell into a pout, but then her eyes narrowed. "Is it because of Brutus? You still haven't told me what happened with him. Did he let you play find the sausage?" She laughed, and Xan had to cover her mouth to keep from spewing her Dr. Pepper.

"You're crazy," she said, chuckling. "He came by to tell me my car was ready. I told you that already."

"You're no fun." She harrumphed. "But come out with me tomorrow night, and I'll make sure you have the time of your life."

"I'll pass," Xan said, turning to watch the game, thankful it was starting back up.

She already had one man she didn't fully understand. She could do without a horde of them falling drunk all over her.

———

BRODY STARED at his computer screen, researching the agents Gauge had found who'd worked Xan's case back in the day. Jack Parsons had been a model employee, excelling on all his reports. He'd worried it was a sign of overachievement to cover the star agent's dirty work, but he was a pessimist and couldn't find anything to even hint at the agent being the mole. Jack Parsons had been a bust, but Brody was actually a little relieved by this. He hated the idea of her current agent being on the take.

Dave Simmons, on the other hand, was shady. He'd been her first agent after Collins got sent away to prison, and after much digging, Brody found out that the guy had actually put her and Scott in Prairie County, Arkansas for her first move. Besides that being a little funny, considering she wasn't much of a country girl, it seemed odd since that was where Agent Simmons was originally from. He'd resigned a couple of years after placing her there, retiring to a farm in none other than Prairie County,

Arkansas. Why put his ward someplace where she could be connected to him? That was only one question. His other question was why did the guy's bank account show a $250,000 deposit two weeks before his retirement? Those two things put the guy on Brody's short list of suspects.

He kept researching the names of guys assigned to her. There'd been ten of them at one time. He'd found enough information on Charlie Bevin, Ezekiel Ramon, Adam Perry, William Bowers, Brian Warner, Mike Shannon, and Henry Walker to feel confident that they'd had nothing to do with Collins finding out about Xan turning evidence. Those guys had either initiated or led major arrests in similar cases and were either now politicians with strong platforms against crime, retired after more years of service, or supervised departments. Of course, arresting members of other crime families could've been a smoke screen, a diversion while working for Collins, but none of those guys had any suspicious money in their accounts or any other links to Collins.

Jeff Coleman, Luke Riley, and Paul Sellers, on the other hand, warranted a deeper investigation. Brody couldn't find any information on any of these guys since Collins' attempt on Xan's life. Realizing he needed help, he pulled out his cell and hit Gauge's number.

"Yeah?" he answered.

"Hey, man. I'm going over these guys you told me about and need some help. I got three targets I can't nail down. Can you see what you can find?"

"No problem. Names?"

"Jeff Coleman, Luke Riley, and Paul Sellers."

There was a brief pause of silence, and Brody assumed it was because Gauge was writing down the info.

"What about the others?"

"They check out. At least enough for me. What about you? Find anything questionable on any of them?"

"Nope. So far, they're clean, but I hadn't got to the three you named or Charlie Bevin and Adam Perry."

"Bevin's a town mayor and Perry heads up the child pornography division at the FBI. I think they're clean. Let's look at these other three."

"You got it. Oh, before I forget," Gauge said suddenly. "Mimi Rochelle stopped by the shop after you left. Said she needed help with her garbage disposal. Wanted *you* to do it." He chuckled.

Brody sighed. "I'll take a look at it tomorrow."

"Be nice to her, man. She's lonely," Gauge chided.

She wasn't lonely. She was a loner. Big difference. She'd come to terms with her husband's death several years ago. "Yeah, yeah. I'll catch ya later."

Brody hung up and stalked to his kitchen for a beer. He didn't have time to fool with a garbage disposal. He had to find those other three missing agents.

And maybe squeeze in a visit to Former Agent Dave Simmons in Prairie County, Arkansas.

CHAPTER TEN

Xan awoke to the sounds of birds chirping and the sun shining through the cracks of her window blinds. She wasn't much of a morning person, but she felt lighter than she had in years. She rolled over, stretching her lazy body and looked dreamily at the clock.

Noon? She jerked into a sitting position. Shit, no wonder she felt good. She'd slept for twelve hours.

She hopped out of the bed, grabbing her robe and rushing to the bathroom. Her car was ready, so she wanted to make sure she looked perfect when she picked it up.

Because she'd get to see Brody. She wasn't in denial as to why she wanted to look good.

She took a quick shower, scrubbing her body, shaving her legs and washing her hair, then threw on her robe and began her search for the perfect outfit. Skirt? No, too obvious. Jeans? Too dang hot. Capris? Too soccer momish. Shorty slut-girl shorts? Hmmm, just right. She paired it with a lightweight, fitted tee to tone down the effect and some comfy sandals. She dried her hair, fixing it just right, hoping the humidity wouldn't demolish all her hard work, and put on some makeup, praying she wouldn't sweat it off before she got there.

She walked down the hall, hearing Scott playing his new video game. She knocked on his door and opened it when he called out.

"Hey, I'm going to pick up the car. You want anything while I'm out?"

"No, I'm straight."

Huh? That was out of nowhere. What did his sexual orientation have to do with anything? She'd already figured out he was straight because he had a girlfriend. Maybe he was overcompensating and wasn't really into girls? She gave him a puzzled look while he concentrated on his game, thinking she needed to have a mother-son moment. "Sweetheart," she whispered, stepping into his room. "I hope you know it wouldn't matter to me if you were gay, though I'm pleased you feel comfortable talking to me about your sexual preference." She paused, waving her finger. "But you're too young to have sex, regardless if it's with a girl or another guy."

Scott's head shot up. "What are you talking about, Mom? I'm not gay. What made you think to ask me that?"

Her brow furrowed. "You just blurted you were straight for no reason, Scott."

He busted out laughing. "You're such a dork, Mom. That means I'm fine."

"Oh," she muttered, feeling a blush tinge her cheeks. "Okay, well, I'm off." No reason to stand around and be the butt of a teenage joke. No doubt he'd be laughing about this with Chad later.

She made her exit and got into her rental, humming to herself as she drove the short distance to the garage. When she arrived, she parked the car next to the overhead doors, noticing Brody's Harley parked under a tree, and got out. Clutching her purse, she strode into the lobby and looked around. She heard the sounds of hydraulic lifts and those air gun thingies she'd seen on NASCAR when the cars were in the pits getting their tires changed. There was also some rock music blaring in the background, someone else she'd never heard of, reminding her of her ride in Brody's truck, making her smile.

She hoped she didn't look too obvious as she scoped out the place, searching for her Viking, but when her eyes connected to Roc's, she quickly jerked away. She didn't know what it was about him, but he made her feel uneasy. She chanced another look at the bays, seeing him walk her way.

Shit.

She took a deep breath and squared her shoulders as he neared.

He stepped up to her, handing her an envelope, which jingled. She opened it and glanced inside. It was an invoice and her keys. Her heart sank as she looked up at him, wondering why he was tending to her and not Brody.

"What was wrong with it?" she asked, staring him straight in the eye. She wouldn't let him see her disappointment.

"Radiator. Among many other things. It's all in the invoice."

She nodded, holding out the rental keys. "Here. Bro—er—Brutus said I could just leave the rental here."

He took the keys and nodded. He stared coldly at her, but then his lips turned into a sneer. "I'll take 'em. Brody's over at Mimi's."

"Mimi?" she breathed, not meaning to, but trying to process the words he'd said.

"Yeah, he goes over there a lot, though I don't think he's been over much since you hit town. Mimi must've noticed the coincidence because she came up here yesterday while he was giving you the news 'bout your car. She left word for him, and he went running over." Roc shoved his hands in his pockets and rocked back on his heels, giving her an evil smile. "He left this morning and ain't been back."

She'd only thought her heart sank earlier. Now it plummeted. Her too-snug shorts made her feel naked in front of this jerk who was obviously trying to get a rise out of her. She had difficulty breathing, but inhaled through her nose to keep her head from spinning.

"Okay, well, if I have any problems I'll let you know."

He was over at Mimi's? Been there all morning? That only meant one thing, and she refused to think about that. She didn't need to be hit over the head to realize he was fucking that skank. It wasn't as if they were exclusive, though she was. Brody was only the second man she'd ever had sex with, and she'd married the first one and gone twelve years since letting the other one have a crack at her.

He was over at Mimi's? She stewed on her way to her car. At least the son of a bitch had it washed. She opened the door and climbed in, realizing the inside was spotless too. It didn't look like a brand-new car, but it looked better than it had in the ten years she'd had it.

He. Was. Over. At. Mimi's. She would not ask Roxie where that skank-whore lived. She drove back home, ignoring how smooth her car drove, fighting the...what? Tears? Anger?

Jealousy. That's what she was fighting. You know what? Fine. He didn't want to be exclusive, then two could play that game.

She didn't need to be jealous of some skank-whore-bitch

sinking her claws into that man. There were plenty of other men in this state. It wasn't as if Xan wasn't attractive. She was fit with highlighted blonde hair and blue eyes. Some might even consider her a catch.

She pulled into her driveway and stalked over to Roxie's house, pounding on the door. Her neighbor opened it immediately.

"Hey, girl. Everything all right?"

"You still going out tonight?" she asked in a terse voice.

Roxie's immediate smile glowed. "Sure are. You comin'?"

"Yeah, count me in." It was time she let some men go fishing. Maybe the next one who caught her would appreciate the catch that she was.

———

AFTER GETTING out of the shower for the second time today, Xan found herself staring at her clothes—the ones she ran out and bought after talking to Roxie. This time, she wouldn't be toning down anything. Short leather skirt? Oh yeah. Knee-high stiletto boots? *Come to momma.* The tight-ass, see-though, nude-color lacy tank top paired with her black demi-bra was just whorish enough to complete the ensemble. She curled her hair and loosely pulled it up, leaving wispy hairs everywhere that accented her big hoop earrings. She gave her eyes a smoky look, making the blue color stand out, and finished up with some shiny gloss.

Taking one last look at herself in the mirror, she smiled, squeezing her breasts. "I know it's been a while since I've taken you out on the town," she murmured. "But we're having some fun tonight, girls. Make me proud." Sometimes, it was great being a woman.

She walked out and grabbed her purse, silently thanking the fact that Scott wasn't home. He'd made plans to stay the night with Chad after they went out with their girlfriends, and he'd left before she'd hopped into the shower. She was not ashamed by the way she was dressed, but there were just some things a boy shouldn't see. His mom dressed like a hooker probably came in second on that list, right after seeing his mom have sex.

Xan jumped when her phone rang. She knew Roxie was coming over here, so she knew it wouldn't be her calling. Xan looked at the number and frowned. It was unknown. She didn't want to take the risk of it being Brody but knew she didn't have a choice but to answer it. It could be her son calling from someplace.

"Hello?"

"Hi, Ms. Bradley. It's Agent Jack Parsons."

She sighed, her hand lifting to her heart and feeling it pound widely in relief at her not having to confront Brody right now. She chuckled at her silly reaction. "I've told you to call me Xan. I really like it, and as many times as my name has changed, that's saying a lot."

He laughed too, so that was a good sign. "*Xan*. Um, I just wanted to check up on you and give you an update."

"Oh, well, I'm good. I had a minor panic attack after the news of Marco's release, but Scott stepped up to the plate and calmed me down. Oh, and some hoodlum tried to run me over, but other than that, I'm good." *Besides the Viking asshole who fucked me and then fucked me over.* Though Xan was pretty sure that wasn't what Jack had been asking about.

"Yes, I'd heard about that, and I'm glad you're okay. As for Marco Collins, your feelings are to be expected." He cleared his throat. "Speaking of him, he showed up in

Michigan and reunited with his father, which was what we had anticipated. He hasn't made a move yet, but I want you to know you're covered. We've got people watching you."

"I don't suppose you'll tell me which FBI agents are watching me?"

She heard a gasp and whirled, seeing Roxie stare at her in disbelief. *Shit, shit, shit.* How the hell had she gotten in? *Scott.* After all these years, the boy should know better than to leave a door unlocked. But right now was not the time to dwell on what a teenager should or shouldn't be doing.

"You know I can't do that, Xan." But she barely heard him over the blood rushing in her ears. How much had Roxie heard?

As Xan watched her, she knew the answer to that. *Enough.* Roxie had heard enough. This was a big clusterfuck.

"Look, Jack. I gotta go. I'll talk to you later."

"Is everything okay?" he asked suddenly. The agent had a nose for danger, but the only danger now was to her cover, and to a woman known to enjoy a little gossip.

"I'm good. If not, I'll let you know." She hung up without letting him needle her. It wasn't as if she could explain what was going on with Roxie standing ten feet from her listening to every word uttered.

She put her phone in her handbag and leveled a stare at Roxie, who was uncharacteristically quiet. Xan could play this one of two ways—she could confront Roxie about the phone call or pretend she hadn't heard anything.

Yeah, Xan liked the second option best. "What? No comment on my threads?" She did her best Vanna impression, waving her hands in front of her body. "The outfit's new."

That seemed to snap Roxie back to the present and out

of her thoughts. "Oh, you look hot as hell, girl." She stepped forward hesitantly. "W-what was that phone call about?"

So much for pretense. She sighed, dropping her hands. "It's a long story. One I'll tell you about after I get some drinks in me." And after she came up with a plan to say just enough to pacify without divulging everything.

"Okay." Roxie still didn't seem too convinced, but she turned and headed for the door. Once outside, they got into her car and Xan buckled up.

"Where is this place anyway?"

"Pulaski County, just before you hit Faulkner County. It's a big club that people drive for miles to come to."

Roxie had called it a honkytonk, but Xan didn't know the first thing about country music. That didn't matter. As long as she got plenty of alcohol in her, she could damn near tolerate anything.

"You look hot too, by the way," she said suddenly, realizing she hadn't commented on her friend's sexy outfit.

Roxie giggled. "Thanks. I might have to cut this dress off me tonight. Gettin' it on was a feat!" Instead of hitting the interstate, Roxie pulled down a dirt road. "Anna Sue's coming too," she explained when Xan gave her a puzzled look.

"Oh, okay." They picked up the other gal and headed to the bar. Anna Sue talked so much that Xan figured she should've gotten her buzz on before leaving the house. The chick talked about everyone. Hmm, gossiping seemed to be a favorite pastime around here.

They parked on the gravel lot and walked up to the bar, Xan being careful not to mar her new stilettos. When the door opened, she was immediately assaulted with twang blaring from the speakers and a chorus of *yeehaws* from some of the patrons.

"Don't look so scared, girl," Roxie said. "They're just hootin' and hollerin' in there. Someone's probably on the bull."

On the bull? Was that some Southern slang metaphor for something? Same thing as *drunk* maybe? Surely there wasn't a live bull in the building. That would just be ridiculous.

When they walked farther in, Xan paled. Nope. It was worse than a live bull stinking up the joint. There was a mechanical bull in the corner with some crazy drunk chick grinding on it, riding it in slow motion.

"That looks like fun!" Anna Sue bellowed. "I'm gonna get me a drink an' get in line. See you gals later."

"In line? You mean people choose to do that?" Xan shoved her thumb in the direction of the mechanical monstrosity, sporting an incredulous look on her face. The damn thing didn't even look like a bull. "I figured that was just some form of punishment for people who lose some kinda bet."

Roxie laughed. "Oh no, girl. The fellas get on it to outdo each other." She waggled her eyebrows, nudging Xan's side with her elbow. "And the ladies get on it to rev up the guys."

"I'll pass. I'd rather do karaoke and I can't carry a tune in a bucket," Xan said, stepping away and heading to the closest bar. She needed that drink...like yesterday. At least there were three bars set up in this place. Roxie followed, and they both ordered their drinks while Xan took in her surroundings.

This place looked like a cross between some hunting club's rejects and a NASCAR shrine. She enjoyed watching the sport from time to time, but the mixture of dead animals mounted everywhere with posters of race cars seemed odd. But that wasn't all. There were lassos and cowboy hats hanging haphazardly on some of the mounts, really confusing whatever motif the owner of this place was going for.

"Let's grab a table." Roxie walked to the side, over by the dance floor. "Oh, this is perfect," she squealed, and practically jogged in her heels the last few steps. Roxie and Anna Sue seemed much more excited about this little adventure than Xan did.

Maybe it's because you'd rather be getting your groove on with your sexy Viking? Too bad he was too busy boinking that skank-whore-bitch Mimi. Xan might be just now reacquainting herself with this whole new sex life thing, but one thing was for certain—she didn't do sloppy seconds. If that maddening man wanted to play the field, then she was bowing out of his game. She'd find another field to play on. If parts of her body protested that idea, she ignored them.

She bit back a sigh when she sat down, finding her inner strength with a sip of her liquid courage, hoping her inner bitch would stay hidden. She didn't want to hide behind that persona when guys started hitting on her. She needed to embrace the attention and enjoy this night on the town. But there was a fine line between inner strength and inner bitch.

Oh Jesus, people where sashaying and kicking their boots in some kind of ritualistic dance. It was like the Stepford Wives on Wild Turkey.

She downed her drink and waved the waitress over, promptly ordering another.

"You wanna dance?" Roxie perked up.

"Not yet." She needed to be on her third drink to even consider it.

"Okay." Roxie slumped in her seat and ordered another drink. They talked about some of the things people were wearing to pass the time and visited with Anna Sue when she came up for air from the dance floor. When their third drinks arrived, Roxie leaned in to Xan. "You gonna tell me what that phone call was about? You were talkin' about the FBI. I heard you. Don't deny it."

Oh shit, she hadn't been thinking of an excuse. "Um, well, I can't really go into the details, but I'm under their protection. My ex-husband tried to kill me."

"What? That's horrible!"

"Yeah." But that wasn't even the half of it.

"So you have some agents watchin' you now?" She turned around, scanning the bar. "Do you know who they are?"

"Yes, I have people looking out for me. No, I don't know who they are." She sighed, really regretting telling her this much. Not that she didn't trust Roxie, but Xan had been a very private person. Until now. "Look, Roxie, you can't tell anybody this."

She waved her hand dismissively as she took another swig of her drink. "Don't even mention that, girl. I may like my town gossip, but I'd never divulge anything serious." She waved over the waitress for another drink, and Xan looked at her glass. When had she finished her third drink? The tingling sensation in her toes told her she'd better slow down. "You want another?" Roxie asked when the waitress neared.

"Sure." Why not? She'd slow down another time.

Well into their fourth drinks, Roxie nudged Xan's arm. "How 'bout now? Dancing's really fun," she crooned with a little slur.

Xan nodded and started to stand, and Roxie giggled, clapping her hands as she hopped up. They made their way to the dance floor though the throngs of people. Where'd they all come from?

"Okay. I'll show you how it goes."

Oh good Lord. She thought she could just come out here and groove to the music, but Roxie was going to make her do this tribal mating dance.

"Step, cross, step, turn, stomp your boots, shake your ass, turn, and start over."

They jumped in at the stomp your boots part, but Xan forgot to shake her ass.

"No, it goes stomp, stomp, stomp, shake, shake, shake, *then* turn."

God forbid she got this stupid shit wrong. She giggled at her manic thought—probably fueled by the amount of alcohol she'd consumed—and renewed her efforts.

They'd repeated the steps about three times when everyone yelled, "Yeehaw" in unison.

"What the fuck?" She jumped at the sudden shouting. Was that their mating battle cry?

Roxie guffawed when she jumped. "They say yeehaw at the main chorus. Don't worry, you can feel when it comes."

She could feel it? Was that some kind of country girl premonition? She ignored her sarcasm and tried to lose herself in the rhythm. Mating dance or not, she was starting to have fun, even if she noticed a few men gawking at her.

By the second yeehaw, she jumped in and shouted with the rest of the crowd, laughing and loving the freedom. She shook her ass and stomped her feet with the best of them, and after the last time she yelled yeehaw, she was completely gone.

"I love this country shit!" she hollered, throwing her hands in the air and giving her ass a bigger shake as the song ended.

"Girl, that was fire," Roxie said, tossing her arm over Xan's shoulder. "Let's get some liquid."

They walked to the bar and grabbed a couple of other drinks before going back to their table. Anna Sue joined them while they laughed and tried sipping at their drinks, rather than downing them like they all wanted to.

But now, Xan was fighting off dance offers from every single man around her. It was easier than she thought it'd be, but it only made her a little sad she wasn't with Brody, which immediately pissed her off. She wouldn't let thoughts of him ruin her fun. Maybe she'd take up the next offer that came her way.

"You ladies see who walked in?" Anna Sue asked, looking over her shoulder. Xan looked around, searching the room, then gasped. "Looks like the three bees of the hive swarmed in for some honey. Bear, Brutus, and Blade."

Well, son of a bitch. Seeing Brody made Xan's blood boil. What? That asshole hadn't gotten enough tail yet? He needed to prowl for more pussy? If she felt used before, she felt downright sick now. What did she expect, really? He seemed to follow the advice of his little head. Men fucking sucked.

She was about to voice that out loud, turning and fuming, when she caught sight of Roxie's expression, stopping her cold. She looked crushed. Very crushed.

Xan inhaled slowly, tamping down her anger and mentally telling herself to ignore the blond asshole who'd just walked in. Her new friend seemed to need something. Consoling? Hell, she didn't know. She hadn't had a friend since before she got married. Anna Sue hadn't noticed. After announcing the guys' arrival, she tried waving down a waitress. When that didn't work, she said she was going to get another drink and headed to one of the bars.

"What is it?" Xan asked, reaching over and touching Roxie's arm.

She sighed, looking defeated. "It's nothing."

"That's bullshit, Roxie. Something's wrong. You went from giggling to moping as soon as those guys walked in."

Roxie stared at her for a while, indecision evident in her heavily made-up eyes. Then she nodded slowly. "Okay. You told me about the FBI stuff, so I'll tell you what happened. You just can't repeat it, okay?"

Xan nodded, rubbing her arm in encouragement. "Of course I won't."

"It's about me and Teddy. You know? Bear. Well, I used to flirt with him all the time, but hell, I flirt with a lot of guys, so he didn't think much of it. Nor did he reciprocate." She hesitated and glanced over her shoulder to the guys. Xan refused to follow her gaze for fear of seeing Brody.

"But he wasn't just one of the guys to you?" she guessed.

"No," Roxie breathed. "I liked him. A lot. Then one night we ran into each other up here. He'd been pretty drunk, but he was flirting with me, asked me to dance, bought me my drinks. It was great." She shrugged and looked down. "I followed him to his house afterward, and we screwed like bunnies."

Xan's eyes got wide. "Oh, wow. Okay, so far that doesn't sound so bad. What happened after that?"

Roxie took a sip of her drink and then looked at Xan. "After many rounds, we both passed out. A few hours later, I woke up because he was hanging all over me, snoring in my ear. I figured I should head home since I was awake, you know, and he didn't actually invite me to stay the night.

"The next day, I didn't hear from him, so I figured he was so drunk he forgot, but then that night, I got a bouquet of flowers—not roses—with a note asking why I'd left. I was tickled he acted like he missed me, so the next day, I went up to the garage. He walked over to me, and I, ugh, I smiled up at him, waiting for him to take me into his arms, wanting to rub my hands all over his bald head. But he just stood there, looking at me like he always did. Like I was some annoying townsperson he didn't know how to talk to. He never once brought up our night or the flowers, so I made up some lame-ass excuse about my check engine light and got the hell outta Dodge. We've both pretended that night never existed ever since."

"Oh God, Roxie, that's horrible. I'm so sorry."

"Yeah, thanks. Anywho, My cousin, Flint, had been at the bar that night. He and Teddy used to be the best of buds, but they had some falling out shortly after...and it seemed to make Teddy more distant. Like, he secretly blames me for ruining his friendship with my cousin. Doesn't help Flint is the sheriff 'round here. Who knows? It's not like I could go up and ask Teddy what his deal is." Roxie shrugged. "All in the past now."

What was it with men? Where they all a bunch of ogres who needed lessons in how to communicate with women?

Unable to resist any longer, Xan turned and glared at Bear, feeling offended for her friend. Only her gaze landed somewhere else.

And boy did Brody looked pissed.

CHAPTER ELEVEN

WHAT IN GOD'S name was Xan doing here dressed as if she was ready to break every heart in this damn place? It took every ounce of willpower not to stomp over there, yank her up, take her back to his place, and fuck her until she remembered who she belonged to. If one more motherfucker put his hands on her, Brody was going to go ape-shit crazy.

He'd missed her when she came to get her car today because he was helping Mimi with her garbage disposal. He hadn't wanted to do it, but the old lady reminded him of a grandma he never had, or didn't remember having anyway. The poor widow had taken him under her wing after her husband had died, and he allowed it, which didn't really jibe with his usual loner lifestyle, but he couldn't turn the lady down. Knowing Xan was being covered by Gauge, he did the Good Samaritan thing only to find out from his colleague that his ward had blown out of her house dressed like a vixen with an agenda.

He didn't believe it. Not until he walked into this bar and saw her. And see her, he did. Through the heavy crowd, he noticed her right away.

So did his dick.

He got instantly hard, seeing her milky thighs hanging out of that fucking short-ass leather skirt. He only had a partial view of her, seeing only her back and side, and if her shirt was as see-through as what he'd seen so far, he might just come in his damn jeans. And those boots? Jesus, was she trying to emasculate him right in front of his buddies? Because he could very easily fall to his feet in front of her if she'd let him lick those damn things. He bit back a groan, then caught Blade's amused expression.

"What?" he barked.

Blade laughed and Bear motioned for the waitress, trying not to get involved. Smart man. "She's fuckin' hot, and you have a hard-on for her." It was an expression. Only Blade didn't know how true it was at the moment.

"You don't worry about how hot she is. You got that?" He shoved his finger in Blade's chest.

"Chill, bro." He threw his hands up and leaned away. "It ain't me you gotta worry about." He hated being this obvious about her, but right now he just couldn't seem to find a reason to give a shit. Let his buddies know. Hell, he was about ready to inform every person with a dick in this room she was taken.

"He's right, Brutus," Bear said. "You like her. That's cool with us, but maybe you should clarify that with her."

He thought he did, damn it. But then after that mind-blowing sex the other day, he'd closed himself off from her. And yesterday, he'd gone to her house and fucked her like a man possessed, but had kept his emotions under a tight leash. If she was pissed about that, tough shit. He'd have to continue keeping his feelings under wraps. He wasn't sure what would happen if he let them loose. He couldn't chance it, though. There was still some kind of history between them, so he had to be careful with her from here on out, but he'd give her what he could. It would have to be enough for her.

"I'll make sure she understands how things are gonna be," he muttered, taking a long pull of his beer.

Blade looked over at the girls' table and winced. "Dude, she must be talkin' shit because even Roxie won't look over here. You know it's bad when a natural flirt won't give you the time of day."

Bear cleared his throat, and Brody noticed how uncomfortable his friend suddenly looked. There was definitely something going on with Bear and Roxie. If not, Bear acted as if he wanted there to be. He could ask, but if Bear wanted to talk about it, he would. Besides, he hated it when he was questioned about stuff he didn't want to talk about. He'd spare Bear that treatment.

"Not that I don't enjoy hangin' out with you two nutheads, but I'm going to find me a lovely lady to spend the evening with, and with any luck, I might get to buy her breakfast when I'm finished with her," Blade said as he got up and headed to the dance floor.

As Brody watched him escape, his eyes traveled back over to Xan's table. *Well, I'll be a son of a bitch.* Some scrawny little jackass in Wranglers and a Stetson was pulling her up out of her chair, guiding her to the dance floor.

He shot to his feet, but Bear grabbed his arm. "Hold up there, hoss. I know that look in your eye, and you can't snatch up that little weasel."

Brody turned slowly. He didn't want to knock out his friend, but he was this close to hitting somebody. "Let. Go."

Bear studied him for a few seconds then sighed, shaking his head and letting go of Brody's arm. "All right."

He stalked to the dance floor, not hearing the people who tried chatting with him. He was on a mission, and if he didn't get over there fast—*damn it*. He was seeing red. He was going to kill that fucking little weasel. He'd just grabbed her ass.

His ass. His. She was his. Yeah, he knew that made him the biggest hypocrite, but he didn't care. Not one iota.

He reached them, grabbed the dude's arm, and yanked it off her body, staring down at him, trying like hell not to break it.

"Brody! What the hell are you doing?" Xan demanded.

The weasel tried removing his arm from Brody's grasp, and when he didn't have any luck, he squared his shoulders and tried to stare down Brody. He had to give the twerp some credit, seeing that the guy had to look up several inches to stare at him. Brody narrowed his eyes and lowered his head, still leaving several inches between them. "Get lost."

The guy blanched and nodded, and Brody let him go, watching him stumble as he fled.

"Real fucking nice!" Xan barked, turning on her heel.

He grabbed her waist and slammed her back into his chest. He felt her gasp at the sudden movement, but he just lowered his head to her ear. "Care to tell me what you're doing out here, looking like this, I might add?" he asked softly, but his anger was barely banked.

"I was trying to have fun," she sneered.

He growled, clutching her hips tighter as she tried to wiggle away. *Have fun?* "Wrong answer." He wrapped one arm around her abdomen and the other above her breasts, keeping her from going anywhere. "Try again."

"Where the hell do you get off?"

"In your pussy or your mouth. Keep this up, and tonight it'll be in your ass after I spank it."

"Ugh! That's not what I meant, you egotistical asshole." She turned her head to the side, looking up at him, staring daggers. "Go find your *other* little playthang. I'm through with you."

What the hell did that mean? He hadn't had sex with another person since her ass twitched into town. Hell, he'd tried going out and getting laid the night he met her and couldn't do it.

"Excuse me, ma'am. Is this man bothering you?"

Brody's head snapped up to see another Wranglers-wearing punk step over to them. Only this guy was bigger, an actual challenge.

"Fuck off," Brody snapped.

"Yes," Xan said at the same time.

The other man stood straighter, crossing his arms. "Let her go, man."

Brody narrowed his eyes at the dark-haired giant, not recognizing him, which wasn't unusual at this place since people came from all around. Squeezing her tighter, he lowered his head to whisper in Xan's ear, but not taking his eyes off the man standing before them. "You be a good little girl and tell this man to leave us alone, or I'm going to beat the shit out of him," he said loud enough for the guy to hear, then lowered his voice, keeping his next sentence for Xan's ears only. "Your ass is mine tonight."

She huffed, a cute little growl that would've had him chuckling under different circumstances. "Fine," she gritted out, then stared at their guest. "I'm fine. Thanks for your concern."

"You're sure?" he asked, stepping closer, pissing Brody off.

He let go of Xan and pushed her behind him, keeping a hand wrapped around her wrist. "Get the fuck out of my face."

Instantly, Blade and Bear were at his side. "You heard the man. There's nothing to be concerned about here," Bear said a little more diplomatically.

Fuck diplomacy. That prick was going to leave this second on his feet or on his back. Brody wasn't going to tolerate a man coming between him and his woman. Yeah, it was a primal reaction. So fucking what?

Xan sighed, and he turned to the side, looking at her. "Can I have a word with you?"

Her request had the intruder nodding in understanding and stepping away. Once he was gone, Blade and Bear retreated as well.

She crossed her arms and glared at him, and damn if that didn't make his dick hard all over again. She was the sexiest thing he'd ever seen dressed like his own personal wet dream. Her anger was icing on that cake. He preferred women with a little spunk because they were more of a challenge. But thinking back on his sexual history left him feeling a little cold. Xan was timid at first, and he'd tried fighting his attraction to her then, making her a challenge to him even when she wasn't trying to be. What was it about this woman that called to him, making thoughts of other women lacking in the worst way?

"Because I let you fuck me doesn't give you the right to go all caveman on me."

He crossed his arms, hiding a smile because he kind of liked the caveman reference. "I disagree."

"Okay, well, after you spent all damn day with another woman, you lost whatever right you thought you had."

Oh shit, was that hurt that flashed in her eyes? It was so

quick, he couldn't be sure. But hell, he didn't want to be the cause of her being upset, for any reason. He relaxed his arms, letting them fall to his sides and took a step toward her. "It's not what you think," he said softly.

She laughed bitterly. "Oh, it never is. You know, I lived with an abusive man who fucked every woman he wanted, treating me like utter shit in the process. I won't go through that again."

Brody could see the walls she was erecting, so he had to do something fast before she walled herself completely off from him. He stepped closer and hesitantly stroked her cheek. "Mimi is a sixty-year-old retired school teacher who lost her husband about five years ago. After I did some work on her car, she kept returning for me to fix minor things. Then she started calling me to fix other stuff besides her car. I understood what it felt like being alone, so I couldn't tell her no. I guess I don't really give it much thought anymore." He hesitated when he saw her slouch. "I didn't think about how you'd misinterpret that."

She narrowed her eyes and shoved a finger in his chest. "I didn't misinterpret a damn thing. Your buddy led me to believe you were fucking her."

Brody's eyes got big. Then his jaw ticked, unable to hide the irritation building inside him. "Who?"

"That guy Roc."

Brody was going to kill him. "What did he say?"

"That you were over at Mimi's." She frowned and shook her head. "It wasn't so much what he said, but how he said it."

He knew Roc could be an ass, but Brody wasn't sure what to make of this. He felt fury boiling inside him and tamped it down. He had damage control to contend with right now. Roc could be dealt with later.

He *would* be dealt with later.

"Is that why you came out in search of a new man?"

She shook her head, but the flush of her cheeks and her eyes betrayed her. "Roxie asked me the other day to come out with her, then brought it up again last night at the game. Since Scott's staying at a friend's tonight, I figured I'd hit the town."

He stepped up against her, pulling her into his arms and lowering his head. "You look so fucking hot, it's making me crazy." That and the vanilla-flavored sex scent seeping out of her pores.

Xan lifted her head to say something, but then burst out laughing. "They're playing a rap song in a country bar?"

Brody half-smiled at her, loving the glow in her eyes now. "Who said this was a country bar?"

"Um, society? If it walks like a duck and quacks like a duck..." She lifted one shoulder.

"Oh, well, let me educate you," he murmured, pulling her head back to his chest. "This place plays all kinds of music. Every forty-five minutes there's fifteen minutes of rock or rap or pop. Most people around here like all kinds of music."

She made this sexy little acknowledging sound in the back of her throat, and his dick throbbed.

She seemed to notice that because she rubbed her belly against it. He groaned and held her tighter, unable to stop himself from grinding up against her. God, she felt so good. He couldn't wait to have her again. If she wasn't careful, they wouldn't make it out of this place without him sampling her. They'd be finding a nice, dark corner.

They swayed seductively to the music. Thankfully, people were too wasted around them to notice they looked as if they were slow dancing to a rap song because he sure as hell wasn't letting go of her right now. He traced his lips down her throat, nipping the sensitive skin where her neck met her shoulder.

"Brody," she gasped.

"Fuck, yeah," he groaned, grabbing her ass and forcing her to rub against his aching erection. He was so hard he was about to bust the zipper of his jeans. Levi's, not Wranglers. But the feel of her softly rounded tummy grinding against him only made him crave her heat, so he lifted her a little more, seeking that needed contact. But he was unable to burrow into her thighs because of that tight leather skirt. Filled with frantic frustration, his mouth slammed down on hers, kissing her with uncontrolled lust. His tongue dueled with hers, and he was about two seconds away from lifting her skirt right up on this dance floor. "Come home with me tonight," he said, ripping his mouth from hers. Now. All night. Right now. All fucking night long. He hadn't missed it when she said her kid wouldn't be home.

Xan leaned back and stared at him, the lust in her eyes waning, weariness taking over. His need was boiling in his veins, and his balls, but he didn't miss her expression. Why was she suddenly blanching at the idea of going home with him? It wasn't as if they hadn't had sex already. More than once.

"Um, I-I don't think so."

He pulled her back in his embrace, burying his head into her hair, trying to calm his raging urge to throw her over his shoulder and take her home anyway. "You know you want to, baby."

"Yeah." But she didn't sound convincing. *Shit.* If she put the brakes on, he'd have his work cut out for him.

"What's wrong? I told you I haven't been bed-hopping."

Then, trying to ease her sudden concern, he said, "Mimi would break a hip if she tried."

A chuckle escaped before she clamped her hand over her mouth, shaking her head into his chest. He smiled into her hair, loving the sound of her laughter. Damn, did she bathe in vanilla? Even her hair smelled like the decadent extract. His cock throbbed. He never would've thought vanilla would be an aphrodisiac.

She sighed and he tried to clear his head of her essence.

"I can come over to your place, but I can't stay."

It was progress, but not enough. "Bullshit. You already said Scott was stayin' the night somewhere. You're free all night." He nuzzled her head to soften his words. Then needing her to understand how much he wanted her, needed her, he eased back to gaze into her sky-blue eyes. "I need all night, Xan, because once I get started, baby, I'm not gonna want to stop."

She licked her lips, heat flaring back to life in her eyes. Oh yeah, she wanted him. He just didn't understand her hesitation. "How about you come back to my place, then?"

Whoa. Maybe he'd read her wrong and there wasn't any real uneasiness on her part. He contained his shock and faked a little casual response. If his dick was vocal, it'd be laughing at his acting skills. If it wasn't so hard it hurt. "Sounds good." He caressed her arm, fighting the urge to pick her up and run out of the place like a raging, horny teenager now that he'd gotten the green light.

She nodded, pulling away. "I rode with Roxie. Did you drive?"

"Yeah. Brought my truck. Go tell the girls you're leaving, and I'll tell the guys."

As he headed to his buddies, Brody watched her walk

away, her luscious body begging to be free of its leather cage.

After he'd taken her like a cherished lover the other day, he'd freaked out and fucked her like a cold madman the last time, fearing his emotions were getting in the way.

Tonight, he wasn't sure how much he'd be able to control either urge.

CHAPTER TWELVE

Xan sat in Brody's truck, listening to the indie rock music he loved so much, counting the minutes it'd take to get to her house. When he'd asked her to come over to his place, she'd worried.

Okay, she'd freaked.

She'd come a long way since the hell that was her life with Marco. He was one abusive bastard, and he'd been her only experience. Until now. Problem was she had a hard time trusting men in general, especially in groups. Until now. And she hadn't had sex with another man. Until now. She was definitely making progress, and even dancing with Robby—Robby? Bobby? Whatever his name was—she'd felt empowered. No, she wasn't attracted to that guy, but she hadn't been scared of him either. She would have done a fist pump when she got finished with that dance if Brody hadn't interrupted her. And yeah, she danced with the guy to make Brody jealous. But dang it, she'd thought he'd been screwing around with another woman. Now she felt bad thinking of old-lady Mimi as a skank-whore-bitch. She'd been hurt by the idea of him seeing another woman, and that pissed her off. She was getting too close too fast.

And she'd freaked when he brought up coming over. Not so much because of the speed of their relationship. Relationship? God, she felt so inept with this stuff. But in one form or another, that was what they had. No, she'd really freaked because she hadn't spent the night at another man's house. Ever. She could accept the idea of spending the night with him, but it had to be on her own turf. Silly, since Brody was still built like a brick fortress and could overpower her with his pinky, but there it was. She felt safer having him stay over with her.

But then that brought up the whole mothering issue. She'd never had a man in her life since Marco, so her son never had to deal with one hanging around. What was right here? Hell, she didn't know. She knew she was winging it, but had done a dang good job under the horrible circumstances she'd been dealt. But she was also a woman. Single moms weren't all celibate. The fact she was delving into this *thing* with Brody was proof she was changing.

Yeah, she'd made a lot of progress since meeting him, but she still had a ways to go allowing herself to fully trust a man again. Who could blame her? Marco was... She shivered, thinking of some of the things he'd done to her.

"You're awfully quiet over there," Brody murmured, pulling her out of her reverie, reaching over and squeezing her thigh. She'd sensed his mind had been busy trying to figure out why she'd almost denied his request for a night of love-making. *Sex.* A night of sex.

"Just coming down from my buzz." She smiled, slicing her eyes in his direction.

"I could stop and get us some wine or beer or something."

"Nah. I have some wine and beer and tequila at the house already. Unless there's something you want that isn't already there."

He clutched her hand and lifted it to his mouth, kissing it gently. "The something I want is right here."

She melted at his words, leaning back and staring at him as he pulled into her driveway.

He cut off the ignition and got out, grabbing a duffle bag from behind the seat, and she raised an eyebrow at him. "Extra set of clothes. Never know when I'm gonna get messy at work and have to run into town. I also have an extra set of gym clothes in here if I get the urge to work out again in the evenings."

"Ah." Work out *again*? Who liked to work out once a day? Heck, she moaned and groaned when she forced herself to stick to her three-times-a-week one-mile walk. The way he looked, she shouldn't be surprised, though. The man must pump iron for hours. She nodded in response, and they met in front of his truck, him taking her hand and glancing at her car parked in her driveway.

"How'd she drive?" he asked, tilting his head at her car, which she lovingly, irritatingly called Bertha.

"Good. Bertha's never been better."

He threw his head back and laughed. "Bertha? She looks like a Bertha."

She chuckled with him, shaking her head. "She looks nice too. I don't think she's ever been this clean," Xan said as they approached the front door.

He leaned against the jamb as she fished her keys from her purse. "Well, I still think you should buy a new car. Technology has greatly improved in the last thirty or forty years."

He smirked and she rolled her eyes. Bertha was not forty. Yet.

"There's only so much I *can* do to prolong Bertha's life."

"Well, I have my reasons for keeping her around. If I ran out and bought a new Honda, she'd be jealous."

Xan opened the door and Brody followed her in, setting his bag down and grabbing her as soon as she closed and locked the door. Her body immediately came alive, loving the feel of his hands caressing her, his lips peppering kissing along her neck. "Honda, huh? What kind?"

What? If her brain wasn't turning to mush from the lust overtaking her system, she might've ignored the question. "Yeah, Accord."

"Mmmm...very dependable." He kissed his way to her jaw, his lips grazing, kissing, nipping along the path. Conversation about the car forgotten. His hands slid down her back and groped her ass. "God, I love your body. If you want to keep me from ripping off this skirt, you better take it off."

He was already pulling it up, which was a feat in and of itself since it was so form-fitting, but the skirt was headed in the wrong direction. It wasn't as if she could pull the dang thing over her head, so she backed away from him. He reached for her, growling in protest as the heat of her body left his.

Her hand slapped his chest to stay his progression. "Let me take it off."

His hands fisted at his sides in an obvious attempt to resist snatching her back into his arms, his eyes boring into her as if his will alone would make her naked. "Bedroom," he grunted.

His control seemed to be hanging on by a mere thread, which Xan found incredibly sexy. She wanted to tease him, but got the feeling that'd be the equivalent of taunting a wild animal.

Stepping back, she decided she didn't mind living a little dangerously. She'd been sheltered for far too long and wanted to see how far she could go.

She looked up at him through her long lashes and smiled coyly. "Wait."

She eased the zipper down the back of her skirt and shimmied out of it, taking her time, drawing out his pleasure, his suffering. Now she stood before him in her nude lacy top, displaying her black bra, matching thong, and knee-high leather boots. Without giving him any time to adjust to the vision of her, she clutched the hem of her shirt and pulled it over her head, mussing her hair in the process. There wasn't a need to go slow since the shirt was practically see-through.

Without saying a word, she turned to walk toward her bedroom. She knew he'd follow, but as soon as she gave him her backside, he groaned a strangled, desperate sound she'd never heard a man make before. It was thrilling, empowering, and it made her ache with need. She couldn't wait to get this man in her bed. As she walked, she felt him right behind her, his breath caressing her exposed shoulder. When she pushed her door open and stepped in, whatever control he was grasping snapped.

She heard his duffle bag hit the floor right before Brody grabbed her by the waist and yanked her up against him, his chest hair abrading her back. Damn, when did he have time to unbutton his shirt? She loved the feel of his hair against her skin.

She loved the feel of it even more when it was against her nipples, so she tried turning, seeking that contact.

He clutched her tighter, not letting her move, and she

felt his hot breath against her ear right before his lips landed there. He sucked her lobe into his mouth, nibbling on it. She shivered and moaned, leaning into him, wanting more, as he whispered hot and dirty words she could barely make out in her lusty haze.

He worked her up quickly to the point she wanted to beg. No matter what, she wanted him inside her. Right now. Any thoughts of teasing him fled. From the way he was acting, Xan knew she wouldn't be able to control this encounter. She'd have to save that for another time. He walked her over to the bed, folding her over the side so that her face was buried in the blanket and her boots were still on the floor. She couldn't see what he was doing, but that only made her hotter, wetter. Her other senses were heightened, her skin alive with electricity arcing through her everywhere he touched. She gasped when she felt him kiss the inside of her thigh above her boot.

"Damn, baby. These boots are staying on." She felt him grasp her leg, spreading her wider, his head lowering.

He groaned, but all she felt was the hair on his head rasping against her knee. What was he doing?

"Mmmm. They taste good too, but nowhere near as good as you do."

Taste? He was tasting her boots? That should've grossed her out. But at the thought of him running his tongue along the leather she wore, spasms rocked her jealous core and she moaned, arching her back, needing his tongue on her flesh.

He answered her silent plea, trailing his wet tongue up her inner thigh while the palms of his hands traced up her back. He deftly unhooked her bra, freeing her swollen breasts. His tongue reached her lace-covered mound, and she almost yelped when she felt it right where she wanted it. But he continued his track up, and she did whimper a protest then. Brody's chuckle was muffled against her thigh, but he caressed her back to ease his denial.

When his hands slid up to her cheeks, she froze in anticipation. Would he stretch this out and make her wait, or would he yank them off? Jeez, she hoped it was the second one. Thankfully, he didn't hesitate to slip a finger under each side of her panties and tug them down just far enough to expose her. She moaned and ground her hips against the air, beckoning him to take what she offered.

"That's it, baby. Show me how wet you are." He licked the crevice where her bottom met her thigh and she wanted to cuss him out for teasing her like this.

"Please," she finally begged, not caring how desperate she sounded. She continued to rotate her hips, feeling her clit swell without any stimulation, orgasmic tingles racing down her spine. She was so close, and he wasn't doing anything but driving her crazy.

He wrapped both hands around her, grabbed the front of her legs, and yanked them wider. The quick action yanked loose one of the strings of her panties, and they fell to the side, still hanging on one leg. She'd have a mark on her thigh and friction burns on her knees tomorrow, but she'd only have to worry about all of that if she survived this sensual attack.

"Brody," she breathed. She needed him to touch her.

"Shhh." So incredibly slowly, one of his hands moved, the tips of his fingers reaching her mound and then sliding over the tops of her lips. She groaned and tried to move her hips, but his other hand held her in place.

"Easy," he said. "I want to enjoy this."

The man was pure evil. She just knew this was punishment for dancing with someone else. She'd try to articulate that if she could actually form words.

Without warning, he separated her lips, exposing her clit to the air. She tried to buck—toward him or away, she wasn't sure—but he still had an iron grip on her thigh. Her legs began to shake and a whimper slipped out. A soft growl was the only warning she got before he released her hip to finger her exposed clit and shoved his tongue inside her. She'd already been so close that the moment he touched her aching body she cried out, exploding in rapture. She rocked against his fingers as his tongue continued to probe her. It felt as if her orgasm lasted an eternity, but probably only lasted seconds. And he stayed with her, coaxing as much pleasure out of it as possible.

When she slumped against the bed, spent, his fingers pulled free from her, and she felt him move away. She'd have looked if she had the energy, but she couldn't muster the strength. She heard him rustling with something, the sounds of cloth and zippers breaking the silence, and she still didn't turn her head.

His hand stroking her side startled her, but then she moaned as she felt him drawing her panties completely off. They weren't finished, not by a long shot.

He kneaded her cheeks, spreading her. She felt vulnerable like this, but it was also a sexy position to be in. One that did nothing but help build her desire quickly once again.

She felt his cock against her entrance and she rocked back. Brody hissed, but kept her from taking him inside just yet. He rubbed along her core and groaned, teasing them both with the anticipation. He continued to rub and shallowly press into her before retreating for several minutes. She ached and moaned, wiggling her hips since she was finally free to do so, trying to encourage him to take her already, but she was driving her own passion higher. Unable to stand it anymore, she balanced herself on one hand with the intention of touching herself.

"Oh no you don't," he said, grabbed her hand, and held it down on the bed. He pushed into her and then grabbed her other hand to keep her in place before thrusting hard.

She screamed, throwing her head back against his shoulder as he pounded into her.

He whispered something to her as he kissed her ear, but she couldn't hear him over the blood roaring in her ears.

Then he released one of her hands, his finger finding her clit, and he stroked it mercilessly while maintaining his forceful rhythm.

Too much. Too many sensations. She ground against his finger to increase the contact with her clit, but her greedy body thrust back what little she could to feel his cock deep inside her.

"Oh God!" She was going to come. She could hardly move since he had her almost pinned between his arm and his body, but that only heightened her arousal, building her orgasm to an explosive level. "Don't stop," she said when she was past the point of no return.

"Never," he growled. "Fuck, Xan. You're so goddamn tight." Then he was moving impossibly fast, his hips thrusting, cock plunging into her. She was helpless, trapped in a sensation so erotic it bordered on pain as he fucked her relentlessly.

"Brody, Brody, Brody," she chanted, unable to make a coherent thought. He lifted his other hand, grabbed her hair, and yanked her up into a sitting position.

"God, look at your tits bouncing for me." She couldn't look anywhere with the tight grip he had on her hair, but she felt them jerking up and down. She could only imagine how erotic the visual was for him. Knowing how much she was turning him on was such a power rush.

"Harder," she breathed. Her body was clenching around his dick and her clit was throbbing. She was so, so close., but it wasn't enough. She needed more. "Harder."

He growled as he obeyed, giving it to her harder with both his hand and his cock. "Take it, Xan. Ahhh. Perfect. You're fucking perfect, baby."

Her orgasm was building. She could feel it. Her muscles were twitching, fisting on him as she rocked back, meeting his thrusts with almost the same intensity as he was delivering them.

"Oh, God..." Then she crashed over that precipice, screaming as he plowed into her.

"Fuck yes! Oh yeah, baby. Come for me." He didn't slow down as she came harder than she'd ever come in her life. Then he roared behind her before biting her shoulder, muffling his growls, as his rhythm faltered before stopping completely deep inside her.

At length, he collapsed on top of her, panting against her skin, crushing her into the bed, and she didn't care. He was on top of her and still inside her, but he wasn't close enough. She felt her heart opening up to him, and she wasn't sure what to do about that.

Maybe, just maybe, it was time to trust her heart to a man again.

CHAPTER THIRTEEN

AFTER EASING Xan's arm off his chest, slipping out from underneath her, and tucking the covers back around her naked body, Brody headed to the kitchen to cook them some breakfast.

But it wasn't his growling stomach he was thinking about. It was the woman he'd just left that controlled his thoughts.

She was an enigma to him. Logically, he knew he should avoid her, but at this point, that was out of the question. It was apparent Xan didn't know him, so he should let that worry go. He wouldn't, but he could focus on other problems. Problems like those three agents he needed more information on and one Dave Simmons currently spending his golden years in Prairie County, Arkansas. The same county he'd placed Xan in when she first went into Witness Protection.

Brody needed to make sure she was safe from anyone wanting to harm her, especially her ex and his people, both for her own sake and his peace of mind. Because if he didn't focus on her protection, he'd just focus on her. He'd already lost the battle to stay away from her, so now he needed to figure out how to temper his need to be with her. Putting his energy on work would help some. Not much, but some. At this point, he'd take what he could get.

As long as he could get some of her in the process.

He rummaged around her fridge, pulling out some eggs and bacon. He found the coffee in the cabinet above the coffeemaker and set it to brew while he scrambled some eggs and reined in his thoughts. He could worry about what to do about her when he wasn't standing in her kitchen wearing his boxer briefs. Turning his attention to food, he wasn't sure how much she ate, but he was a big man, so he used all the eggs in the carton, then set it aside to fry up the package of meat.

Mmm...pork. He was starving. Last night, he'd worked up an appetite, one he fully intended to satisfy before working it up again with Xan. Very, very soon. He'd just finished frying the bacon, shoving several sizzling pieces in his mouth and letting the rest drain on a paper towel, when he heard the sleepy shuffling of feet. He smiled at the sound as he cleaned the pan to use it for the eggs, then setting it aside to grab a cup from the cabinet.

"Good morning," he said, pouring her some coffee, not looking at her.

He heard her yawn and grumble something before the lazy foot shuffling started again. He turned to hand over the coffee he'd just poured, and the air locked in his lungs. She was leaning against one of the chairs, waiting for her coffee, her hair a tousled mess. Her robe barely covered her thighs, and it gaped open at the top, giving him a luscious view of her mouthwatering cleavage. She was fucking beautiful.

And he was toast. No way around it, this woman had him by the balls.

He cleared his throat and gave her the coffee, but he couldn't not touch her. He wrapped an arm around her waist in a sideways hug while she sipped her coffee and he brought his lips to her ear. "Sleep well?"

"Mmm." He wasn't sure if she was talking about the coffee or answering his question.

"I'll take that as a yes." God knew he had. He'd slept like a rock, and he couldn't remember the last time that'd happened. Not with a woman, that was for damn sure.

"It was," she croaked. Damn, but her voice even had a sexy rasp to it first thing this morning. She set her cup down and looked at him. "You didn't have to cook. I'd have fixed us something."

He wrapped both hands around her and she hugged him back. "It was my pleasure," he murmured as he lowered his lips to hers.

He was just going to kiss her. One little *good morning* kiss. But as soon as his mouth captured her lower lip, her taste exploded in his mouth, and he lost all sense. Groaning, he deepened the kiss, his tongue stroking into the wet heat of her mouth. He didn't know what it was about this woman that made him lose all control, but he was through questioning it, fighting it. His hand slipped into the gaping opening of her robe and found a taut nipple, which he rolled between his thumb and forefinger. She gasped into his mouth and he swallowed it up, returning a growl when he felt her bare leg slide against his.

Fuck it. He grabbed her and set her on the table, her moan throwing fuel on his fire, making him rip her robe open as he shoved his underwear down just enough to spring his cock free. He was so hard he was already leaking pre-cum when he clutched it, squeezing the base to keep from coming as soon as he entered her like some teenager unable to hold back his load. He plunged into her and her head fell back with an erotic sound that made his balls ache.

He took her with a feral intensity that should have surprised him for being so early, but around Xan, he couldn't contain his lust.

"Brody!"

He loved the sound of his name on her lips. "Yeah, baby. Say my name again."

He plowed into her and she gasped, screaming his name as her pussy fisted around his cock so tight he knew he wouldn't last.

"Xan! *Fuck*." He buried his head in her hair and groaned as he came, feeling her milk every last drop of his cum.

Right into her pussy.

Without a condom.

Son of a bitch! What was wrong with him? That was twice now. He didn't want to come off as an inexperienced kid, but that was exactly how he felt.

He held her close as the last of her spasms around his cock diminished, caressing her back with one hand and rubbing her head with the other. Then he eased back and kissed her temple, her cheek, her lips.

"Sorry," he breathed into the kiss. "I didn't mean to attack you first thing this morning." He hesitated, knowing he had to confess, but figuring she already knew. "Without a condom."

She chuckled softly and he smiled. Even though he felt like an idiot, he loved the sound of her laughter. "I didn't mind. And, er, maybe we can discuss skipping the condoms altogether."

His heart raced. No condoms meant a commitment. He knew he didn't want her seeing any other guys, but he also knew he couldn't think about a future with her. But the fact that she'd brought it up made pride swell inside him. It meant she wanted a relationship, and no matter how irresponsible that might be, he couldn't help wanting to pretend for a little while.

"We'd have to agree to be exclusive." If even just for the duration of their relationship, no matter how short that time might be.

"That won't be a problem on my end. It's been a while for me anyway." She shrugged and looked away. Brody knew it had been a while for her, but wondered if maybe that meant she hadn't had sex since Collins. Her response didn't stroke his ego any, though, since it didn't necessarily mean she wanted to be exclusive because she wanted only him, just that she hadn't been playing with any other fish in the sea lately.

Whatever. Her reasoning didn't matter. Only her willingness did. "It won't be a problem with me either." He leaned down and kissed her to seal their deal, fighting the urge to giggle like a giddy schoolgirl. He was really fucked.

She chuckled against his lips and he drew back. "You started eating without me. You taste like bacon."

He laughed. "I did no such thing." He gave her an innocent look, shaking his head. "I had to make sure the bacon tasted okay. I can't serve you poisoned meat."

"Oh, we can't have that now, can we?" She giggled when he nuzzled her ear. "And did it taste okay?"

He smiled, leaning down. "You tell me." Then he kissed her again, a full-on assault of the mouth.

She broke away, panting. "Yeah. You're making me hungry."

"You're making me horny," he groaned, but pulled away from her to tend to the eggs.

She squeezed his butt cheek before sitting down and wincing when her knees bent.

He turned sharply, looking at her. "What's wrong?"

"Is it carpet burn if it was caused by sheets?" she asked as she caressed one of her knees.

"Oh God, baby." He stepped over to her, leaning and wrapping his arms around her. "I'm sorry, Xan."

She reached up and stroked his face. "I'm okay, Brody." She chuckled. More than okay.

He sighed, shaking his head as he leaned back. "Yeah, well, I could've been more considerate."

"Uh-huh," she mumbled, nodding as she took a sip. Shit. He didn't like hurting her. She looked up at him, her face softening. "I'm fine."

He made a noncommittal sound as he cooked the eggs and plated the food. He was a big man, and she was a small woman. He needed to be more careful with her. The knowledge that he'd been rough enough to cause her lingering pain stabbed him in the chest. She needed to be cherished, not treated like some crack whore. He'd make the effort to be gentler with her.

With that settled, he sat down to eat, placing Xan's plate in front of her first. They ate in comfortable silence, but Brody had to touch her. He slid his hand on top of her bare leg above her red knee, letting it rest there as he ate.

"So what do you want to do today?" He wasn't ready to leave her. Not yet.

"Um, I hadn't given it—" She stopped when the front door opened, her eyes flying open wide as heavy footsteps jogged to the kitchen. Exactly where they were. He was about to grab her and shield her from the intruder, but then he realized the pale look on Xan's face wasn't a result of fear for her life.

"Mom!"

Well, son of a damned bitch. She was sitting in this kitchen in her robe, and he was in his fucking underwear, no shirt.

And her son was about to walk into the room.

Fuck, fuck, fuck!

At least he was sitting, facing the door. It'd be obvious he didn't have a shirt on, but the kid wouldn't see just how little he actually had on. His old rule of not dating single moms filtered through his brain. Funny how it didn't bother him that he considered it an *old* rule.

Scott came barreling into the kitchen. "It's smells good in here. I'm starrr—oh shit!" He halted, his eyes darting back and forth from his mom to Brody and back again to his mom.

"Language, Scott." She glanced at Brody. "Sorry, he gets that shit from me, but I'm trying to do better."

"Sorry, oh crap. Um, nope, oh crap just doesn't cover it." He stared in shock, eyes now staying longer on his mom with sly glances at Brody every few seconds. After what felt like a long moment of torture, the kid finally started fighting a smile.

Why the hell did Brody feel as if *he* was the teenager staring at his girlfriend's dad?

"Um, am I interrupting something?" Nope, no longer fighting that smile. His face was glowing like the damn cat that ate that stupid canary.

Brody wondered if he should say something or just wait for Xan. This was her kid, and he didn't want to step on her toes. Just when the silence was getting deafening, she fidgeted in her seat.

"Did you eat breakfast at Chad's?"

"Yes. But I could eat again." The wide smile stayed on

his face as his hands propped on his hips. "I came over to get my football. We need to run some plays." He paused, glancing over at Brody. "How are you, Brutus?"

"I'm good, kid. How are you?" Brody hid his smile. The little man was actually doing a little posturing with him over being here with his mom. If he didn't already like the kid, he would've started liking him now. He appreciated the fact that Scott was being protective of his mom.

"Same here. Say," he said, tilting his head as if he just had a novel idea. Brody didn't buy it. "Would you like to come out and throw the pigskin around with us?"

"Oh, Scott, he doesn't—"

"I'd love to." He didn't think the kid really wanted him to play football with them. He probably just wanted Brody away from his mom. It didn't matter. He'd enjoy a little football and male bonding with the kid. But he wasn't backing down from the taunting. He had to show the guy that, while he was around, he'd be the one protecting his mom. She might still be his mom, but Xan was Brody's woman. "I have to get dressed first."

Xan groaned, trying to bury her face in her coffee cup. That was okay too. She didn't understand male dynamics.

Scott's smile disappeared, his eyes narrowing. "You do that." He walked over to his mom and kissed her cheek. Xan reached up and patted his head, not looking at him. Her mortification was rather quite adorable. But Brody didn't have kids, so he really didn't understand what she was going through.

Scott turned to leave and Brody smiled, watching. The kid had spunk.

"That was horrible."

He leaned over and took her hand in his, rubbing soothing circles on it. "It wasn't ideal, but it wasn't horrible.

He's a young man who needs to understand his mother has needs like everyone else. Just like he does, unless he's a eunuch." He picked up his cooling coffee and gulped it down.

"Oh God, that's even worse. I don't want to think about *his* needs." She sighed, shaking her head. "I know you don't have kids, but did you ever walk in on your parents having sex?"

Since he couldn't remember his childhood, he didn't remember if he had. But that wasn't really the point. Xan was freaking out and he needed to help her chill. And he could do that by playing down the incident. He stood, clutching the side of her head and kissing her hair. "We weren't having sex. Now, if he'd come home thirty minutes ago..." He chuckled as he pulled away.

"Oh shit. He could've walked in on us having sex!" she hissed.

"Right. And he didn't. So no worries." She started to speak again, but he halted her efforts. "I'm getting dressed. I'm not sure what you're doing today, but I have a couple of kids to beat at football."

He left her gaping at him, and he stifled a chuckle. He quickly threw on some shorts, a muscle shirt and tennis shoes from his bag, grateful he had those workout clothes with him. He and the guys from work got together on occasion to play a little, so Brody was glad he wouldn't make a complete fool of himself out there. He pulled out a hair tie to hold his hair out of his face. When he stood to leave, Xan walked in.

"You're really playing football with my son?"

Uh-oh, were those unshed tears in her eyes. What did he do to upset her? Did she feel neglected that he wasn't going to be spending time with her? He stepped up to her and pulled her into his arms. "It'll only be an hour or so, baby. I promise we can do whatever you want after we're finished playing."

"Oh, no." She shook her head against his chest. "It's not that." She eased back and tried to free herself from his embrace. He wasn't having that. He squeezed her tighter, grasping her chin and lifting her face so she'd be forced to look at him.

"Then what is it?"

"It's silly." She waved a dismissive hand and tried to look away, but he held firm.

"Xan." His tone was reproachful.

She took a shuddering breath and reluctantly looked at him again. "It's just that...um, that Scott hasn't had any adult male role models around. Ever. So it's nice, er, sweet of you to spend a little time with him. That's all."

"Baby," he breathed, leaning his forehead against hers, not knowing what to say. He wasn't a role model. He couldn't remember his past, but knew he'd been a contract killer once upon a time. Even though he didn't do that now and had no memories of ever doing that before, he had some shady dealings with his side job under Colonel. Granted, it was within the realm of law enforcement. Mostly. But just thinking about being there for Scott gave him a warm feeling inside, gave him a sense of pride. Even if he'd only be in Scott's life for a short while.

"Look, I know you're not his dad or anything. Oh God. I can't believe I just said that." She tried getting away from him again. When he pulled her back, she struggled with him, obviously embarrassed.

"Stop fighting me, Xan," he murmured. "I'm flattered you think he'd benefit from spending time with me. He's a great kid, and I'd love to hang out with him." That seemed to help because she relaxed and let him hug her to his body.

"W-why don't you ever ask me about his dad?"

Oh shit. What was he supposed to say? He'd better think of something fast. "I figured you'd tell me about it when you were ready."

She hummed against him and pulled away. "I'm glad you want to hang out with Scott."

Why was she looking at him like that? She seemed distant, and he hated that. He wanted to do something to lighten her mood. "Yeah, of course I'd much rather play with you in the sheets, but we can always do that later. We can play *find the pickle*."

She laughed and he smiled, just the reaction he wanted. God, he lov—um, no. He cared for this woman. He wasn't in love with her. He quickly, forcefully shoved that thought away.

"I'd better go before I get razed by the kids for being held up by a mommy."

She popped up on her toes and kissed him before he jogged out to play some pigskin with the young folk.

Love? No way. No how.

Right. He was in deep, deep shit.

CHAPTER FOURTEEN

Xan sat on her front porch sipping her hot cocoa late that evening, wondering why in the world she was drinking this hot stuff when it was still well over eighty degrees outside.

Brody'd left over an hour ago after spending the first part of the day playing football with the boys. They'd run drills and gathered some of the other neighborhood kids together for an impromptu game of touch football. Even Roxie and Scott's and Chad's girlfriends had come over to watch the game. She'd noticed how Scott lit up when Malorie Kimber arrived and remembered Brody's little comment about Scott's needs. Maybe it was time for another talk with her son. She tried to have them regularly, and it'd been about six months since the last one.

But Xan wasn't the only one to notice Scott's reaction to his girlfriend. Brody'd eyeballed him and had even pulled him aside a few different times to talk one-on-one. It could've been about anything, but Scott kept glancing at Malorie when he was talking to Brody. Xan got the feeling Brody was talking to him about his girlfriend, but she wasn't sure about what. She'd had every intention of asking, but Scott was always around.

Well, except when Brody had tricked her into following him in for a glass of lemonade and pulled her into the pantry, slipped her shorts off, and took her from behind while covering her mouth to muffle her cries.

Yeah, except for that one time, there hadn't been an opportunity to ask him, and at that moment, she'd been too caught up in lusty pleasure to think straight.

The day had been great, really wonderful. She'd had fun visiting with Roxie, watching Brody keep up with the young men, then hanging out with Brody and Scott all afternoon.

But in the last hour since he'd left, she couldn't stop thinking about her conversation with Brody this morning when she'd asked him why he hadn't asked about Marco. He'd stiffened slightly before giving her a perfectly good response. If he hadn't flinched like that, she probably wouldn't have given it another thought. She figured she hadn't dwelled on it since then because of her obsession with Scott and his interest in his new girlfriend, but thinking about it now made the hair on the back of her neck stand on end. She had that itchy feeling that something wasn't right. But why?

She tried reasoning with herself. Seriously, she hadn't known Brody for very long. She already knew he was mostly a loner, so maybe he didn't pry into her life because he felt as if it wasn't any of his business. But they were sleeping together. And she cared about him. How much, she didn't like to consider because she'd start trembling, breaking out in gooseflesh.

Which brought up another point entirely. Why break her abstinence streak now? Why Brody? And why was he reluctant at first? Why did he really have a change of heart?

Her neck kept itching as the questions swirled around in her mind. She rocked on the porch swing, sipping her cooling cocoa, trying to make sense of her apprehension. With the exception of her FBI agents, she hadn't trusted a man since Marco. Maybe this was just new to her, and she wasn't used to accepting male companionship.

Or maybe something was off.

Jack had told her that the FBI was watching her, and she'd already encountered them. Her heart stuttered. Or him? Was Brody an agent on her case? Was that why he'd fought his attraction to her? Oh God! Or was he not even attracted to her at all? Was getting close to her just a means to an end?

Wait, wait, wait. She was just being silly. If that was the case, then he wouldn't have been hesitant in the beginning. He'd have taken his opening without reservation. Her experience with agents had shown her they were ruthless professionals.

She chewed her nails, considering. She could make guesses all night, but there was only one way to find out. She got up and walked into the house, heading for the kitchen since Scott was at the other end of the house in his room playing video games. She pulled out her cell phone from her purse and called Jack. He answered the first ring.

"Hello?"

"Hi, Jack, it's Xan."

"Yes, I recognize your number. Is everything okay?"

Maybe she should've thought this through before picking up the phone and just calling him. Too late to worry about that now. "Um, well, I'd like to talk to you about the agents you have watching me."

He hesitated, and Xan wasn't sure if she should say something else. "What about them?" he finally asked.

"Who are they?"

"You know I can't divulge that information."

She took a steadying breath while she considered another tactic. Best to just come right out with it. "Look, Jack. You told me after I arrived that I'd already encountered the person or people watching me. At that time, the options were limited to the people at my work, in my neighborhood, and at the garage where work was done to my car."

"I never said the person or people in question were people you'd met. I said you'd encountered them. That could've been a person in a gas station, at Walmart, or many other locations where you ran into them in passing."

Damn. He had a point there, but she wasn't giving up. "Tell me what you know about Brutus?"

"Brutus, AKA Brody Jackson, is a mechanic for Sheppard's Garage. Mid-thirties, blond hair, blue eyes, drives a late-model Harley Davidson Cross Bones motorcycle and a late-model Ford F-150 crew cab truck—I believe Harley Davidson Edition. The man likes Harleys."

Why would Jack know so much about Brody? Surely this wouldn't be that easy. "You spilled that much information when I just asked you about a man named Brutus. How could you have known who I was talking about? Do you know all this because he's working for you? Is Brody the guy, or one of the guys, you have watching over me?"

He chuckled and she felt her face flush in anger. Why did he think this was funny? This was only her life they were essentially talking about. Before she got a chance to dig further, Jack responded.

"Some of the people I have watching you were at that little honkytonk you went to the other night. Saw you leave with him. It's my job to know if the people in your life are a threat to you."

Well, that made sense, she thought reluctantly. She strummed her fingernails on the kitchen counter, trying to think of another way to find out the identities of the people watching her. He hadn't come out and said that Brody wasn't part of that team. "You're evading my questions."

"You're right. Because I can't tell you shit, and you know it. We're protecting you, so please don't worry about that, but if you get suspicious about anything, call me immediately."

That gave her pause. "How close are you?"

"My proximity is irrelevant. But I may be closer than you think."

She guessed that was good. If he was near, then he could be here at a moment's notice if something happened. Not that it helped answer any questions she had about Brody. Realizing she wasn't going to get anything concrete out of her super-secret agent man, she mumbled her understanding and got off the phone.

Brody Jackson. Xan hadn't even realized she didn't know his last name until Jack had told her. Maybe she was overreacting to Brody's reaction to her bringing up Marco. So he hadn't asked about Scott's dad or her past in general. She hadn't even asked him for his last name. Or about his past. Maybe things were progressing normally for their budding romance. But she really had no idea if this was normal for a couple who were falling in love.

Love? Hmm. Maybe not love. Lust. Yeah, falling in lust. But if she was going to open her heart up to Brody *eventually*, maybe she should get to know him a little better before her heart overruled her brain.

But getting to know him meant she had to open up

about herself too. And she wasn't looking forward to telling him about her past. Too many painful memories. Though if she expected him to open up to her, she needed to be prepared to talk about Marco.

And Tess. God, even after all these years, that wasn't a subject she enjoyed.

If Brody had no feelings for her at all, he'd probably run screaming when she opened up her baggage for his perusal.

And if he did have feelings for her and became concerned for her safety when she spilled all the grueling details of her life, her heart just might overrule her brain before she was ready.

Because she already felt as if that was happening.

————

FIRST THING MONDAY MORNING, Brody pulled his Harley into the garage's parking lot. Colonel should be pleased that he'd actually be early for this meeting. But he wasn't here brown-nosing or seeking brownie points. No, he needed to talk to Gauge about his research.

Brody tried getting more information on Paul Sellers, Luke Riley, and Jeff Coleman last night after leaving Xan's house, but he just kept hitting a brick wall. Wall? A fifty foot brick fortress was more like it. And he was frustrated as hell. Something wasn't adding up right, and he needed answers before bad things started finding their way to Xan's and Scott's front door.

He killed the engine and stalked into the bays. Gauge was already there, waiting for him.

"Thanks for gettin' here early, man. I appreciate it." They shook hands and Brody patted his buddy's back before crossing his arms over his chest. "I've got squat, and it's pissing me off. Tell me you got something."

"Yeah, I got something." Gauge nodded his head to the side to motion Brody over to their makeshift conference room. Since no one was here yet, it'd be private, so he followed. Once inside, Gauge turned to face him. "I had to call in some major favors and sell my soul for this shit, so I'd like to keep it on the D.L. Unless it becomes necessary to tell Colonel, this stays between us. Got it?"

The words should've sounded grave coming from him, but Gauge actually sounded pissed. Brody didn't know what to make of that, so he just nodded, wanting to hear the news.

"Paul Sellers and Luke Riley are still agents, but they're deep undercover. From what I hear, we're talking years. No specifics on their assignments, but my contact told me those guys are so involved in their own shit that they couldn't possibly have anything to do with what's going on with Alexandra Collins, AKA Xan Bradley, or the Colleoni family." Gauge shifted and glanced behind Brody, making sure they were still alone, Brody figured, and lowered his voice. "Jeff Coleman is a little trickier. I'm still gathering intel on him, but apparently, he's the guy who was the head agent on her case before Dave Simmons. He orchestrated her extraction from the Collins estate, but was injured before he could follow through with it. After he was retrieved and treated, he disappeared. Whether that happened on his own or if he got too close and is now under FBI protection, I haven't figured out."

Laughter flowed in from the other room right as the front door opened to the shop, meaning some, if not all, of the other guys were here, and this conversation was over. "Okay. Thanks."

"No problem. Just remember, keep your trap shut unless this info becomes necessary to spill. The identification of undercover agents is serious shit, and I don't want to lose a valuable asset over it."

"You got it. Thanks, man." Brody patted the guy on the back and took a seat as Blade and Bear strode in.

"Well, looky looky here," Blade said with a smirk. "I can't believe you got your big ass outta bed this early. Usually, you ain't strollin' in until right at eight."

"Fuck off, Blade," Brody growled.

"Ahhh, did we interrupt your little bromance with Gauge over there?" Hunter teased as he walked in, chuckling. Roc was right on his heels.

"Don't be jealous, Hunter. C'mon over here and I'll let you suck my dick." Brody groped himself and flipped the bird.

"Seems like you're getting enough action. You don't need that pussy over here too," Roc muttered as he sat down, glancing at Hunter.

Brody glowered, remembering the bullshit Roc had fed to Xan about Mimi. And he sure as hell didn't like Roc's tone, but he had to be careful and not show too much emotion, otherwise the guys'd rake him over the coals. Luckily, he didn't have to worry about a comeback that wouldn't insult Xan or implicate him because Hunter stomped over to Roc.

"I ain't no pussy, you dickweed."

Bear stepped in between them. "Enough, you two. We don't have time to referee a fight that Hunter'd lose." He chuckled.

"Eat shit, Bear!" Hunter stormed over to the other side of the small room and sat. Stewed, really.

But even through the horsing around, Brody felt his blood pressure rise as he stared at Roc, arms crossed over his chest. The idea of keeping quiet sounded like a good plan, but he was having a really hard time sticking to it.

"You've got somethin' to say to me, Brutus?" Roc barked.

Brody's arms dropped to his side as he took a step toward Roc. That mouth of his was going to get him in some serious trouble, starting right now. Brody was fucking pissed, and he didn't want to hide it. Blade noticed the look in Brody's eyes and stepped over, immediately coming to his aid. The other guys looked confused and started to gather around as Colonel came rushing into the room, not paying any attention to the gathered men.

"Sit down, sit down, everyone. We need to make this quick."

With narrowed eyes pinned on Roc a few seconds longer, Brody turned and took a seat, wondering what the hell had crawled up Colonel's ass this morning, while both relieved and irritated he didn't get to set Roc straight on a few things. Oh, if Roc kept that shit up, he'd get his chance. Brody wasn't going to sit back and let that SOB cause problems for Xan.

"How's the Bradley watch coming, Brutus?" Colonel asked, gulping his coffee and wincing. Hell, Brody could see the steam coming off it from where he sat.

He cleared his throat, wondering how best to respond. He didn't want to come out and talk about his personal relationship with Xan, but he *was* on an assignment. "Good. No signs of any shadows or any unwanted interest from suspicious parties."

"Good. Good. So you're staying on her, then?" Brody

hesitated, and Colonel looked up from his coffee, pinning him with a stare.

Fuck.

"Yeah, I'm staying on her. We've been gettin' close."

A knowing smile kicked up on Colonel's face briefly before it went back to an all-business facade. At least it seemed as if he was letting it go and wouldn't be pressing for details because Brody refused to let what was happening between him and Xan be analyzed and ridiculed by a group of horny ass-wipes.

"Good. Fortunately, we have a bead on that little shit we think is in Marco's camp, Dale Adams. Apparently, he laid low for a while after beatin' the shit out of you two,"— he quirked an eyebrow at Blade and Brody—"but he's resurfaced." He looked at Brody. "I need you on this. He's staying at a campground out by Lake Conway. Take whoever you want. But maybe you shouldn't take Blade this time since he sucked at watching your back last time." He chuckled and shook his head.

"Hey, hey. No fair. We were ambushed." Blade's face fell in a pout, gaining laughs from the other guys, then he looked to Brody for confirmation. "Isn't that right, buddy?"

Brody just grunted and looked over at Colonel. "Blade can come again."

"Thanks for the love, man." Blade sat back with a shit-eating grin.

"It's not like he does any fuckin' work around here anyway," Brody said.

"Dude! I thought you loved me?" Blade and that damn fake pout. Brody hid his smile and waved him off, avoiding eye contact with Roc.

When he looked back at Colonel, he didn't have to fight

that smile anymore. His boss looked seriously distraught about something. Brody studied him, trying to figure out why he looked the way he did and why he was trying to cover it up with humor. Maybe it had something to do with regular work and wasn't relevant to the assignment they were on.

Then Colonel's eyes met his, the worried look turning to one of sadness. And Brody knew he was wrong. A chill slid down his spine at the realization that Colonel knew something he was reluctant to share.

"You need to make sure you watch the boy too, Brutus."

Of course he'd keep an eye on her kid. They were both under their protection, so that was a given, but why was Colonel stating the obvious and looking at him with such a grim expression? He nodded, hoping his boss would elaborate.

"I've received information that Marco might make a play for the boy. Apparently, he wants him to be his protégé and follow in the family business."

Over his dead fucking body. Brody wouldn't allow that. Scott was a great kid, loved sports, video games, and just being a kid, and Xan would be devastated if anything happened to him.

Colonel shook his head, sighing. "If he can't take him alive, he'll kill him. He's done it before."

"What do you mean he's done it before?" The words were out of Brody's mouth and he was on his feet before he realized it. Brody knew Marco was a ruthless man, but something was way off here.

"Sit down, Brutus," Colonel said sternly. "What I mean by that is Scott was their second child. Their first, Tess Collins, died during infancy. I have reason to believe it wasn't SIDS like the medical examiner stated in the autopsy."

Brody sat down, turning over Colonel's words. He was implying that Marco killed his own child. How sick! If he'd done that, he'd definitely do it again. He had to make sure that both Xan and Scott stayed safe. He couldn't lose either one of them. How had they become so important to him in such a short amount of time? He didn't know.

He didn't care. The fact was his responsibility of them exceeded this assignment, and he'd make damn sure they were protected.

"Okay. How's the minivan rebuild coming?" And just like that, Colonel switched gears to shop talk, but Brody couldn't follow. He wanted this meeting over, so he could question Colonel about what he knew.

When the meeting finally came to an end, Brody stood casually and told Blade to warm up the wrecker so they could check out this Dale Adams prick on Lake Conway. Then he blocked Colonel's exit from the meeting room.

"How did you find that out?" he barked, knowing his boss understood just exactly what he was referring to.

"Stand down, Brutus." Colonel leaned up against the wall as if he carried the weight of the world on his shoulders and rubbed his hands wearily across his face. "That wasn't all. And it's bad," he mumbled into his hands and then looked up, facing Brody. "Real bad."

"What?" He didn't want to hear this, but he had to know. If it involved Xan and Scott, he didn't have a choice. Whatever it was, he'd be able to help them better if he knew everything.

"I've been digging into your association with Collins."

Brody's blood turned to ice. "You said I was a contract killer," he said woodenly.

"Right. Because Collins didn't do the dirty work himself unless he had a personal vendetta like when he tried to kill his wife." Colonel sighed. "I'm sorry, man, but apparently, you know Marco Collins, and have flashbacks of his wife, because...he hired *you* to kill their daughter."

CHAPTER FIFTEEN

"No way! No fucking way did I kill a baby." Brody was screaming in Colonel's face. His whole body was shaking, rejecting the lies his boss just spilled.

"I know this is hard to hear, I—"

"It's bullshit!" Brody backed away so he wouldn't strangle his boss, and paced like a caged animal, head shaking, fury consuming him.

"You think you were a hired gun with a heart?" Colonel asked mockingly.

"*Shut up.*" He whirled, stomping back toward his boss. "Shut the fuck up!" He refused to believe it. He would *not* believe it.

"Brutus, I think—"

"I've got work to do." He had to get away from here, away from the lies. Lies! He slammed the door on his way out, not meeting the stares of the other guys, who no doubt heard his fervent denials. Only they didn't know what he was denying.

He made his way to the wrecker, swallowing the bile that rose in his throat, clenching his fists to stop his hands from shaking. He climbed into the driver seat of the wrecker —already started by Blade—and threw it into reverse.

"You okay, man?" Blade asked as Brody peeled onto the two-lane highway.

Hell no, he wasn't okay, but Blade wasn't in the garage when Brody was yelling at Colonel, so he had no idea something was up. "No," he gritted out.

"Did somethin' happen after I left?" Blade's eyes narrowed. "Did you attack Roc? I saw the murder in your eyes earlier. What was *that* about?"

"He led Xan to believe I was fucking Mimi." His lips said the words, but his brain was still wholly focused on Colonel's words, not Roc's actions.

Blade guffawed. "He said...that you...and little ole—"

"Knock it off!" Just thinking about Roc pissed Brody off even more. He needed an outlet for his anger, and if he let Blade work him up, Brody would pummel Roc as a means to alleviate what Colonel had said. He would not believe those words. "He's a fucking liar."

"Er, I know that. No one believes you bumped uglies with Mimi."

"I'm not talking about Roc. I'm talking about Colonel."

Brody could see Blade studying him from the corner of his eye. Then he shifted in his seat. "What happened? You're about to snap, and I'd like to know if I need to take cover."

Brody took a deep breath and twisted his neck from side to side, trying to relieve the tension, trying to rein in his anger.

It wasn't working.

"You heard him mention in the meeting that Collins and Xan had another baby that died." Brody hesitated, finding the strength to finish. "And he seems to think I'm the one who did the deed."

"Oh shit," Blade breathed. "Why would he think that?"

Brody relayed the info Colonel had found out about his past along with this new little tidbit of *unreliable* information, not liking the understanding in Blade's eyes. "You better not believe this shit. I didn't kill a baby. I wouldn't do that."

They were pulling into the campground of the lake when Blade found his voice. "I don't know what to believe. But I know exactly what you need, and we'll get it right after we're through here."

"Yeah? What's that?" Because Brody was at a total loss.

"Whiskey."

———

"I'M NOT'S A BABY KILLER," Brody slurred into his fourth, rather large glass of Jack Daniel's.

Blade patted him on the back. "I know, man. But saying it ain't gonna make it go away. We need to get to the bottom of this."

"How? I can't fuckin' think straight right now, and you enlist...in-insist that I drink this shit." He downed the last of that fourth glass, and Blade filled it back up.

"You couldn't think straight before, man. You need to numb your brain, so you can think straight tomorrow."

"I'll have a damn hangover tomorrow," he mumbled into his glass. "It'll hurt too much to think then." He took a drink. "Besides, I'm, er, supposed to be watchin' over Xan and Scott. Can't do that when I'm lit."

"Don't worry, Brutus. I've got your back. I know you've

been staking out from the north side of that empty rental next door to Roxie's house. I'll check things out tonight."

Brody groaned. He was fucked. Really and truly fucked. He didn't have the resources to verify what Colonel had found out. No. What Colonel had *told* him—Brody refused to believe him. Yet, somewhere in the pit of his stomach, he knew the possibility existed that everything was true. Oh God. How could he face Xan if he was the reason her baby had died? He finished off his fifth glass, and Blade promptly refilled it.

"Look, what we found earlier at the campground will help."

"We found a whole lotta nothin', asshole," Brody mumbled into his fifth glass. Or was it his sixth?

"Not true. We found where that prick Adams is staying. Found his arsenal of weapons and ammo. We know he's dirty. We just need to find out more about him. I'll call Colonel—"

"No." Brody sat up, glaring at Blade. "I don't want to talk to that jerk."

Blade sighed. "You can't punish the messenger, Brutus. He's your boss, and he's trying to help keep Xan alive while researching your past to find what your connection is to her. We've all done things we're not proud of, man. Look at it this way—you don't have to remember the shit you pulled in your badass days." Something dark flashed across Blade's normally easygoing face, but Brody was too fucked up to process it.

"Fine," he breathed. "We need help, but I just don't want to face Colonel right now. Call Gauge. He's been helping me on the side anyway."

Blade's brows furrowed. "You've been working on this without me?"

"Don't get your panties in a wad." Brody downed the last of his whiskey. "And get me some water, so I can be ready to talk to Gauge."

Blade got up and made the call while getting Brody a glass of ice water. After downing half the glass, he rubbed it against his head, trying to clear it, but all he could think of was Xan. Her beautiful face, light-blue eyes, hair with streaks of gold, her damn vanilla scent that drove him crazy whenever he was within a few feet of her. She was a remarkable woman who loved her son, who probably loved her daughter too.

The daughter he'd killed.

He didn't want to accept it, but as time moved on and he slumped deeper into a drunken stupor, one thought kept looping in his mind—if he wasn't the one to kill her, then why did he know Xan?

It was the only thing that made sense. He'd known for many years that he'd been a contract killer. If he hadn't known this before, he might've been able to deny the accusation, but knowing what he knew, he couldn't. And he didn't have the memories to either confirm or deny what he'd been told.

His chest ached so bad he could barely breathe. Thinking of causing Xan that kind of pain tormented him in ways he never thought possible. His skin crawled; his eyes burned suspiciously. He hadn't had a reason to cry since losing his memory. Realizing he was about to create that memory now was damn near killing him. He cleared his throat, shook his head, and took another swig of the water he'd been clutching like some kind of lifeline he didn't deserve.

He was a piece of shit, the worst kind. For him to have been able to kill an innocent baby, that'd make him a monster. He was no better than Marco Collins. Thinking otherwise would make him a hypocrite.

What do you think killers do, dumbass? They kill people. Maybe he justified that before by thinking he was eliminating other criminals. If he'd killed other killers, drug dealers, human traffickers, and similar scum, he was ridding the world of losers who caused people harm. But thinking he killed a defenseless baby? Oh God. He jumped up from the chair he'd been sitting in at Blade's kitchen table and bolted for the bathroom, dropped to the floor, and hurled his guts.

"Brutus?"

Brody heard Blade at the door, but couldn't stop vomiting to answer. Once he started, the roaring in his ears seemed to purge his brain as his stomach purged its contents.

"Gauge will be here in two minutes. I'll, er, find you some crackers or something."

As Brody retched, the burning in his eyes escalated to full-on tears. He gasped to catch his breath and sobbed just before puking again. He continued the cycle of vomiting and crying until his stomach was empty and he was dry heaving. He'd never be able to face Xan again, and that knowledge was almost as painful as realizing Colonel was right. He slumped to the floor, covered his face, and tried to take deep breaths to calm down. Under any other circumstance, he'd feel like such a pussy right now, but all he felt was revulsion.

He grabbed the counter and hoisted himself up. He washed his face and finger-brushed his teeth with some of Blade's toothpaste, refusing to look at himself in the mirror. Then he pulled the thong from his hair and retied it before joining Blade.

And Gauge, he saw once he entered the living room.

"You okay? Stupid fuckin' question. Of course you're not." Blade sighed. "I've got some crackers and Sprite in the kitchen."

He turned and Blade and Gauge followed him to the table. Brody didn't deserve to feel better, but he knew he still had a job to do, so he picked up the soda and started drinking it.

"I've already filled Gauge in on what happened."

"You mean that I'm a baby killer? Good. One less thing to talk about." He picked up the crackers and slumped into the nearest chair.

"Brutus, man, we'll get to the bottom of this," Gauge said, taking the seat next to him. "I've already told Blade everything."

Brody raised an eyebrow, wondering if everything included the info he'd found on the undercover agents.

Gauge nodded in response. "Yeah, everything. He knows everything we do." He locked eyes with Blade. "And it stays between us. Not that I have a problem with authority. I know I'm the new kid on the block around here, and I sure as hell don't want to piss off the boss man, but this is sensitive shit we're dealing with. It's nothing personal."

"Got it," Blade said, picking up the beer he'd been nursing while pouring Jack down Brody's throat. "So what all do we know?"

"We know that Xan discovered incriminating evidence against her husband and turned to the FBI. We know that sometime between her seeking help and getting shot, Collins found out. After that, it's just speculation. We think that one of the FBI agents was dirty and ratted her out to Collins."

"The only suspicious ones at this point are Dave Simmons, her agent at the time she went into witness protection, and Jeff Coleman, her contact agent up until the night she was attacked," Brody said after finishing his cracker.

"Simmons is retired and living in Prairie County. Coleman is still on the lam."

"That still doesn't make sense that Simmons would place Xan and Scott in his hometown," Blade said, leaning forward. "That alone makes him suspicious."

"I need to go out there and check it out," Brody mumbled. Damn, his head was pounding from the alcohol in his bloodstream and violently puking.

"No good, Brutus. Your assignment is to stay on Xan and Scott," Gauge said, shaking his head.

But Brody couldn't bring himself to see her now. Or Scott. He knew he had a job to do, but he needed time to deal with this new revelation.

"You can do it." Gauge slapped Brody's back, obviously reading the reluctance on his face. "I still have people working on Coleman's location, so we can't do anything about him tonight. I'll check out the farm. You,"—he looked over at Blade—"help keep an eye out on the Bradley house tonight. Brutus is in no condition to do it himself."

"You got it."

Oh God, Brody wasn't ready to see Xan. His stomach churned, so he grabbed more crackers.

It was going to be a long night. *Better get used to it.* He had a job to do and a woman to avoid. Any attraction he was allowing himself to embrace before was now off-limits.

She deserved better than the likes of him.

———

XAN PASSED by the Sheppard's Garage wrecker on her

way back home Saturday morning after grocery shopping. She saw the long, blond hair and sunglasses concealing those deep-blue eyes she knew all too well. Yet, Brody didn't even so much as look at her when she waved at him.

Her Viking was avoiding her.

She had half a mind to whip this old Pinto around and follow him, demand some answers. They were not an item, but they'd been intimate, and now he was just brushing her off? That didn't make sense.

Unless Brody really was part of the FBI team watching over her, and Jack tipped him off about her suspicions regarding him. Wouldn't that just suck? It wasn't as if Jack owed her any loyalty. He was on the job, and if Brody was tasked with watching over her, then he was on the job too. If she was both of their assignment, then they had an obligation to share notes.

Oh Jesus, she hoped those notes didn't include how she liked to scream when Brody was pounding away inside her. She felt her face flush at the thought of him sitting around, talking about the intimate details of their lives.

But even if Brody was an agent—and that was a big if—he was also a man. She'd already deduced that if he stuck to her like glue because she was a job, he wasn't wearing his FBI hat in the sack. That was purely the man, not the agent, or hired help of her agent, whatever the case may be. But she'd like to know.

Boy, would she like to know.

And maybe he wasn't sticking to her like glue now because he didn't have anything to do with her case. Maybe he'd just gotten his fill of her. Ugh, the man was infuriating.

Resisting the urge to follow, she turned down her street and parked her car. She carried in and put away the frozen foods first, then came back out for the canned goods. She noticed Roxie supervising Chad putting a spare tire on her car.

"Hey," Xan called as she started to grab the last bag.

"Hi, girl. Come on over." Roxie motioned for her to join them, so Xan left the lone bag in her car and headed across the street.

"What happened? You get a flat?" As if that wasn't obvious.

"Yeah," Roxie sighed. "Chad's changin' it now. Don't know what happened. I guess I hit some glass last night or something coming from the game 'cause it was plumb flat this mornin'."

"No telling. At least you didn't get stranded somewhere."

"No lie. I'm glad Chad was here this mornin' to fix it. So, whatcha been out doin'?

"Shopping."

"All done, Mom. You should head over to Sheppard's and get them to replace it. You don't need to be drivin' around on this donut."

"Yes, son," Roxie said, chuckling, then turned to Xan. "Wanna come? I could use some girl talk."

Xan stiffened at the idea of running into Brody. He'd been avoiding her, and the last thing she wanted to do was go crawling around him like some stray dog, begging for attention. "I-I don't think—"

"Oh, c'mon now. Please? I don't wanna sit up there all by my lonesome. They don't even have a TV in the waitin' room."

Well, Brody did leave in the wrecker, so he should be gone a while. That thought gave her the encouragement she needed to say yes. She didn't mind going if she didn't have to face him and the humiliation of an in-person rejection. "Sure. Just let me get the last of my bags in."

"Goodie!" Roxie clapped her hands and Xan shook her head with a smile as she walked across the street back to her car. She grabbed the last of the bags, shut the hatchback, and carried it inside. She yelled to Scott that she was going with Roxie to get her tire fixed and headed back outside. Roxie was already in her driveway.

Xan climbed into the car and turned down the awful country music.

"What's goin' on with Brutus? He still avoiding you?"

They'd just had this conversation last night at the boys' football game. "Nothing's changed since last night, Roxie."

"Well, I've been thinkin' about your little predicament," Roxie said as she tucked her hair behind her ear. "That night we went out, you told me about people watchin' you. Maybe he knows something about that?"

Hmm. That was what Xan wondered too, but why would Roxie consider that a possibility. "I don't know who it could be. Why do you say that?"

"Because he always kept to himself, except when he banged some bimbo, but even then he tended to go out of town to pick up some chicks. Then you come to town, and he's on you like bees to a daffodil."

Xan smiled. "Maybe he's just trying to pollinate me."

Roxie giggled. "I know, right? Men. Always thinking with their peckers." She waved her hand and turned up the air conditioner even though they were about to pull into the garage. "It's already September, you'd think it'd cool down already. Anyway, what I'm sayin' is that maybe he has a reason for, um, for—"

"Fucking me?" Xan prompted, and Roxie blushed. "Honestly? I thought about that, but I can't be sure. It doesn't really matter now since he's treating me like some diseased outcast."

"Oh, hush up. He is not. He's a man. Didn't I just say that men think with their wee-wees? You just need to speak a language he understands," Roxie said as she turned off her car in front of the empty bay.

They both got out and entered the lobby. Colonel walked over, wiping his hands on a grease cloth. "Hello, ladies. How can I help you?"

"Hey there, Colonel. My tire's flat. Chad changed it and threw it in the trunk. Can you fix it for me?" She handed him her keys. Xan didn't miss her glancing at the bays, probably seeking out Bear. Except for the one time Roxie had confessed what happened, she never spoke of him, but knowing the truth, Xan could see the hurt in Roxie's eyes.

"Sure thing. It may be a while. We're shorthanded at the moment."

"That's okay. We'll wait."

Xan followed Roxie to the couch and sat beside her, figuring she shouldn't bring up Bear and instead thinking about the last thing Roxie had said before getting out of the car. "What do you mean I need to speak his language? He's a man, not an alien."

Roxie leaned back, crossing her arms over her perfect body and raising an eyebrow at her. "How long has it been since you've been with a man?"

"Umm, a week?" Xan shrugged innocently, knowing that wasn't the answer Roxie was looking for.

"I don't mean with Brutus, you dork. I mean before him."

"A while." She was *not* going to be specific. Oh hell no.

"Okay, look. Maybe you're just out of practice then. I do know you're under some kind of protection—"

"Shhhh." Xan swatted Roxie's shoulder. Jesus, why didn't she just take out a dang ad in the paper? *Xan Bradley, prude, is on the run from her ex-husband, Marco Collins.*

"Sorry," she whispered. "Any-hoo, I think maybe you haven't had too many opportunities to keep from getting rusty."

Lord have mercy. Xan needed to find the exit to get off this horror ride right now. "Get to the point."

"Seduce him." Roxie smiled crookedly at Xan.

"Seduce him? How?" They'd already had sex. If she threw herself at him and he turned her down, she wouldn't even take the time to go find a hole to crawl in because that'd take too long. Nope, she'd just dig one where she stood.

"Remember the night at the club? You went out and bought a kick-ass outfit, and he couldn't keep his hands off you."

"I can't afford to run out and buy something sexy every time I want to get him into bed. Besides, if he doesn't want me for *me*, then I'm not interested." Her vagina was calling foul on that.

"Oh, honey. You don't have to do that every time. Just every now and then to remind him what he's missing. Besides, I wasn't really talkin' about *outer* clothes. I was thinking more along the lines of lingerie." She wagged her eyebrows, biting her lower lip.

"Good grief. How in the world would he see me in that if I can't get him alone? I've only seen him on the road a few times. I can't exactly drive around in a teddy."

"Invite him over—"

"No." Xan was already shaking her head.

"Scott can stay the night with—"

"Uh-uh."

"Chad. And you can have the house all to—"

"No way."

"Yourself. Why? You can't tell me you're chicken? *Bwok, bwok.*" She put her hands in her armpits and started flapping her arms. "*Bwok, bwok!*"

"Shut up," Xan hissed, grabbing one of her arms before Roxie stood and did the damn chicken dance in the middle of the garage lobby.

Roxie giggled as she relaxed back into her seat. "C'mon. Give it some thought. It's not like either of you are goin' anywhere. Mark my words. You wear the right thing, and you'll have him eatin' right out of your hands, girl. Besides, you could use a little some-some."

Xan sighed and started to say something when the door to the lobby opened. She turned and stared right into her Viking's dark-blue eyes. His sunglasses were resting on his head, sweat trickling down his brow. Damn, she wanted to get up and lick it off his body. But knowing that was a really bad idea no matter how much her vagina was seconding it, she couldn't seem to tear her eyes away from him.

And he just stood there, staring back, his eyes dilating so quickly the blue bled to black before her eyes, the heat in them unmistakable. Oh yeah, he wanted her, so why was he resisting?

But as he stood there, the passion in his gaze shifted to sadness, and then something dark, almost devastating. He swallowed a few times, licked his lips, then looked at his feet and rubbed his nape under the hair tie, mussing the sweaty strands that clung to his neck.

"Everything all right with your car?"

It was obvious he was speaking to Xan, but the fact that

he looked away from her hurt. She tamped down that unfamiliar feeling and cleared her throat. "Yeah. Roxie had a flat, and she wanted me to keep her company while it was fixed."

He nodded and looked up—at Roxie. "You've been waitin' long?"

"Not too long." She shrugged.

"Um, I'll go see if anyone's started on it. If not, I'll take care of it."

And then he left the lobby without another glance at Xan.

"Hmmm. That boy is fightin' some major demons. Did you see that face? Bless his heart. I don't think it's anything you did, honey. I think you need to comfort him. And the best way to do that is to wrap your pussy around his cock," she whispered.

"Roxie!" Sheesh. "He hardly looked at me. Kinda hard to offer comfort when someone is avoiding you."

"Oh, now don't be a sourpuss. You know what they say —you catch more flies with honey than you do vinegar."

Xan took a deep breath. Maybe she really did need Roxie's advice. At the least, she needed to get Brody to talk to her about his change of heart. "Fine," she relented. "How do you propose I do that?"

"Easy. Douse yourself in honey and go catch that fly. Let him spend all night licking it off your body."

If only it was that easy.

CHAPTER SIXTEEN

Brody watched as Roxie and Xan pulled out of the garage, a heavy feeling in his chest. He'd busted ass to get a new tire on Roxie's wheel, get her tires balanced, and get them the hell out of here. God, he'd missed Xan like crazy, and seeing her was like pouring a pound of salt on an open wound, one he'd created himself by denying any contact with her.

One he'd created years ago by killing her daughter.

That was still a bitter pill to swallow, but he had no other choice than to face the facts. It was the only conclusion that made sense because the only memories he had of her was when she'd been all dolled up, and from Gauge's, Blade's, and Brody's research, the only time in her life when she'd dressed in designer clothes like that was when she was married to Collins. Add that to the fact Brody had been in some mysterious accident that by all accounts should've left him for dead, rather than with a case of amnesia, that could've happened around the time of Xan's marriage to Collins—it really didn't bode well for Brody. Collins could've tried to ice him after he killed the baby to cover it up. He tried every angle to refute those possibilities and came up horribly short. And disappointed.

And utterly devastated.

He'd been a wreck this past week, growling around the garage like a lion with a sore paw. And the truth was he was a man with an aching heart. He couldn't deny his feelings for Xan anymore. He was in love with her. And he'd fucking destroyed her life. He didn't deserve to be in the same room with her, much less buried in her body. Hell, he didn't even deserve to fantasize about her. His ass should be locked up on death row, if not already gassed.

He hadn't allowed himself to look at her even when he was keeping an eye on her place. He'd seen her car in the driveway and knew she was home, but he kept to the shadows and watched for any signs of unfriendly activity at night, and made sweeps of her house during the day while she was at work and Scott was at school. And he thought just being in her house was the worst form of torture. Hell, seeing all the places he'd touched her body and smelling her lingering vanilla scent was bad. But seeing her just now? That was pure agony.

He hoped it'd get better as time went on, but being forced to see her today proved that wasn't possible. He obviously couldn't remember for sure if he'd ever been in love before, but he knew he hadn't been since losing his memory. Until now.

He'd spent these years seeking sexual release with willing women and without emotional attachments, not because he was afraid of falling in love, but because he didn't know how to be in love with someone. And he still didn't know how to accept it, deal with it.

It didn't matter. He didn't deserve to be in the same room with her, so he sure as hell didn't deserve to be in a relationship with her. As he thought about her, he knew he'd never love another woman again. She was the only woman fully suited for him, but he wasn't suited for her. So now he had to learn how to live life without the one woman his heart demanded. If he was man enough, he'd confess to her what he'd done.

But something like that needed to be discussed in person, and he knew if he was alone with her, his cock would overrule all rational thought. To touch her would be succumbing to the darkest sin, one there was no redemption for. He was already damned, and he'd do his best to keep from dragging her with him.

So he was doomed to live a life of hell, knowing he hurt the woman he loved. It didn't matter that it happened before he fell in love with her. He was a monster, and he couldn't change his past no matter how much he wished it.

Colonel dropped some lug nuts and cursed, yanking Brody out of his depressing thoughts, though he knew he'd never truly escape them, only be granted brief reprieves.

"Where the fuck is Gauge? That little shit knows better than to take off on a Saturday. His ass is the lowest on this totem pole. He should be working overtime to ensure he stays welcome at this job." Colonel grumbled as he picked up the items he'd dropped.

"He'll be in later," Brody said, stepping over to help Colonel. He didn't want to tell his boss where Gauge was—in Prairie County, Arkansas, doing some digging on Dave Simmons.

"Colonel's right, that punk is new, so if anybody gets a Saturday off, it shouldn't be him," Roc said from across the shop.

It'd been a week since Brody found out about Roc feeding innuendo to Xan about Mimi, and he'd been avoiding him because Brody knew he'd knock out that jackass if given the opportunity. But keeping his distance didn't help him to keep his mouth shut. Brody knew he'd been snapping at Roc all week, but Colonel acted sympathetic, probably figuring that Brody's mood was specific to the baby-killing news and not something personal, so he hadn't chided him over it.

"He's been here for two fucking years, asshole. We all get days off now and then," Brody growled.

Roc slammed down his wrench and pointed his finger at Brody from over the car he was working on. "I wasn't talkin' to you, motherfucker. You can back off my ass any time now. I'm sick of your shit. I ain't done nothin' to you!"

That was it. Brody shoved off the ground and stormed over to Roc. "You haven't done anything to me? You haven't *done* anything to me? Is that right?" Brody reached the black-haired jerk, grabbed a handful of his shirt and pushed him into the side of the car. "How the *fuck* do you explain Mimi?" Brody yelled in his face.

Roc blanched briefly, then narrowed his green eyes. He put his hands against Brody's chest and shoved, but Brody was much bigger, and so pissed he couldn't be moved.

"Get off! I didn't do anything to Mimi."

"I'm talking about what you said to Xan about her. Your punk-ass practically told her I was fucking Mimi!"

All work in the shop stopped and a couple of the guys gasped. "Dude, that ain't right," Hunter said.

"What the hell's wrong with you?" Bear shook his head as he headed over to break up the impending fight. "She's like our den mother. Brings us cookies and shit."

"He likes stirring up trouble, that's what," Blade muttered.

"I never said you were doing Mimi," Roc spat. "I told

her you were over at Mimi's house and had been there all morning. It ain't my fault she assumed the worst."

"You lyin' sack of shit!" Brody's fist connected with Roc's face once, twice, before Bear threw his arms around him to pull him away.

He wasn't strong enough, so Hunter and Blade jumped in to help. The three were finally able to peel Brody off Roc.

"It ain't my fault you're sweet on her pussy," Roc yelled as he threw a punch. Brody blocked it, but not before it made contact with his jaw and slid away.

Getting sucker punched by a prick who was bad-mouthing Xan made Brody's blood boil even hotter. He roared and dragged the three men holding him back in Roc's direction and hit him again.

"Enough!" Colonel ordered as he grabbed Roc and pulled him away from the group. It was easier to move the smaller man, and it seemed as if Colonel was going to let it go. But then he got in Brody's face. "Get the hell out of here. Go cool off at home." Then he turned to Roc. "You too. And if you want a job to come back to, you'll watch your fucking mouth in the future. Got it?"

Roc grunted and nodded before looking away. Brody stalked off to his motorcycle, revved it up, and shot out of the parking lot. He was so pissed he was shaking. So much for not acting on that rage. When he'd snapped, there was no going back. Roc deserved every hit, and then some. Brody should've pushed the other guys off and pummeled that jackass. Misguided anger or not, Roc needed to be taken down a peg or two, and Brody was just the man to do it. If that man so much as breathed wrong around him, he'd take him out.

He wasn't ready to go home because he knew he'd drown his frustrations, anger, pain in more alcohol, so he drove to Gauge's house, hoping he was back and had found something about Dave Simmons. When he neared, he saw Gauge's truck, so he pulled in. After parking, he strode up to the door and knocked. He heard the chain rattle just before the door opened.

"Hey, man. C'mon in." Brody followed Gauge back into his living room where he had a laptop open and papers strewn about. They both sat on the shabby couch. "Whatcha doin' here so early? I figured I wouldn't see you for a couple more hours."

Brody swiped his hand over his face and then over his hair. "Got sent home for fighting with Roc."

"Ah, well, that was bound to happen." Gauge chuckled. "He needs a good ass-whipping anyway."

"Yeah," Brody grunted. "It was stopped before it really started." He sighed as he sat back and ran his hands over his jeans. "Any luck today?"

"Yes and no. We still can't count Simmons out as a suspect, but he hasn't been hiding anything. He was there at the farm today, and I spoke to him. I flashed him one of the fake identification badges Colonel had made for us. Told him I was an FBI agent working the Collins case." Gauge wagged his eyebrows. "He hadn't seemed uneasy with that and answered the general questions I'd asked. But when I acted like the questions were over and pretended to be shootin' the shit with him, I asked him about his retirement and he clammed up. Didn't volunteer any information and promptly escorted me off the property."

"Hmmm, that could be taken a couple of different ways. Either he's dirty and was covering his ass, or—"

"Or he's just a former agent who answered questions to help another agent out and wanted to keep his personal life off the table."

Either way, Simmons was still a suspect. "We need something more concrete before we decide if he's a real threat to her."

"Yeah, I've been following the money. So far, that big deposit is the only one that doesn't fit. It came out of nowhere, and he hightailed it out of the agency as soon as that puppy cleared the bank. Short of asking him outright, which we can't do, it's taking longer than I wanted finding the source."

"Thanks, man. I appreciate you doing all this."

Gauge sat back and stared at Brody for several seconds. "She means a lot to you."

It wasn't a question, but Brody felt like answering anyway. "Yep." As hopeless as the situation was, his feelings were not questionable.

"Look. I know I've told you this before, Brutus, but you shouldn't take what Colonel told you at face value. Think about it. He's getting intel from sources that are shady. Those guys have their own agendas. Who's to say the Tess Collins story wasn't fed with a specific outcome in mind."

Part of what Gauge was saying was true, but Brody couldn't afford to hope. And yet...

"What would anybody gain by leading me to believe I'd killed Xan's baby?"

"The very fact that you're questioning yourself is reason enough. Who knows, man? These guys could be looking for a score and would know Collins is looking for his ex and his kid. We still haven't cornered that Dale Adams rat. Someone knows Xan and Scott are hiding out here, and we don't know how close that someone is to Collins. If Adams worked for Collins, he'd be here by now. So I think Adams is some third-party player. He sees you hanging around Xan, feeds this to his boss. Colonel asks questions about your past to people who'd have been around during that time—people like this Dale Adams character. The right person has his ears open, and he can figure out how to play everything to his advantage. If they can't get to Xan because you're always around, they take you out. They can't get close enough to you physically, so they mess with your head, hope to trip you up, catch you off guard."

Brody chuckled, the first time he felt genuine humor since learning the dreadful news. "That's some story you've conjured up. Unfortunately, you have no proof except to show me the ass you pulled it out of."

Gauge smiled and punched Brody's shoulder. "My point is we don't know what happened. If it makes you feel better to distance yourself from Xan, then I'm not going to argue. But I think you should be critical of anything you learn about your past. No matter how good or bad it seems."

Brody felt a little better looking at his situation through Gauge's eyes. He made sense, and maybe Brody should be a little more leery of what he'd learned about his previous life. But even if there was the slightest possibility that he killed Xan's daughter, he had to live with it if that was the case. It didn't change anything about his relationship with Xan. It only gave him motivation to seek the truth for himself.

"Thanks, man. I'm gonna head out. Let me know if you find anything about Simmons' money."

"Will do."

Brody left and let the thrilling hum of this bike soothe his muscles. He was still pissed at Roc and fighting the urge to demand answers from Colonel on his informational sources, but now that he had a glimmer, a sliver of hope, his mind was fighting to recall Xan's beautiful body spread out beneath him. He couldn't allow that because nothing had truly changed. But as soon as he got a few beers in him, his moral fiber would dissolve and he'd find himself wrapped up in a Xan fantasy so hot, he'd be jacking off all night.

A few minutes later, Brody was pulling into his drive-way. He killed the engine and walked into his house, heading straight for his kitchen. It was time to get started on drowning his morals so he could dream about the woman he loved, doing very naughty things to his body. He yanked the fridge door open, grabbed a beer, and twisted off the cap. He downed half before he turned and almost choked on the last bit.

Because, in his haste, he hadn't noticed he wasn't alone in his kitchen.

Xan sat in a chair at the far end of the table, facing him, wearing the sexiest, purple-and-black negligee he'd ever seen. His dick was already half hard with images of Xan's beautiful body. Now it was painfully erect. Thankfully, he was too shocked to groan at the sight of her because he'd definitely be making some noises. He took two steps in her direction before he realized what he was doing.

No. He stopped and squeezed his eyes shut, blocking out the vixen before him. He couldn't touch her, but she didn't understand why.

And he wasn't going to tell her.

Evidently, he wasn't man enough to break the news to her. But he didn't have time to chastise himself right now. He needed to be a dick—not think with it—and throw her out. He'd been rude to her in the beginning, so he could do it again.

He opened his eyes and the air locked in his lungs. God, she was a vision. How could he turn her away without crushing her heart? He'd already done enough damage to her. He didn't want to just keep adding to it.

"Xan," he breathed. Whatever else he was going to say

was forgotten, if it was ever clear, when she stood. That damn teddy had tiny purple lace covering her tits and scrunched black lace that clung to her body, ending just below her pussy where garters tipped with purple bows hung to hold up her sheer, black stockings. She even wore stilettos strapped at the ankle.

She was a fucking knockout.

"Xan," he tried again, but had to stop to clear the catch in his throat. Jesus, he wanted her. He clenched his hands, fisting them and stretching his fingers several times as his body fought his brain for control.

"Brody," she murmured, stepping toward him.

A groan slipped out, but he bit it off as he took a step back, retreating like some scared newbie.

"Where are you going, lover?" she purred as she advanced on him.

He was a goner. He couldn't think straight with all the blood rushing to his cock. His balls were aching, sweat beading on his brow. He had to get her out of here, so he could jack off. If he could just beat one out, he could remember the reasons why he needed to avoid her.

She stepped up against him and he instinctually grabbed her arms to push her away. But she quickly flicked the button of his jeans and unzipped his pants, giving his cock a little relief. Only he didn't have time to relish the additional room his growing dick needed because she dropped to her knees and licked the pulsing head.

He hissed, grabbing her hair. "Xan, this isn't a good—"

Oh for the love of God. She took him into her mouth and his objection died the death it deserved. No way in hell could he find the willpower to stop her now.

"Shit, baby," he groaned as she sucked just the head, her tongue teasing the ridge just the way he liked it.

She hummed around his cock and his knees started to buckle. She arched her back, exposing her bare ass. *Bare.* Shit, she wasn't wearing any panties under that devil's wet dream. His hands fisted tighter in her hair as his control snapped. He held her still while his hips thrust, fucking her sweet little mouth, watching the globes of her ass sway as she churned her wanton hips. And still she sucked him with greedy enthusiasm.

"*Fuck.*" He wasn't going to last. He pumped faster and she grabbed his balls, squeezing them almost painfully. "*Ahh*, I'm gonna come, baby."

He pushed into her two more times, feeling his balls tighten. If he could think straight, he'd be embarrassed by how fast he was ready to blow. Because he *was* ready. Oh yeah, he was about to shoot down her throat and would relish every second of it.

She pulled away suddenly, and he howled in frustration, feeling the impending orgasm hover as if on a knife's edge. She stood, her mouth swollen and wet with her effort. Brody panted, staring at her, wondering why she stopped, keeping himself from shoving her back to her knees to finish like some selfish prick.

"You want to come, you have to fuck me first. Then I'll let you come whichever way you want."

CHAPTER SEVENTEEN

Xan watched Brody's eyes, already glazed with lust, narrow with her demand. She knew she wasn't playing fair getting him all worked up and stopping, but she didn't care. He'd been avoiding her for a week now, and she wanted answers.

And, by God, if she didn't get answers, she was going to make him regret his actions by showing him what he'd been missing. Because she'd been missing it—him—too. She'd lain awake every night fantasizing about him. It'd been extremely hard stopping just now, but she had to embrace the bigger picture here.

She wanted him. In bed. In her life. Maybe getting answers wouldn't be possible, but she'd do what she could to open up to him and encourage him to do the same. But if he didn't want a relationship, she'd take what she could get. She wasn't going another twelve years without sex if she could help it.

And if she had to be a cock-tease to get her way? So be it. She knew the outfit was a hit the moment his eyes widened. The bulge in his pants? Oh yeah, that was another indicator.

"You'll let me come however I want?" he rasped.

"Mmm-hmm." She ran a finger along his neck, inciting a subtle shiver in response. Her Viking seemed to be holding back still, and that was unacceptable, so she mustered up the gumption to continue her seduction. "What's wrong, big boy? You know you want to feel how wet you make me," she crooned, running her hand down his abdomen and lightly clutching his cock.

He groaned and swayed toward her. His movement was automatic, but she didn't care. Since he was leaning her way, she seized the opportunity. Already in ridiculously high heels, she nudged up on her toes with ease and captured his open mouth with hers, sliding her tongue into the heat. She kissed him hard as she squeezed his cock, and he broke. Brody grabbed her ass, lifting her and turning, slamming her against the nearest wall. *That's what I'm talking about.* Her arms went around his neck, legs instinctively wrapped around his hips as she rubbed her weeping pussy against his cock.

He took control of the kiss, ravishing her mouth, nipping at her lips, massaging his tongue against hers almost desperately. Xan continued to rub herself against him, loving the animalistic sounds rumbling in his chest and tearing from his mouth and into hers. He squeezed her ass cheeks with such force he'd leave marks, and that only made her hotter. The idea of him marking her as his ignited some primal instinct in her that should've been reserved for men with cavemen mentalities, not a woman who'd suffered what had to be the longest dry streak in history.

And she didn't care. He could grab her by the hair and

drag her wherever he wanted at this point, and she wouldn't protest.

Unable to wait any longer for him to possess her, Xan reached down and guided his dick to her aching opening. As soon as the head nudged her, Brody grabbed her ass to hold her still and plunged home, driving to the hilt.

Xan gasped.

Brody growled.

And he was pumping into her with no hesitation. She threw her head back, hitting the wall, panting for breath as he fucked her hard. He released one hand from her ass and grabbed her hair, bringing her face down to his.

"Is this what you want, baby? Damn you." He kissed her again, groaning into her mouth as he plowed into her with passion, with anger, with desperation she still didn't understand.

But it didn't matter. Electrical shocks traveled down her back, settled at the base of her spine as her orgasm started to build. She dug her fingers into his hair, pulling it free of the thong, and clutched it as she moaned into the near-painful kiss.

Oh God, she was about to come. Her core fisted around him and she knew she was about to go over. She could feel it rushing toward her like a runaway train, and it would crash over her in seconds.

Brody's thrusts became frantic, and she screamed into his mouth just as her climax detonated. His mouth ripped from hers, his head burying in her neck as a roar released from him. Then he bit her shoulder hard to stifle his cry as he came with her. She winced at the power of his continued thrusts into her oversensitive body and his teeth locked on to her skin, but the pain only intensified the pleasure.

Long moments later, his grip on her ass eased, his teeth

unclenched, and his thrusting stopped. She was panting, sweat trickling down her cheek. He was moaning, rubbing his forehead against her shoulder.

"Sorry," he breathed. "I shouldn't have taken you so hard." He actually sounded upset by that, and Xan couldn't allow that. She wouldn't.

"You shouldn't have waited so long to take me," she said softly, stroking his hair.

He chuckled and she smiled, pleased he wasn't going to dwell on it. He eased her down and stared into her eyes, stroking her cheek. The emotions she saw were unfathomable. Roxie was right—Brody was fighting something. Before she could ask, he leaned down and kissed her forehead, the tip of her nose, and then her shoulder where he'd bitten her, where she was sure a bruise was forming if not already there.

"I intend to make up for lost time," he mumbled against her shoulder. Then he kissed her neck and bent down, hooking his arm behind her knees and lifting her to him. He carried her down the hall, into his bedroom, and through the master bathroom door. He gently eased her to her feet and turned to the whirlpool tub, turning on the water and gauging the temperature until he was satisfied with the heat, then flicked the stopper. "As much as I love this outfit of yours, baby," he said as he trailed a finger along the thin strap. "It has to come off."

Even after that mind-blowing orgasm, her body tingled with awareness, but she was suddenly struck with a small case of shyness as he peeled the negligee off her body. She'd had to give herself a major pep talk to show up at his house in this thing, but she knew the benefits far exceeded any urge to be bashful. She'd never before put forth effort like this to attract a man. Hell, after getting free from Marco, men freaked her out. She'd done everything in her power to avoid those Y-chromosome carriers, and here she was tempting the biggest, sexiest man she'd ever laid eyes on.

When she was naked save for her stockings and stilettos, Brody kissed her chest...right over her heart. And it raced at his tender attention. Then he pulled away and caressed the skin where his lips had just been, gazing into her eyes. She inhaled quickly, not quite a gasp because she was too mesmerized to react suddenly.

And then, as if the intensity was too much for him to bear, his eyes blinked away and back before looking down at his hand over her heart. The emotion pouring from him was like a living thing in the room, and Xan swayed as if physically impacted. Emotionally, she was already too far gone. Brody grasped her hips as he knelt before her, keeping her steady. Slowly, so slowly, he removed her shoes and slid her stockings off, following the path with his lips, kissing her inner thighs, knees, the arches of her feet. Xan had never felt this kind of attention from another man. It was as if she was the most precious thing to him, as fragile as spun glass, and she didn't know how to define—or even embrace—the warmth surrounding her.

He followed the path back up her body, his mouth lingering on her nipples, and her head fell back on a moan. Okay, she could attempt definitions later.

He kissed a path up her neck to her ear. "It's ready," he breathed, and before she had the chance to acknowledge him, he swooped down and picked her up, eliciting a screech out of her.

Brody chuckled as he stepped over to the bathtub, and she tried to fight the heat creeping up her throat from her shocked outburst. He gently placed her in the hot water and turned on the jets. Reaching past her, he grabbed a washcloth and some soap, which reminded her of an outdoorsy scent. It didn't really smell like Brody, but it was definitely not a girlie fragrance. He lathered up and then started washing her.

Her head fell back, eyes closing. *This* was heavenly. Pure ecstasy. She groaned when he massaged the shoulder closest to him, rubbing harder than necessary for just washing her. Not that she was complaining.

"If you come over to my house every night and do this, I'd be at your mercy."

"Hmm, I think that can be arranged."

Xan opened an eye, glancing at him without turning her head. He was concentrating on her bath-massage, working her tight muscles and washing her skin, but even with him touching her like this, he still felt too far away from her.

"You should join me. I could return the favor."

He looked at her and gave his head a quick shake before continuing with his sinfully delightful ministration.

"Why not?"

"This is for you," he said, keeping his eyes on his task.

"Then you should get in because that's what I want." She stuck out her lip with a fake pout, and he smiled crookedly at her.

"You don't play fair?"

"What gave that away? The fact that I showed up here half naked?" She winked, and a chuckle slipped out of him before he could stop it.

"Okay. You win."

Brody stood and removed his pants. His shirt had disappeared a long time ago. She scooted forward when he stood straight and stepped back over to the tub. She turned her head, watching as he stepped in behind her, trying not to smile when he winced while settling in.

"Jesus, it's hot."

"You're the one who ran the water." She giggled as she leaned into his chest. "Don't be a crybaby."

"Crybaby?" he murmured, picking up the cloth and washing one breast as he kneaded the other one with his free hand. He bent his head down to her ear and nuzzled it. "I'll show you crybaby."

He gave her nipple a sharp tweak and she cried out. "And to think *you* said that *I* didn't play fair. That's cheating." He laughed as he soothed the pain, rolling her nipple between his fingers. The pain quickly turned into a pleasure she couldn't hide. With a soft moan, her head rested on his shoulder, her knees falling slightly apart. Brody dropped the cloth and gave her other nipple the same attention. The dual assault was too much to take, so she writhed in the water, her motion causing more waves within the jetted bliss.

He nipped her ear, his breath coming hot and hard against her skin, and her hips kept churning, seeking contact with something, anything. She backed up against him and he shifted down into the water so that his body was at more of an angle. Her buttocks rubbed his erection and he growled into the ear he was ravishing. She rose, leaning all her weight against him, and grabbed his cock from between her legs.

"Oh God, Xan," Brody groaned as she stroked him. But it still wasn't enough. His mouth was on her flesh. His hands were on her breasts, and he was rocking that hard-as-steel cock in her hands, but she needed so much more. She moved and angled his cock at her entrance. She had to have him. Again. "Baby, it'll hurt you in the water. Give me a sec, and I'll—"

She didn't wait. She leaned forward and took his cock

inside her halfway. It registered somewhere in the back of her lust-filled brain that he was right—his cock didn't slide in easily. She didn't have time to process that even if she could break through the passionate fog that consumed her because Brody's breath caught, and he snaked one arm around her belly as he hoisted them out of the water and onto the ledge of the tub. He propped himself against the corner of the wall, his feet still in the water, and she sank all the way down, taking him to the hilt.

He clutched her hips as she rode him reverse-cowgirl style. If she wasn't so turned-on, she'd find the whole cowgirl concept funny considering her previous dislike for all things country. But she was already close to coming so that thought fled as soon as it entered. She braced her hands on his knees and she bounced on his dick with greedy abandon, grinding against him. His panting echoed off the tiled walls, and she could tell that he was close too. He shot up, pressing his chest against her back, wrapping an arm around her, while the fingers of his free hand sought her clit. "You feel so good, baby. So fucking good."

He thrust up, meeting her on each downward stroke while he fingered her aching nub. Her orgasm built. Tingles licked her spine and she knew it was over.

"Brody," she panted, reaching back and grabbing his neck. "I'm gonna come."

"Yes, baby. Ahhh, fuck!" He slammed up again and she screamed. Explosions of colors, lights danced before her eyes as she continued to ride him, ride out her climax, ride out his joint release. Wrapped up in passion so strong, she trembled.

She was so relaxed she was vaguely aware of him lowering them back into the tub, him crooning softly in her ear. While she was curled into his body, fighting unconsciousness, he washed them both quickly, but thoroughly. Then he shut off the jets, pulled the plug, and dragged them from the bathtub. He dried them both and carried her to his bed.

He eased in beside her, pulling her into his arms, gently tracing lazy patterns along her hip, and she realized she'd never felt this protected. This loved. Brody may not be in love with her, but she couldn't deny the fact she was in love with him. She wasn't sure when it had happened. Maybe that first time she saw him at the garage when her body had recognized his importance to her before her brain had. Or maybe it was the first time they'd kissed and she'd never felt that kind of desire from another man. Or maybe it was the first time they'd made love, which was why it'd hurt her so much when he'd immediately rejected her. She didn't know when she crossed the point of no return with Brody Jackson. She just knew she had.

It didn't matter if Brody would ever feel the same way about her. She learned the hard way there were no guarantees in life, but she wanted to make the most of their time together.

And she wanted to lift the cloud that'd settled over him during the last week or so. She didn't know what was bothering him, but she wanted to help him.

That was what people did for those they loved.

She rolled over, startling him, catching him lost in his own thoughts.

"I thought you were out," he murmured.

"Almost. You wore me out."

He smiled and her heart melted. His long hair unbound, fanning over his shoulders, made her want to run her fingers through it just to feel him, soothe him. "I'll take that as a compliment, darlin'."

"You should." And she couldn't help it—she smiled back. "So tell me something about you?"

And just like that, his smile disappeared, and those storm clouds rolled into his eyes. She hated to see his happy and relaxed demeanor change, but she wanted to help him with whatever was bothering him. And she had to start by getting to know him better.

"What do you want to know?" he hedged, and she didn't like the fact he was guarded.

She reached up and stroked his cheek and gently brought his head down to hers, kissing him lightly. He didn't respond right away, but he couldn't resist her for long. No matter his reasons for his recent avoidance, he still wanted her. He kissed her back but let her control it. When she pulled away he grunted and she smiled, loving that his need was so transparent where she was concerned. "Where did you grow up?" She figured she'd start with something easy and continued stroking his cheek, encouraging him to answer.

He sighed, shutting his eyes and giving his head an infinitesimal shake. Okay, maybe that wasn't an easy question to start with, but when he opened his eyes and gave her a sad smile, she knew he was going to answer.

"I don't know."

"What do you mean?"

He shifted, bringing her closer to him. He cupped her hand against his face, holding it to his cheek. "I mean I was in a bad accident many years ago and don't remember anything that happened before then."

"Oh." Wow. He really didn't know where he'd grown up. "How long ago was that?"

"Um, I'm guessing around thirteen years. My early memories are vague. I just remember bits and pieces of being in a hospital. I know it wasn't more than thirteen years ago because that was when *that* hospital opened."

"What happened?"

"Not really sure. I was told it was an accident, assuming it was a hit-and-run, but there were no vehicles. Colonel, my boss, found me and helped me out, then gave me a job once I was able to work."

"And you like working for him?"

He smiled. "Yeah. It's cool. I'm good with cars and stuff, so I figured I at least tinkered around with them before my accident."

"You seem to get along well with the other guys."

"Blade and me are tight. Bear's a good guy. Helps a lot, but doesn't take any shit from anybody. Hunter grew up around here and moved back after something went down. I think he's here licking his wounds or somethin'. Roc is an ass—"

"That's the one who told me about you and Mimi."

Brody's eyes narrowed. "I know. We sorta got into it. I'd whip his ass if it wouldn't cost me my job. Hell, I just might do it anyway if he pisses me off again." He sighed, shifting and bringing her closer. "Anyway, Gauge's the newbie. None of us are itchin' to trust people, so he's still kind of an outsider where the other guys are concerned. But I ain't got any problems with him, and he's been helping me... Er, I mean, he's helpful, eager to be a team player, so I cut him some slack."

This was good. Brody was opening up to her. Of course, he wasn't spilling anything heavy yet. But it was a start. She liked the casual chitchat, especially doing it naked in bed, but she had an objective here, and she needed to get to it. "You wanna tell me what happened? Why you started avoiding me again all of a sudden?" She posed her questions casually, so she couldn't come off defensive and hinder her shot at an honest response from him.

He looked at her, and the light in his eyes dimmed. His jaw ticked as he clenched his teeth, but his expression wasn't one of anger or even avoidance. It was more like shame, and she immediately regretted asking. Sure, she wanted to know his reason, but not if talking about it would cause him more harm than just letting the topic go.

"I, er, I'm sorry. You're right, I was avoiding you. But I want you to know it had nothing to do with you." He leaned up, braced himself on his elbow, and gazed into her eyes. "You are perfect. An angel. And I'm...I'm not. There are things in my past I'm not proud of. I wish I could change them, but I can't."

He looked desolate, so alone, and it didn't make sense, but she wanted to help ease his pain. It was, after all, the real reason for getting him to open up to her. "We are who we are because of the things we went through."

"You have no idea, Xan. I'm a monster, a mur—"

"It doesn't matter to me what you are."

"It should." He fell back onto the bed, rubbing his eyes. "I have to tell you something, and I'm not even sure how to do it."

CHAPTER EIGHTEEN

Xan got a sinking feeling in the pit of her stomach, but even the prickling foreboding didn't stop her from wanting to comfort him. "My ex-husband tried to kill me," she blurted. She wasn't sure what she was going to say, but it wasn't that.

Brody's hands fell away from his face as he gaped at her. Great. Now that she'd dropped that little bomb on him, there was no going back.

"I got married very young. Marco was..." She trailed off, remembering how charming he was to her at the beginning, and smiled at the memory that was a lifetime ago. "I don't know. He was larger than life." She pinned Brody with a stare. "And he wanted me. See, my parents died when I was ten. They had me late in life, and my grandparents had died when I was younger. My uncle on my mom's side was in a nursing home, and my aunt on my father's side was all I had. She was retired and tried to help me as much as she could, but she had a heart attack a year later. That's when I entered the system."

Brody stroked her arm, and she felt his encouragement

through his gentle touch. She took a deep breath, drawing in the strength she needed to continue, inhaling his scent and immediately recognizing the strength he presented. And not physical strength. No, just having him near her seemed to feed her needs, whatever she needed, when she needed it, and right now, she needed that strength. She couldn't explain, but she relished it, figuring this was normal for someone in love. Well, normal for *normal* people.

"I met Marco when I was in high school. He was a few years older. In college, or so he said. After a few years of bouncing from one foster home to the next, being treated by someone like I was the only person in the world who mattered was nice. Really nice." She stopped to gather her thoughts. This was harder than she thought it was going to be, but she needed to forge ahead. If she wanted an open, honest relationship with Brody, he needed to know everything about her.

"The fact that he was rich didn't play into it," she continued. "I mean, I thought it was cool not having to worry about stretching my money because he bought me all kinds of stuff. But it was the little things, like if I was out of soda and didn't have time to stop on my way home from my part-time job, I'd find a fresh Dr. Pepper with a rose on the counter when I got home." Her lips flattened as she thought about how obvious the bad signs were now that she was looking back. "I fell hard and fast and then got knocked up. We married right away."

"And then he changed," Brody said, stating the obvious when Xan didn't continue.

"And then he changed." She nodded. "But it was nowhere near as bad as it was after I'd given birth to a girl. He was pissed." She chanced a look at Brody, his eyes squinted as he worked his jaw furiously. He was angry for her, and that thought melted her already warmed heart. Yeah, she was head-over-heels in love with this man. "Anyway, he beat me and raped me until I gave up fighting back. It's weird how someone could see a person and know right away what kind of mood they're in. I could walk into the same room Marco was in and instantly know if it was going to be a bad day."

"Did you try to leave the bastard?"

"No," she said quickly. "He'd have killed me." And then she laughed bitterly. "I knew he'd try to kill me if I ever left on my own, but after I had Scott, I found my ticket out of that hellhole."

"Which was?" Brody asked as he stroked Xan's hair.

"Evidence against him. You see, he was so filthy rich because he was into organized crime. I found a flash drive containing information on contracts and contacts he'd secured along with some information about some human trafficking job that went to shit. I turned it over to the FBI. But he found out and tried to off me."

Brody leaned in and kissed her temple. "He didn't succeed."

"No," she breathed, snuggling into him. "But the evidence disappeared, so the only thing they had on him was an attempted murder charge. He was convicted, and I was put under protection. But he recently got out, and I think he'll come after me. Or Scott." She looked up into Brody's eyes. "I can't let him take my baby." Her voice cracked, and Brody squeezed her to him.

"That'd never happen. I won't allow it." And he said it with such conviction that she almost believed him. Almost.

She gripped his shoulders, her nails digging into his skin and hitting steel muscle. "You don't understand. He'll stop at nothing. *Nothing*. Until he gets what he wants."

"I'll stop him," Brody growled. "Consider it already done, baby." Xan searched his eyes and saw that he truly believed this. She knew it wouldn't be that simple, but the fact that he cared this much helped soothe her, making her want to seek more comfort from him. "I don't want you worrying about this. In fact, this is part of what I tried to tell you earlier. I—"

"Shhh." She put two fingers over his mouth. She appreciated his effort to convince her she didn't have anything to worry about, but she knew better. Talking about it wouldn't make it go away, and she'd succeeded in opening up to him. More than succeeded. She felt this warm blanket of protection surrounding her from Brody's words. He couldn't make Marco disappear, but he could be her moral support, which was more than she'd had outside of the FBI agents assigned to her case. It made her love him even more, want him desperately. "No more talking." She heard his breath catch as her mouth descended on his.

———

BRODY KNEW he should push her away and finish this conversation. She'd opened up to him, and by God, he wanted to do the same with her. He wanted to come clean with his past, hell, with his present too, since technically, she was an assignment.

He knew she'd stopped being an assignment from practically the very beginning, but that didn't stop him from wanting to bear his soul as she had done. Until there were no secrets between them, they couldn't be a couple.

And when she found out the truth, she'd cut his balls off.

Nope, no hope for them being a couple. So why couldn't his heart accept what his brain already knew?

If he was a gentleman who thought with that organ and not his dick, he'd push her away, confess his sins, and await her wrath. But as Xan's tongue licked the seam of his lips, probing for entry, any logical thought process disintegrated.

On a groan, he opened for her. Her tongue delved into his mouth, seeking his, and more of his control slipped. He flipped her, landing on top as he took over the kiss, his tongue plundering the moist, hot depths of her mouth. She was a fucking drug to him, and there was no detox. She was air for long-submerged lungs. Water for a man dehydrated. She was everything to him, and even though they didn't have a future together, he'd love her forever.

Yeah, he was a lovesick fool, and he didn't give a damn. He'd have to give her up one day, but he just couldn't push her away any longer.

He trailed hot kisses along her jaw to her neck, nipping and licking the path and grinding his aching cock against her wet pussy. He wanted to slam home—they were already naked, so it'd take all of two seconds—but he needed to take her slow, love her with his body as he loved her with his heart, his soul. He wasn't worthy of her, but she'd always be the other half of him.

And he wanted to touch, kiss every inch of her, worship her body as she deserved.

As he continued his loving attention, trailing a hot path downward, his lips found a puckered nipple. Xan gasped and arched, thrusting it into his mouth, the sound of her pleasure fueling him on. He worried it with his teeth before sucking it hard, bringing that sweet nub to the roof of his mouth. And he still couldn't get enough of her.

He would never get enough.

He rolled her other nipple with his fingers as he devoured her. God, she tasted so good. Like the sweetest candy. He alternated, swooping over to the other nipple with a groan as his hand raked over the wet one he'd just deserted. But he couldn't stay on one for long, so he moved between the two, licking, sucking, nipping one while he pinched, pulled, rolled the other. And he moved back and forth, ratcheting up their desire. Xan was a wanton, writhing goddess beneath him, moaning her ecstasy and clutching his hair, not really guiding him—just holding on while he feasted on her.

And then the scent of her musky, spicy arousal mixed with the hint of vanilla that was her essence called to him. He left the pleasure of her breasts and peppered kisses along her softly rounded belly. When he reached her sex, he nipped her upper thigh, her inner thigh, and continued trekking south, brushing his lips on her knee, calf, foot. She let out a little frustrated whimper when he skipped over her swollen pussy, and he smiled, loving the sounds escaping her. He continued his caresses, kissing a path back up her other leg. And this time, he hovered over her core as her legs trembled in anticipation. He blew his hot breath over her drenched folds.

"Please," she moaned, and his sudden intake of breath at her begging for his touch flooded his senses with her intoxicating scent.

He lowered, lightly licking her seam. "Tell me what you want, baby."

"You. Just you, Brody." Fuck! His cock jerked at her admission. He'd just wanted her to be vocal about her sexual needs, and she'd hit him with something deeper. And he loved it. Hated it because he wanted her too, and he knew they didn't have forever, even though she'd own his soul forever.

But right now, right here she was his, and a primal urge enveloped him. "Mine," he growled, and then he devoured her pussy like he'd done with her breasts. He licked, sucked, nipped along her slit, his tongue swirling circles around her clit, and the hands in his hair that were just lazily holding on became more demanding. She tugged on him, trying to get him to direct his sensual attention to her most sensitive part. Instead, his tongue stabbed into her quivering pussy, and she jerked up with a gasp as her hips flew off the bed.

She was about to come apart, and his cock was throbbing so painfully in anticipation that he was about to embarrass himself and shoot all over his sheets. He needed to end her torment right now and send her over that precipice he'd had her on. He drew her clit into his mouth and sucked lightly as he batted it with his tongue and shoved two fingers into her. She screamed. Exploded. And he couldn't continue his ministrations to bring her back down. He had to get inside her right fucking now.

He lunged forward, bracing his weight on his forearms, taking her mouth with his in a searing kiss as his cock slipped slowly inside her. Oh, going slow was killing him, but if he pounded into her, he'd come, and then he'd really be embarrassed.

"Ahhh, yeah, baby," he breathed into her mouth, fisting her hair, as he started thrusting in earnest.

"I can taste myself on you."

And if that wasn't the sexiest thing she'd ever said, he didn't know what was.

He reached down and grabbed her thigh, pulling her leg up and anchoring it at his hip. Jesus, he wanted to rest it on his shoulder so he could lick her dainty ankle, but he'd save that for another time. Right now, he wanted his mouth melding with hers as he took her.

She lifted her other leg, hooking it against him like the one he'd positioned, effectively opening her up to him, and he pounded into her, finding depths he'd never experienced. It was heaven to his heart. Her hands circled him, nails digging into his back to force him as close as he could possibly get.

And then she gasped, fingers biting into his skin as she thrust her hips up and exploded in his arms. The sounds of her cries, the feel of her clenching around him, her nails breaking his skin, the smell of her sweat and arousal, finally broke his last thread of control. With a roar, he plowed into her as he came, barely registering Xan flying into a second orgasm, giving her everything he had to give.

Long moments later, he eased off her and walked into the bathroom to retrieve a washcloth. As he turned, he noticed blood trickling along his side and smirked. His little hellion marked him. And with that thought, another surge of possession swept through him. One he damn well should get used to. He quickly cleaned up his battle scars and returned to Xan, gently cleaning her. He tossed the cloth into the hamper and crawled into bed next to her. She was almost asleep, and he'd love to keep her here all night, but because he loved her, her priorities were also his. He was a selfish bastard, but he knew he'd never be the number-one man in her life. That position was already filled, and Brody would happily take second place for as long as she let him.

"Baby? Where's Scott at? Do you have to go home tonight?"

She groaned and snuggled into him. Those damn warm tingly things crept over him, and he figured he'd have to get used to that too. He just didn't have the willpower to deny his need for her. The guilt of what he might've done to her all those years ago would eat away at him as his love for her continued to grow, but that was a burden he would bear all by himself. A secret he could never confess. Because it would destroy the woman who mattered most to him.

But he would also take what he could get. He didn't know how long he had with Xan, but the memories would get him through the rest of his life.

They'd have to.

"He's staying at Chad's tonight," Xan whispered.

"Mmmm, that's great news," he murmured as he hugged her tighter to him.

"You don't mind keeping me all to yourself tonight?" she asked, but she was drifting under and barely coherent.

"Forever," he breathed, but she was already asleep.

CHAPTER NINETEEN

Who was ringing her doorbell at the butt crack of dawn?

Xan groaned, rolling over to glance at her clock. "Holy shit," she muttered. "It's not even five o'clock."

She definitely hadn't had enough sleep. She'd stayed up until midnight watching Scott play *Battle Warfare* with Brody and Chad before Scott left to spend the night at Chad's house.

Over the last few weeks, Brody had been a constant figure in their lives. He'd taken them both out to baseball games, movies, dinner, and when they weren't all going out, he'd come over and have dinner with them and they'd play board games, watch TV, and hang out like a normal family. It was nice.

Hell, who was she kidding? It fucking rocked. Okay, it *freaking* rocked. She was really trying to do better on the cussing thing. She had her good days and bad ones. She was woman enough to admit there were some things she couldn't change about herself, and that was one of them. Not that Brody tried to change anything about her. He seemed to love her just the way she was. And yes, she got a sneaking suspicion that he was in love with her. Thinking that melted her heart and turned her on big time. If he was anywhere in sight when she'd think about his feelings, she'd jump him. Not that he was complaining. When she'd initiate sex, he'd get so hard and come like a raging beast. It was hot as hell—heck. Yeah, that just sounded stupid.

Grumbling, she grabbed her robe and stalked toward the door. Brody had just been here a few hours ago, and she missed him like crazy. He normally stayed the night when Scott stayed over at Chad's, but he said he had to get to work early. As for Scott, he was old enough to understand that Brody was her boyfriend, so maybe it was time to ask Scott how he felt about Brody staying over. They'd talked about her relationship with him in general, and Scott loved Brody. He hadn't admitted that, but she could tell in the way he talked about Brody when he wasn't around and acted around him when he was.

Of course, she'd have to talk to Brody about it too. This relationship stuff was hard...but worth it.

As she reached the door, she froze. A manila envelope was on the floor beneath the mail slot. Living a life on the run from people who wanted to kill her, she knew a thing or two about not accepting things at face value. This couldn't be good. Tip-toeing toward the door, but not taking her eyes off the package, she looked through the peephole anyway. Unable to see hardly anything, she flipped on the porch light, illuminating half her small yard.

Still nothing. Whoever had been here only wanted to leave the envelope. For now anyway.

She leaned down and picked up the thin package before turning off the porch light and double-checking that the door was still locked. She walked back to her bedroom because she felt safe there. Maybe it had something to do with being able to hide under the covers. Or maybe it was the gun she kept in her nightstand. Either reason worked for her. When she reached her bed, she sat on the edge and opened the package, pulling out what was inside.

Her heart stopped.

She couldn't breathe, and she felt as if she was going to pass out from lack of oxygen. Her hands trembled as she held up the lone item from inside the envelope.

A photograph.

A picture of Marco and Brody...*Brody*...with their arms slung over each other's shoulders, smiling and laughing. It was an old photograph, but it was them. They looked like the best of friends.

Her ex-husband who wanted to kill her. And her lover. Together embraced in shared camaraderie.

No fucking way.

She was going to be sick, so she swallowed convulsively to stave off the urge, but the lump that quickly worked its way up her throat turned into a sob instead.

She cried as if she was in mourning. And she was because, in a heartbeat, she'd lost the man she loved. The moment she'd opened this package, her life changed.

As she stared at the photo, her tears dripped on it, and she hastily wiped them off with shaky fingers. This could be evidence, so she needed to hand it over to Jack with the FBI in pristine condition.

Jack. She needed to call him. She didn't know for sure what this meant, but she had a damn good idea. Marco wanted her dead, so he must've sent Brody to watch over her, make sure she didn't run when Marco got his ass out of prison. She bet the story about Brody's amnesia was a lie to draw her in, which wasn't necessary because she was already in love with him by then.

"Oh God," she cried, throwing herself into another round of weeping sobs. She was in love with one of her ex-husband's cronies. He'd played her for a fool, and she was too stupid to see it coming. Twelve years since Marco tried to kill her and she hadn't trusted another man. When she finally opened her heart to one, it was to one who'd had no intention of protecting it.

She reached for her cell phone as she continued to sob. Jack answered on the first ring, and she was shocked he was able to understand the story as she relayed it to him because it barely made sense to her. It still didn't. She didn't want to believe it.

"Fax me a copy of that photo. And you stay put. Leave Scott at the neighbor's. I'm contacting the closest team to you. They'll be there in five."

Xan mumbled her agreement and listened again while he barked orders and repeated himself twice as she turned on the fax machine and sent him the photo. He really did worry for her well-being. But once the call was over, she was all alone again with just her thoughts, and as the seconds ticked by, she felt the walls closing in.

She had to get out of here, find a new place to hide. Maybe that would cure her anxious feeling. She could call Jack once she picked up Scott and got them to a secure location. But as she jumped from the bed and threw on a ratty old pair of jeans and flip-flops, all she could think about was confronting her lover. Did Marco tell him to fuck her, or had Brody ventured down that path all on his own? Her emotions were all over the place. First she was shocked, then devastated, now pissed all within minutes of each other. She figured she'd cycle through them over and over because her heart was breaking, and she didn't know how to deal with that, but right now, rage was taking over.

She'd run with that.

Before grabbing her keys, she took her gun and shoved it in her purse. She was too emotional to think straight right now, but she'd be damned if she allowed herself to walk right into the lion's den without protection. She stomped outside and into her piece-of-shit car. After several tries, she finally got it to start, then peeled out of her driveway—well as much as this old four-banger would. Her breath hitched from her crying fit, and the action caused her to inhale a concentrated scent of Brody's masculine aroma. She looked down at the culprit and moaned. She'd slept in one of his t-shirts and still had it on. Her lip started trembling, but she couldn't start crying again, so she punched the gas. She had to confront him now, or she'd lose her nerve and never do it.

She was at Brody's house in record time. As she stalked up to his door with the picture in hand, she remembered the last time she'd surprised him at his door, which he'd returned the favor by shoving a gun in her face. And why did he have a gun if he was just a mechanic? God, the signs were just adding up. She wished she could attribute her gullibility to her inexperience with men, but the truth was, she'd lived a very cautious life.

There was no excuse.

She knocked on the door and braced herself with a steadying breath and a mental pep talk. She soon realized neither worked when she heard his heavy footfalls inside the house.

The door swung open, and Brody's sleep-tussled hair caressed his face like a lover. His drowsy eyes became alert as he took her in. Then he reached for her.

"Baby? Is everything all right? Where's Scott?" The concern in his voice did her in, and the momentary anger she was clinging to dissolved into another sob. "Sweetheart, you're scaring me." He pulled her into his house and shut the door, not letting her go.

But she pushed him away. Startled, he eased away from her.

"Xan?" His tone was reproachful, and that was just what she needed to cut through her devastation and grasp on to a spark of anger.

She pulled the picture up with both hands, showing him. "Care to explain this?" He gasped, stepping closer, but she backed away. "Stay where you are." She shoved her hand in her purse and pulled out her gun. Brody was as big as a fucking house. There was no way she could get away from him if he restrained her, so she had to protect herself as best she could. But as he stared wide-eyed at her, she was beginning to realize how incredibly stupid she was being. She'd been given direct orders to stay and here she was standing in front of the enemy. Really, what was she thinking? When she got a taste of stupidity, she really lapped that shit up.

The look in Brody's eyes went from concern to his own form of devastation. But why? More games? She didn't know, but she wasn't leaving here until she got some answers.

No matter how much they were going to hurt her.

———

SHIT, shit, shit, shit! This was bad. When Hunter had called him to say Xan had left her house and was headed in his direction, he had no idea it was going to be about this. He should've told Xan about his past and the possibility of his involvement with Marco when he'd had the chance. But he'd hoped to gain irrefutable evidence that either pinned him to Tess's murder or proof that it wasn't him. Yeah, he could've just told Xan about everything and let her judge for herself, but he was just too chicken-shit to do it. And now here she was, standing in his living room with wet, swollen eyes, tear streaks down her face, clutching a pretty damning photo with a piece aimed at his chest.

For weeks he'd hoped what Colonel told him about killing Xan's daughter was a lie, and he, Gauge, and Blade had investigated other possible scenarios, hoping that some other thug had done the deed. And here she was holding the fucking smoking gun. Now there was no mistaking his connection to Marco. He'd be sick if he wasn't standing before the woman he loved, watching her heart break, knowing it was all his fault.

Fuck.

He slowly dropped his outreached hands and backed away, taking a seat on the couch. He propped his elbows on his knees and buried his face in his hands.

How the hell was he supposed to start explaining? Jesus, this hurt. "Why don't you sit down? This could take a while."

"I'd rather stand."

His head popped up at her shaky voice. She sounded as if she was about to collapse, but she was putting on a brave front, standing with her feet apart, weapon trained on him with one hand and clutching that picture with the other.

"Please," he begged, looking into her eyes with what he hoped was a no-threatening look while motioning for her to sit. "I'm not going to hurt you. I won't even touch you. I lo— I, um," he cleared his throat, "it's a long story, baby. I promise to tell you everything."

She looked as if she didn't trust him as far as she could throw him, and that fucking hurt too. But he waited patiently. He wanted to find out where she'd gotten that picture, but he knew he had no right to demand anything from her. She needed answers first, and he had to find the words to give them to her.

Slowly, as if she was afraid she'd spook him, she crept over to the opposite end of the couch and perched on the edge. Her poor little knuckles were white from fisting the objects she held, and he had to fight the urge to grab her hands and massage the tension away. She was keeping her distance and using a weapon to protect herself. The last thing he wanted to do was make her feel any more threatened than she already did.

"What I told you about my amnesia is true. But what I didn't tell you is that I'd remembered you from somewhere. I have these little glimpses of memories, flashes of you I couldn't explain. You see, Colonel did some digging into my past and found some things out that I'm not very proud of."

"Like what?"

He sighed, rubbed his hands over his face, and leaned back into the sofa. "Like I was a contract killer."

She stiffened, but thankfully, didn't bolt. Brody didn't want to have to stop her if she tried leaving, but he needed to tell her everything. He couldn't afford for her to leave without telling her what he could.

"I don't know much about that. Like I said, I have no memories of that life, so I've been living my life like that never happened. But those ingrained skills do come in handy with my work."

"Your work? You're a mechanic, *Brutus*. You don't need to know how to kill someone.

"Please don't call me that. I—"

"I'll call you whatever the hell I want," she gritted out. "Now explain what you mean."

"Fair enough," he sighed. "I mean, we do side projects. I led you to believe those projects were related to the garage, but they're not, not usually anyway. We take on missions from private and government clients, doin' jobs they either don't want to do themselves or can't. I'm not allowed to tell you anything specific, but I will tell you that you were an assignment. At first. That and the fact that I had memories of you were the reasons why I tried to avoid you in the beginning. We were hired to protect you since Marco was up for parole."

The color drained out of her face. "The FBI hired you?"

"Shit, Xan, I'm not allowed to talk about this." If Colonel knew Brody was spilling their secrets, he'd have his ass. But this was Xan, and he'd answer whatever he could. "But yeah, we have contacts with the FBI."

"So you knew about my husband coming after me?"

"*Ex*-husband. And we don't know that. It was my understanding we were hired just to watch over you. I don't think the FBI knew for a fact Collins was coming for you. But why wouldn't he? I guess they didn't have concrete proof at the time, so they did what they could to keep you safe. But I don't know. I didn't ask questions. Just did what I was told."

"And what were you told?"

She wasn't making this easy on him. "You and Scott were to be watched twenty-four-seven, but I was told to stick close to you. In the beginning, I staked out your place, followed you around." He averted his eyes. "Later, I didn't have to be so covert to watch out for you."

"No wonder you weren't shocked when I opened myself up to you and told you about my past. You already knew. God, I'm such an idiot."

"No, I mean, yes, I knew, but no, you're not an idiot,

baby." He shifted a little closer to her. "I had a job to do, but I was attracted to you from the very beginning. Once we became involved, the line between my job and my love life became very blurry. Yours and Scott's safety became a very personal issue for me."

"Then why not tell me? Because you knew me from somewhere and were ashamed of your past? Damn you, Brody! I told you I was beaten and raped by the man you're buddy-buddy with in that picture. How do you expect me to feel about that?"

"After we became involved, I learned of a possible connection to Collins, and I've been investigating it. Until you brought this picture here, I haven't been able to find anything concrete linking me to him."

"Why would you? If you were a killer working for him, I'm sure you didn't leave a bunch of evidence lying around. You should have told me this. Why bother trying to verify it first?" she yelled, jumping to her feet, and Brody jumped up too.

"Because I love you, and it scares the shit out of me that I could've done something to hurt you!"

She stared back at him, working her mouth as if she was trying to speak. "You love me?"

Oh shit. He hadn't meant to blurt that out. He'd been trying to keep a lid on his feelings until he knew he was free to love her without worrying if he was the one who'd killed her daughter. Up until she'd shown up here with that photo, he was starting to believe that maybe Colonel had gotten his information wrong—their intel wasn't always foolproof when dealing with unsavory characters—and that the baby had actually died of SIDS. He took a step toward her. "Yes, I—"

"Don't." She lifted her gun to halt his progression and

took a step back. "Just stay where you are. I-I need to think about this."

Instead of retreating, he sat on the couch where he'd been standing. If she sat back down, at least they'd be a little closer. He steepled his hands over his mouth and watched her, waiting. He knew this was a lot for her to take in and he had to give her time, but he'd give anything to be able to pull her into his arms without her freaking out.

"Let me make sure I'm clear here. You work with the FBI, but you were a contract killer who worked for my ex-husband. And you expect me to believe that you had no idea who I was when I moved to town?"

"I didn't say that. I said I didn't know of my possible connection to Collins until after we became involved. The moment I saw you, I recognized you from somewhere but couldn't place you. I was informed of our responsibility to watch out for you after we met."

"I see. And what are you not telling me?" Her eyes narrowed.

Oh fuck. He swallowed. "I, er, Colonel told me something about our past I've been trying to confirm one way or the other." He shut his eyes because he just couldn't look at her and see the disgust on her face when he spilled the rest of this. "He, um, told me I knew you because Collins had hired me to kill your kid."

She gasped and his eyes flew open. "What the fuck? Marco wanted Scott dead?" She backed away, shaking her head. "Why? He wanted a son to begin with. Th-that doesn't make sense."

"Not Scott," he breathed.

Xan's brow furrowed in confusion, then her eyes slowly opened wide as the color drained from her face and she wobbled on her feet. He started to get up, but she grasped the side of the couch, dropping that photo. "No." She shook her head. "She, she died of SIDS. I-I saw the autopsy report." Her voice cracked as she fought not to cry.

"Xan." He stood slowly.

Her trembling hand covered her mouth and she whispered, "Are you telling me you killed my baby?"

That was it. He couldn't take it anymore. He stepped over to her and clutched her arms. "I don't know. God, Xan, I don't know. After I found out, I tried staying away from you, but I couldn't. And I've been doing my damnedest to find some answers. I don't want it to be true."

And then she wailed—a sound that'd haunt him until the day he died—and beat her weak little fist against his chest as she screamed and cried. The force of her blows not enough to hurt him physically, but he felt each strike clear to his soul. And because she didn't try to pull away from him, Brody held on to her arms and let her take out her pain on him.

"I'm sorry, so sorry," he murmured over and over, and she finally stopped her assault and collapsed into his arms, bawling. He held her and stroked her hair, whispering his apologies over and over. Long moments later, she finally relaxed into his embrace, and he squeezed her tighter. He'd give anything to take her pain away.

Then she seemed to remember what he was apologizing for because she pushed him away and took several steps back, heading for the door. "Stay the hell away from me," she croaked as she waved her gun at him. "Don't come to my house, don't call me, don't you fucking drive down my road."

He followed her. "Xan, you have every right to be—"

"Don't say another word! You killed my baby. *You.* The man I...the man I've been sleeping with. You better pray we don't run into each other again because I'll kill you. And that's not some idle threat."

She stomped out of his house, slammed the door, and fired up that rusty old car of hers, and he just sat back down and stared at the floor where the photo of him and Collins had landed. He bent over and picked it up, staring at it with burning eyes. He blinked a few times and felt a suspicious wetness trail down his cheek. The last time he'd cried, he'd been drunk off his ass.

Now he just had a hole in his chest.

He took a deep breath. He knew his relationship with Xan was going to end sometime and he couldn't dwell on what he'd lost because he still had a job to do. The fact his heart was splitting didn't matter. He couldn't do anything for her if he let his emotions consume him. Clearing his throat, Brody got up and grabbed his phone. He dialed first Blade and then Gauge, asking them both to meet him at Colonel's house. They were both grumpy being woken up so early, but neither complained about helping him. He had a major problem to contend with and he needed help. Someone had left a photo where Xan could find it, and the reason could not be good—either Collins' men were closing in on her, or someone wanted her to think that.

It was time to bring the boss man up to speed.

———

"JESUS, Brody, you do know what time it is, don't you? What if I was curled up next to a lovely lady all nice and sweet-like in my bed?" Blade asked, sipping his coffee as he leaned against his truck parked outside of Colonel's house.

Brody could've retorted with some macho comeback about how Blade never brought women home, but he wasn't in the mood for banter. Instead, he shut his truck door and walked toward Blade. "I called Colonel on the way over here. He's expecting us," Brody said as Gauge pulled in behind him. Thankfully, Gauge just nodded without bitching about the hour, and they all walked up to Colonel's door. He opened it before they got a chance to knock.

"If y'all are done pussyfooting around out there, get in here and tell me what's so damn important it couldn't wait."

Colonel didn't wait for a response. He turned and stalked toward his living room, and Brody and the other guys followed. After Colonel served up some coffee and they all took seats, Brody brought Colonel up to speed on everything. His research into Xan's past agents and any possible people who'd sell her out to Collins, leaving out the two undercover agents who'd already been excluded—no need to divulge that information. Colonel sat quietly, listening, but Brody could tell his lack of comments wasn't a good sign. Oh yeah, Colonel was definitely not happy.

"Why am I just now finding out about this?" he exploded.

"Because we haven't found anything conclusive on Jeff Coleman or Dave Simmons," Brody said. "Plus, Dale Adams is still lurking around, and we don't know how he fits into this either."

Colonel let rip a litany of curses as he stood and paced, and Brody waited him out. No need to piss his boss off even more. Finally, he faced Brody. "Why'd you tell me now? If you've been keeping this from me then something must've changed for you to be singing like a little fuckin' bird all of a sudden."

Brody reached behind him and pulled out an envelope he'd stuffed in the back of his jeans and under his shirt. Then he handed it to his boss. "Someone sent this to Xan or left it for her where she'd find it. I'm not sure. I didn't get a chance to ask."

Colonel yanked the photo away from Brody and scowled. "I see."

"What is it?" Blade asked, bobbing his head to the side to get a look.

Colonel passed it to Blade. "A picture of Brutus with Marco Collins."

"What?" Blade's eyes got twice as big as he took the photo. "No fuckin' way," he breathed.

Gauge whistled. "Not good, man," he said as he leaned over and looked at the picture while Blade held on to it.

"I know," Brody sighed, glancing back at Colonel. "You see the problem here? Either Collins is on to her or someone wants her to think he is."

"Or someone is really handy dandy with Photoshop, man, and wants to cause you some trouble," Blade said.

"Doubtful," Gauge argued. "They'd have to know about his past for that to be the case, which would seriously limit the suspect pool."

"Only the guys at the shop know about me," Brody said, picking up his cup of coffee for the first time and sipping. He hadn't considered the possibility of someone trying to sabotage his credibility with Xan. Even if that was the case, it didn't make that picture a fake.

"Son, do you honestly think the FBI doesn't have a bead on you? I've been accepting contracts from them for years. We may hit dead ends when looking into your past, but I'd bet my life the feds know how often you take a shit now and could compare it to how often you did before your accident."

And that was true too. Brody'd tried every avenue to find out about his past once he knew he could do it without drawing unwanted attention to himself. He hadn't had much luck, but Colonel had found some old connections who'd pieced some of the information together. And when he'd tried getting info from the feds, he hit a brick wall. So it'd make sense that they wouldn't mind knowing everything about him without sharing.

"You have a point, boss, but what about Xan? And Scott? They're not safe. Someone got close enough to her to leave that photo."

Colonel pulled out his cell phone and dialed a number. "Hunter had night watch," he said to Brody, and then into the phone "Where are you?" He pulled his cell phone away and fumbled with it to put it on speaker so everyone could hear.

"Lost him and just got back. Xan Bradley was MIA when I returned."

"Repeat that, Hunter."

"Followed suspicious vehicle leaving the Bradley house shortly after oh-four-hundred. Lost him and just got back. Xan isn't here."

"Description?" Brody barked.

"Black SUV. Called Bear with tags, and he ran them. Vehicle was stolen."

Shit, this wasn't good.

"Stay at her house." Then to Brody, "Do you know where she could be?"

"She was upset when she left my house this morning. Hunter had reported that Scott was staying over at a friend's house, so she could be anywhere."

"I'll call Roc to scope out the town to find her," Colonel said into the phone.

Brody growled. He still was pissed at Roc for his behavior, and he didn't care if Colonel knew it. His boss's gaze cut to him and he shook his head in warning. Fuck that. Roc had been an even bigger asshole lately. It seemed like the more time Brody had spent with Xan, Roc got more irritated. Brody hadn't lashed out since he'd only been around him at the shop, but what Brody wouldn't give to find that punk in a dark alley. "You tell him not to engage if he finds her," he spat.

Colonel sighed, but nodded. "Report back, Hunter, if you see anything out of the ordinary or if Xan returns."

"Got it."

Colonel killed the call and looked at the men in his living room. "I'll contact the feds and see what they know, but I have to be careful because I have a bad feeling about this. We were pulled on the case as soon as her ass showed up in town, then Adams pops up here, now this. Collins is good, but this is fast work even for him. I think he still has a man on the inside."

"You don't think it's a former agent?" Gauge asked, scooting to the edge of his seat.

"Hell, with deep pockets, it could be a combination of past agents, current feds, and even plants in this town. He could've orchestrated her every move and identity change for all we know. Bottom line, she's in danger."

But Brody would kill anybody, fed or not, who so much as touched her.

XAN DROVE AROUND TOWN AIMLESSLY, trying to get a handle on her emotions. She'd cried until she couldn't cry anymore and then she'd called Jack. Of course he'd freaked about her leaving and lectured her about not staying put like he'd ordered, and when she told him where she'd been and that she'd left the damning photo at Brody's house, he'd really lost it. She knew it was dangerous confronting Brody, but she was shocked and pissed and upset and had gone through those emotions over and over in the last hour, in no certain order. Jack wasn't a woman scorned, so he didn't understand her logic, but said he'd take care of it, whatever that meant.

When she finally pulled into her driveway, she couldn't go in. She knew if she did, she'd be cooking up a storm. She didn't want to be alone with her thoughts anymore, so she killed the engine, stowed the gun in the glove box, and walked over to Roxie's house, hoping she'd be up and have coffee made. Xan knocked on the door and her neighbor opened it a few minutes later with a concerned look on her face.

"Hey, girl. Everything all right?" She tugged her robe closer to her body and smoothed her bed-rumpled hair.

"Sorry I woke you—"

"No, no. I was awake. Just bein' lazy, you know. Readin' in bed with some yummy coffee. Wanna cup?" she asked as she stepped aside and let Xan in.

"Sure. I take it the boys are still asleep."

"Um, Chad is, but—hey, have you been cryin'?"

"Long story," Xan sighed, knowing she'd have to tell Roxie everything, but actually feeling a little lighter knowing she'd get to vent her feelings, rather than leaving them all bottled up to fester. At this rate, they'd eat her insides. "What about Scott? Surely he's not up?" She almost chuckled at that ridiculous thought.

Roxie furrowed her brow. "I don't know. He's not here, hon."

Xan froze. "What do you mean, 'he's not here'?"

"I went to bed early last night while the boys were

playin' video games. When I got up around two this morning to make sure they'd turned off the TV, Chad was in bed and Scott wasn't here. I figured he went home last night when they got through."

Oh God! Xan took off in a sprint. She bolted out the door, across Roxie's yard and into hers. She never thought their houses were so far apart until this very moment.

Xan would've heard Scott come home. She knew she would have. Being a light sleeper on the run from a killer tended to make that a necessity.

When she finally busted through her door, she yelled for Scott, screaming his name repeatedly as she ran to his room. When she opened his door, her heart sank. "Oh God, oh God, oh God."

He wasn't here.

CHAPTER TWENTY

Xan screamed Scott's name again as she ran through the house, out the back door, and around her yard. He wasn't here. Her baby wasn't here. Roxie came running up to her. She'd put on some jeans and a t-shirt. "What's goin' on? Is he not home?"

Xan couldn't answer. She kept scanning her yard, turning in circles. Then out of the corner of her eye, she saw a man dressed in all black running up to her. She gasped and prepared to run, but then recognized him.

"Hunter? What are you doin' here?"

"My turn to watch you. What's wrong?" He was pulling out his cell phone when he asked and put it up to his ear. "I've got her," he said to the person he'd just called.

What the hell? *I've got her?* Had Hunter taken Scott and was now here to take her? She blanched and started to turn around to make a run for it, but he grabbed her arm as he spoke into the phone.

"She's freaked out about something, running around screaming, so I had no choice," he barked into the phone. Then he looked at her. "What's wrong?" he asked gently.

"S-Scott's missing," she croaked. It didn't matter that she'd already been crying this morning and would probably cry at baby kittens because this was her son she was talking about. Her *son*.

"*Shit*. Okay. Um, she said Scott's missing. I'll look around." He hesitated and nodded, glancing at her. "Got it." Then he hung up the phone.

"Who was that? Who were you talking to, and why are you here?"

He rubbed her arm where he'd been holding it. "That was the boss. The guys will be here any minute. And I can't tell you why I'm here, but I think you know."

She yanked her arm out of his grasp and started for her porch. Roxie followed quickly behind her. After all these years, Marco had finally caught up with her...and he'd only been out for a couple of months. Oh, she didn't have proof this was his doing, but she didn't need it.

"We have to call the police," she said frantically. "W-we have to call them right now."

"Wait until everyone gets here, okay?" he said calmly. Oh, he was out of his damn mind if he thought she was waiting around.

"What in Hades is going on here?" Roxie asked, pulling Xan around to face her once they were inside and distracting her from her impending meltdown. When Xan turned, she noticed Hunter had followed her too.

She took a deep breath and quickly relayed everything to Roxie, who'd already known some of this, but now she knew everything. Hunter stood to the side, arms crossed, watching her like a hawk.

Roxie started to respond when Xan finally paused, but the roar of an engine and squealing tires outside caught Xan's attention, and she turned toward the door where Brody came barreling through like a charging bull. She hadn't expected to see him again so soon, and looking at him broke the final thread of her control. She covered her face and sobbed, and Brody rushed over to her and took her in his arms.

"I'll find him, baby," he murmured. She knew she should push him away and get to that killing thing she'd threatened him with just a little while ago. Hell, she should've just killed him and been done with it when she had her chance. This was just one more reason why she should continue to avoid men. They made her crazy. But even as she considered what she should be doing, she couldn't seem to muster the energy to let go of him. So she held him and tried to rein in the waterworks. Crying wouldn't bring Scott back.

She nodded into Brody's chest as she eased away from him. She wiped her eyes and faced the other guys in the room. There were more of them now. "What's the plan? I mean, I know this just happened, but we have to do something. Hunter wouldn't let me call the police until you got here."

"Roc was already out looking for you, so I called him, told him to look for Scott," Colonel said. "Gauge is making some calls. I told him to contact your agent, and he'll notify the proper authorities. When was the last time you saw Scott?"

Roxie stepped forward. "He was at my house last night. I thought he went home, but I'm not sure."

"Where's Chad?" Bear asked suddenly, and Xan didn't miss the way Roxie's eyes lit up at Bear's attention.

"He was sleepin' when I left."

"Go get him," Colonel ordered.

Xan saw Roxie turn to leave as Bear watched her closely.

"Tell me how you found that photo."

Xan looked at Colonel with narrowed eyes. What did that picture have to do with Scott being gone? She didn't want to think about that photo, but she understood why he wanted to know. It couldn't be a coincidence, so she tamped down her irritation and relayed the story—without looking at Brody. Bringing that damn picture back up ignited her anger toward him.

Colonel looked away from her when she'd finished and to the other guys. "We've got to find Dale Adams, Dave Simmons, and Jeff Coleman."

Xan grabbed Colonel's arm and turned him to face her. "Who the hell are Dale Adams and why are you looking for Dave Simmons and Jeff Coleman? They're former agents, right?"

"Dale Adams is—"

"Brutus," Colonel cut him off. "I don't think it's smart to go into this."

Brody squared his shoulders and started toward Colonel, but Xan was just as pissed at the blatant dismiss. "I don't give a damn what you think, Colonel. We're talking about my life here. My *son*. So back off or start talking."

Brody looked at her. "Dale Adams showed up in town shortly after you did. We think he's connected to Collins somehow, but we haven't been able to find him."

"Well, except that one time he and some dude beat the shit out of us..." Blade said, but trailed off at Brody's warning look. "Never mind," he mumbled.

Brody turned back to Xan. "Dave Simmons and Jeff Coleman worked on your case. We've been looking at everyone who could possibly have motive, opportunity, *balls* to sell you out. Those two haven't been cleared as possible suspects yet."

"That's ridiculous. I haven't seen or heard from Cole since the night Marco attacked me. And Dave's retired."

"Cole? Is that what Jeff Coleman went by?" Blade asked.

"Yeah." She shrugged. "He was my primary contact once I was assigned some agents, but I never met him in person. I didn't start meeting my contacts in person until after I got away."

"So you've seen Dave Simmons then?" Brody asked.

She turned to him and suppressed the urge to fall into his arms again. She was hurt. But she was scared, and looking at him gave her a little bit of security. She hated that. She did *not* want to feel safe in the arms of the man who'd killed her daughter. He might not be that same man anymore, but he couldn't erase his past—even with amnesia. "Yes," she said a little too tersely. "He retired after his wife settled some medical dispute from some botched surgery. The bills were paid, and she was given a lump sum for pain and suffering. He was close to retirement anyway, so left to be home with her."

"I'll check that out," Blade said. "If Simmons' wife settled out of court, the doctor could've had those records sealed as part of the deal, which could be why we hadn't made that connection."

"And then we'd only have one suspect," Brody mumbled.

Blade nodded and turned to leave as Roxie came running through the door, clutching her cell phone. "C-Chad won't wake up. I've called an ambulance."

Xan gasped and started for Roxie as she turned to leave and head back home. Why was Chad not waking up? What had happened to him? Xan was a nurse, so she needed to check on him and do what she could until help arrived. But Bear damn near knocked her over as he shoved away from the group of people circled around each other and bolted through the front door, heading to Roxie's house.

Everyone followed suit.

As soon as Xan saw Chad, she went into clinical mode, checking his vital signs. He was breathing, but his heart rate was slow. She asked Roxie if Chad was allergic to anything as she continued her examination. From all accounts, he was a healthy boy. Nothing like this had ever happened.

Then she shifted his body and noticed a little dried blood on his shoulder. There was only a tiny bit, which looked suspiciously like...like a needle prick. "Oh shit," she gasped. "I think he was drugged."

Roxie staggered and Bear caught her, stroking her arm and murmuring something into her ear that made her breath catch.

"Whoever took Scott must've done this," Colonel said as the ambulance sirens got louder as it neared the house. No one commented because there wasn't a need. It was obvious to Xan that what he'd said was true, so she knew the others felt the same way.

Bear left Roxie to escort the paramedics in, and everyone stood back and watched as they loaded Chad on the stretcher. Xan relayed what she'd discovered while they started an IV. When they carried Chad out to the ambulance, Roxie started for her car. Then cursed. "My tire's flat."

"Again?" Bear asked as he walked over to her.

"What do you mean 'again'?" Roxie asked, her voice heavy with suspicion.

Hmm, that was right. Bear hadn't been at the shop that

day Roxie took her car in. Xan had ridden with her, so she knew this for a fact. Great. Now she was getting paranoid. Surely, one of the other guys had told him about her car.

"I do get a log of everything done in the shop, Roxie," Bear said, clearly reading Roxie's and Xan's thoughts, since they seemed to have been on the same page.

"I'll take you," Xan said, walking up to her and rubbing her arm. Jesus, she was shaking like a leaf. But Xan was probably shaking just as badly.

"No," Bear said, slicing his hand through the air with an aura of finality. "I'll take her. You have to stay here in case Scott comes home."

Xan glared at him, but he was right. She wanted to be with her friend because that was the nice thing to do and because she felt as if she was to blame, but inside, she was screaming her own agony. Her son was missing and she needed to comb the streets to find him.

Brody stepped over and rubbed his hand along Xan's shoulder and she stiffened. Moving away from him, she walked up to Roxie and hugged her. "Call me when he wakes up, okay?"

She nodded, pulled away, and followed Bear across the street to his truck. Xan followed because everyone had parked at her house.

After Bear and Roxie had left and Brody, Blade, Hunter, and Colonel had followed her inside, Colonel pulled out his phone again.

"I'm going to call in some help to sweep these two houses for any clues."

When Colonel walked back out to make the call, Xan walked into the kitchen for a glass of water...and to get away from Brody's probing eyes. He was watching her as if he expected her to keel over, or run, or shoot him. Yeah, she was ready to do any of those things, but she couldn't take being gawked at. She was under enough pressure as it was.

After getting her water reprieve, she numbly walked into the living room. Brody and Blade had been whispering, but promptly stopped as soon as she entered. "Don't mind me," she said sarcastically.

"Baby," Brody breathed.

"Don't!" Her hands flew up as she cut him off. "Don't call me that."

Brody sighed but nodded.

She squared her shoulders. His pitiful look was not going to affect her. It. Was. Not. Instead, she looked around the room and noticed a minor change. "It seems you're missing a crony." Hunter was no longer here.

"Yeah, Hunter left to research Jeff Coleman. We still don't know anything about him, so anything he finds will be an improvement."

The front door swung open and Colonel stalked in. Brody and Blade jumped to their feet. "Roc called. He found the boy. He was sleeping in a parked car outside Walmart in Conway."

"Is he okay?" Xan asked timidly. *Oh God, please let him be okay.*

"Roc got him to come to. He said Scott's still a little groggy, but he's talking."

She walked to the table and grabbed her purse on impulse. "Is he taking him to the hospital?" She'd just meet them there.

"Yes, but you're not going." Colonel stepped up to her and blocked her exit.

"Bullshit." She might have reservations about killing Brody right now because her love for him was still too strong, but she didn't mind one bit killing this prick if he kept her from going to her boy. Her mother-bear instincts were roaring.

"I'll go with her," Brody said. "Keep her safe."

Colonel turned to him. "You can go. Someone needs to protect him, and I'd rather you do that and let Roc contain the scene until I can get more people out there since he was the one who found him." He turned to Blade. "And I need you to hunt down that Dale Adams asshole. If Dave Simmons' story checks out, that's one less person we have to worry about. We don't know where that Coleman guy is, but we know Adams is here. Find the punk." He turned to Xan and took a deep breath. "Help is on the way. Once the feds get here, they'll want to question you. Once they're through with you, you can go see your son. I'll stay with you until your agent gets here to make sure you're protected."

Xan hated the idea of staying here when her son was going to the hospital, but she knew Colonel was right. Jack would want to talk to her and look around. It didn't make any sense that Scott would be taken and Chad drugged. This could be all one big setup. She could go running to her baby boy right now, but she wouldn't be any help if Marco got her while she was on her way to the hospital. For all she knew, he was here, sitting back, waiting for his opportunity to take her. She wouldn't be any use to Scott dead.

And she didn't know how to feel about Brody being the one to protect her son. When he could've been the one to kill her daughter. How could a man take the life of one of her kids but protect the other? She couldn't wrap her head around that. Unless Marco still had some crazy-ass idea about having an heir to take over the family business and was still using Brody to make that happen. Could Brody be one of Marco's minions? She didn't know what to believe, who to trust. She looked at Brody and his eyes softened. He was staying away from her, but she got the feeling that he didn't like it. Too bad. What they had was damaged and when this mess blew over, she'd probably be literally sick with the idea of loving a man who'd done something so vile. "Don't you hurt him," she choked.

"Never," he breathed. She nodded and he walked toward the door, stopping when he was beside her. "I'd die before I let anything happen to either one of you. I know you're hurting right now, but you have to know that."

Her breath hitched and she swallowed to stop the sob that was building as she watched Brody and Blade leave.

He'd said that to comfort her, but the thought of Brody dying was just one more devastating thought in this horrible day.

———

BRODY PARKED his truck in the hospital parking lot and rushed into the ER. After asking a bunch of questions and lying about his relationship to Scott, he finally found out that he'd been admitted into the hospital and was given his room number. He took the elevator to the appropriate floor and walked down the hall to Scott's room. When he pushed the door open, Roc had been hovering over Scott in the bed and jerked around to look at him. *What the fuck?*

"What are you doing here?" Roc spat.

"Get away from him," Brody ordered as he stalked into the room and over to Scott, looking at all the wires and shit for anything out of the ordinary as if he had a clue what was *ordinary*. "What the hell were you doing?"

"Nothing." Roc crossed his arms and stared at Brody. Yeah, he liked the fact that his coworker had to look slightly up at him. It was a male thing.

"Didn't look like that to me."

Roc pointed at Brody. "You've been on my case since the whole Mimi thing happened, and you can get the hell off it at any time, bro."

Brody growled. "That doesn't answer my question. What. Did. You. Do?" He was reaching for the nurse call button, so someone experienced could check out Scott's setup, make sure everything was copasetic.

"You're one paranoid motherfucker, Brutus. I didn't do a damn thing. It sounded as if the kid was wheezing a little and I leaned in to hear his breath better."

Brody was about to respond when Scott stirred, so he focused on Scott instead. "Hey," he crooned. "How are you feeling?"

"Sleepy," he mumbled. "Where's Mom?"

"She'll be here later." No need to tell him why she wasn't here right now.

"Doc said that he'll be sleeping on and off all day. They gave him something to counter the medication, but whatever. That's what he said," Roc said, shrugging.

Brody wanted to haul off and pop that jerk in the face. But he schooled his expression instead. "Colonel wants you back at Walmart, checking out the scene. He'll be sending someone over to help."

"Thank God. I hate hospitals." Roc left, moving faster than Brody had ever seen, but he didn't really care. At least he didn't have to look at him anymore.

Scott had fallen back asleep, so Brody sat down and waited.

And waited.

Two hours passed before Scott woke up again, thirsty. Brody poured him some ice water and watched him sip it. "What's taking Mom so long?"

Brody didn't know for sure. He knew the feds liked to be thorough and could question people for days and days if they wanted to, but he figured once her agent showed up, he'd bring her out here and question her, and protect her, while she mothered Scott. "What do you remember?" Brody asked instead of answering.

"Nothing. Last thing I remember was kicking Chad's ass in *Battle Warfare.*"

Brody figured as much, but he had to ask anyway.

His cell phone vibrated, and he breathed a sigh of relief. Maybe now Xan was on her way and he wouldn't have to stall.

Damn. It was Blade's number. "Yeah?"

"Got him. But he ain't talking."

"You found Adams?"

"Yep. Hog tied him and brought him back to the shop. I tried calling Gauge to see if he could help interrogate this ass-wipe, but he ain't answering his phone."

Brody sighed, rubbing his head with his free hand. "Did you get *anything* out of him?"

"A little piss. He's shakin' like a dog shittin' peach seeds right now. I think he's working for someone. Just a hunch, but he didn't seem too scared about being found, but once I was able to grab and tie him, his behavior changed. I mean, sure, anybody would be scared being tied up, but it seemed a little odd. Kinda like being captured was worse than being killed."

"Maybe he doesn't like torture." Because if Adams had anything to do with what was happening to Xan and Scott, that was what would happen when Brody got a hold of him.

"Maybe. Oh hey, Roc just pulled up. Maybe together we'll be able to get this shithead to talk."

"I thought he was supposed to stick around Walmart.

Surely, the feds aren't done there yet." What the hell was Roc up to?

"Don't know, bro, but I'll be in touch. Holler if you hear from Gauge. It's not like him not to answer."

Yeah, that was very odd. But everyone was stretched thin right now.

He pocketed his phone and looked at Scott.

Asleep.

He didn't know if he was relieved by that or not. It'd buy him some more time, but he hated that the drug was taking as long as it was to get out of his system. At least he was alive. And he'd stay that way if Brody had any say in the matter.

Another hour went by as Brody fumbled his phone, willing it to ring, and watched the door, hoping Xan was too pissed off to call him ahead of time and would just walk in. No luck.

But another fifteen minutes later, the door did open, and Bear walked over to him.

"How's Scott?"

"Okay. How's Chad?"

"Better. He's in and out of consciousness. Roxie's still with him."

"Have you heard from Colonel?" Bear was his number-two man, so maybe he'd called him instead of Brody. He was going insane just sitting here, not knowing what was happening with Xan.

"Nope."

That was it. He pushed Colonel's number on his cell phone. "I'm calling him," Brody said unnecessarily. "I know the feds like to take their sweet-ass time, but a little update wouldn't kill him." Brody listened as the phone rang. And rang. And rang. Shit! "He's not answering."

Bear frowned. "That's not like him."

No, it sure as hell wasn't. "Can you stay here with Scott? I'm going to Xan's."

"Sure." Bear nodded as he sat on the windowsill.

"I mean watch him, man. Don't let anything happen to him." Brody hated leaving him with anybody else, but he trusted Bear.

"This isn't my first day on the job, Brutus. Go. Call me when you find out something." He made a shooing motion with his hand, then crossed his arms as he settled into the seat.

Brody grunted, but didn't say anything else. He hurried out of Scott's room and out of the hospital. He tried calling Gauge on the way, but he didn't answer. He called Blade and he did answer, but said that Roc was busy convincing Adams to spill what he knew. Roc had been on Brody's bad side since Xan had shown up in town, but it seemed his badass attitude was finally coming in handy.

A few minutes later, Brody was pulling onto Xan's street and a chill ran down his spine.

He'd expected the area to be hopping with feds at both Roxie's and Xan's houses, but there weren't any marked—or unmarked—cars around. And no one was walking around conducting a typical investigation. What the hell?

He pulled into Xan's driveway behind Colonel's car. Xan's car was still here too. He got out and ran up the porch stairs and knocked before turning the knob. He was too impatient for a formal invite.

"Xan?" he called out as he stalked into the living room. No answer and no sign of either one. Shit, this wasn't good. He called her name louder as he ran into the kitchen. Still no Xan or Colonel. He let out a frustrated growl as he rubbed his hands over his face and into his hair, pulling some strands loose from the thong holding it back. Then he started down the hall. Just as he started to yell her name again, he heard a faint sound coming from Scott's room. He turned the doorknob, but it was locked. He held on to the handle and shoved his weight against the door, busting the flimsy thing open.

And froze.

It took him about two seconds to process what he was looking at. Colonel, tied to the bed, gagged with blood running down his cheek. Brody ran to his boss and gently rolled him onto his back. "What happened?" he asked as he removed the cloth covering Colonel's mouth.

He groaned. "What does it look like?" he panted. Then he sighed, shaking his head. "Bradley said she had to pee and went to the bathroom. She was gone several minutes, so I walked down the hall to see what was taking her so damn long. Someone got me from behind, knocked me out. I didn't see who. When I came to, I was like this." He gestured to his restrained body. "Will you fucking untie me already?"

Brody cursed as he set his boss free. He'd be pissed at Colonel's attitude, but he knew he would've acted the exact same way if he was in his boss' shoes. And if the woman he loved wasn't missing now. Shit! He wanted to hit something.

Colonel winced as he sat up. "Sorry I was short with you, son. I'm mad they got through me. I don't like fucking up."

"You didn't. We should've never left you alone with her. In fact,"—he pulled out his phone—"Scott needs more protection." He dialed Blade's number. When he answered, Brody gave him the bad news and asked him to hightail it over to Scott's room to backup Bear. He trusted Blade the most, and now that Brody had to put all his attention on finding Xan, he knew he could focus more on Xan and less on Scott if Blade was there. When he got off the phone, he turned back to Colonel, who'd gotten out of the bed and started pacing. "Call Roc. Tell him to lock up that weasel, Adams, and get over here. We need Gauge and Hunter too. The four of us will look for Xan." Brody stared at his boss, practically daring him for saying something to contradict his orders. Brody wasn't the boss around here, but right now, he damn well was.

Colonel just nodded and pulled out his phone to make the calls. Within minutes, he'd issued the orders to the other guys. Except for Gauge. He still wasn't answering his phone.

"Did you hear anything?"

"No." His tone was clipped.

Brody needed any information Colonel could provide, so he took a deep breath and tried another route. "What are you thinking?"

"I'm thinking Scott's abduction was a fucking diversion. One of those *make some noise over here while we swoop in and take the real prize* kind of things."

That was what he was thinking too. It was the only thing that made sense. But why now, and how had Collins been successful? Plus, Colonel looked as if he was mulling over something else as he chewed on his fingernails and paced. Brody didn't have time to think about that for long because he heard someone pulling into the driveway. He and Colonel walked into the living room as Hunter walked in the house.

"I didn't find anything on Coleman."

No shocker there. He turned to his boss. "What'd the feds say when they finished?"

"Nothing. They dusted both the houses, asked her a few questions, and left. Her agent never showed."

Brody heard another vehicle pull up, and several seconds later, Roc walked in. Brody tamped down his instant need to hurt him because he needed the prick's help.

Colonel brought the guys who'd just entered up to speed, then he turned to Brody. "Remember when I said that I thought Collins had a man on the inside? What if that inside man isn't working for the feds?" He shook his head. "I mean, I'm sure he has someone on the inside with the FBI, but what if he had an inside man in another organization."

Brody's brow furrowed. "What? Like the CIA?"

"No. Like Sheppard's Garage."

Brody's heart dropped and the other guys stared wide-eyed at Colonel. "What the hell does that mean? You think one of us works for Collins?" Brody didn't want to believe that, but his eyes shot to Roc. If anybody worked for Collins, it'd be that motherfucker.

Roc scowled at him. "Hold up there, hoss." He tapped on his chest. "I'm not working for no one but Colonel."

"I didn't say anything about you, Roc," Colonel said, and then pointed at Brody. "You need to stand down."

He gritted his teeth to keep from lashing out and nodded.

"I was talking about Gauge."

"*What?*" Now that was fucking ridiculous.

"Where have you gotten your information? You know, when you were investigating Xan behind my back."

"We weren't—" Brody sighed, not finishing that statement. "Gauge did provide a lot of it."

"He's the newest guy here. If Xan's agent is on the take —which who the hell knows since he hasn't shown up—he could've worked to plant Gauge here. If that's not the case, then where the hell is he now that the shit's hit the fan?" Colonel asked, sitting down and wincing, rubbing his thigh.

Hmm. He did have a point. But they'd discounted her agent as a possible suspect a long time ago. Brody figured it'd be best not to dismiss anybody now without properly weeding them out of the running as the mole. *Oh no.* What if it was Blade or Bear? They were alone with Scott right now. Either one could take the other if an attack was unsuspected.

He shook his head to clear it and get it on the right path because that thought was insane. He trusted both those guys. He was just too worked up and feeling as if he was spinning his wheels when he should be out looking for Xan.

"What do you propose?" Brody finally asked.

"I think you three should look for Bradley. I could help, but if it came down to a fight, I'm not up for it," he growled, seemingly pissed again that the guys had gotten to him and through him to get to Xan. "I'm going to look for Gauge. If he is our mole, he needs to be stopped." With that, Colonel stood. "Call me if you find out anything. Good luck, guys."

The boss man hobbled out the front door, and Brody was left facing Roc, who he couldn't already stand, and Hunter. "We scour the house, then the neighborhood, then the town. We start small and expand our search area," Brody said before turning to Roc. "Did you get anything out of Adams?"

A sickening smile formed on Roc's face, and Brody wondered why women flocked to him. His black hair and green eyes might be considered attractive on a woman, but Roc just looked mean as hell. "Yeah. Collins hired him. He's been here since two weeks *before* Xan moved to town."

"Fuck," Brody breathed. That settled it. Collins definitely had someone on the inside. He pulled out his phone and called Blade. He told him the news and the theory about Gauge. He seemed a little hesitant to believe it too, but agreed that anything was possible at this point. After Brody warned him not to let any feds near Scott, he got off the phone and faced Roc and Hunter. "Let's get to it."

The guys spent the next hour tearing apart Xan's house, which was where the fucking FBI put her. And with someone on the inside working for Collins, that asshole probably knew everything that'd happened in this place.

Including the nights he'd spent here in bed with Xan. Collins' ex-wife and the woman Brody now loved. If that man so much as breathed on her, Brody was going to rip him to shreds.

He just might anyway.

Might? Oh hell no. He was definitely going to tear that man limb from limb. All the damage he'd caused in Xan's life, Collins deserved to die. Painfully.

The sound of a car pulling into the driveway pulled Brody out of his musing. He turned around and saw Hunter easing the blinds from the window to peek out. "Well, I'll be a son of a bitch. It's Gauge."

Hunter stepped away from the window as Gauge came barreling in without knocking.

"Where the fuck have you been?" Brody barked. "You have a hell of a lot of explaining to do, man."

Gauge looked frazzled, tunnels running through his curly brown hair, making it look as if he'd been running his fingers through it repeatedly.

"I've been looking for Jeff Coleman." He shut his eyes briefly before giving Brody a haunted look and turning his eyes to Roc. "Sorry, man. I thought it was you."

Brody didn't see anything wrong with that suspicion

because he'd already considered Roc as the mole. It may have only been a brief thought, but he'd had it.

"Sorry to disappoint," Roc drawled, and if Brody wasn't mistaken, Roc seemed to be amused by the negative attention now that it seemed he was in the clear. But as for Gauge...

"Yeah, well, Colonel seems to think you're the mole, Gauge. You've been able to find out a lot of helpful information, but when it was time to tussle, you weren't around."

Gauge shook his head. "Sorry, I'm not the mole, but I haven't been honest either." He hesitated, and Brody wished Gauge would just spit it out already. "I work for the FBI. I mean directly. I'm an agent."

Okay, Brody didn't think he'd say *that*. "But you've been here two years."

"We've known Collins has had people on the inside, so I was placed here when communication coordinating Xan's next move was intercepted between Collins' people and several burner phones pinged in town. Someone in the know understood how the feds operate and knew she would've been moved around the time he was up for parole."

"It could've been any current agent who knew the game plan," Hunter said.

"Or any *former* agent," he said to Blade, and then turned to Brody. "Jeff Coleman."

"Former? We hadn't been able to find out if he was still with the FBI or not."

"We know now. Jeff 'Cole' Coleman is Cal Sheppard."

The blood roared in Brody's ears. No way. No fucking way did he hear Gauge right.

"That's right," Gauge said, answering Brody's unspoken denial. "Our very own Colonel is the mole."

CHAPTER TWENTY-ONE

Everything hurt.

As she came out of some kind of foggy state, Xan wasn't sure where she was at or what had happened to her, but her body was screaming. And her throat hurt.

Maybe she *had* been screaming.

"*Mi sei mancata!* Oh, how I missed you."

Her body might've been aching, but at the sound of that evil voice she hadn't heard in over twelve years, it went completely numb. "Marco," she breathed. She didn't have to ask. She knew exactly who was standing near her, even though she couldn't see.

Or move her hands and legs.

She was blindfolded and tied up. Her body started trembling. This was so not good. He'd wanted to kill her all those years ago, and it seemed now he'd get his wish. She couldn't let herself think that. Not yet. There had to be a way out of this.

"Yes, *tesoro. Mi hai mancato?* Because I missed you," he sing-songed, taunting her.

Hell no, she didn't miss him, and if she got free, she

wouldn't miss him then either—because she'd plant her foot right in his crotch. Yeah, she was big and brave all tied up and helpless, but if she let herself believe for one minute this situation was hopeless, she'd lose it. And she had to keep her wits about her.

"No answer, Dria? Are you ignoring me?" he growled.

Okay, best not to piss off the psycho ex who was hell-bent on doing a little killing and a little torturing—in no particular order. "Er, how did you find me?" Her voice cracked and she cleared her throat as she tried to shift up so she wasn't lying on the floor. God, she hoped it was the floor of some house because it felt—and smelled—as if she was in a barn. This town had grown on her, but she didn't want to be cozying up to livestock.

"You were never lost, *tesoro*. I've had eyes on you since the day you crossed me. One doesn't get to this station in life without a few men in his pocket. And I have several. Your precious Agent Cole has been an employee of my father's since before I started taking on some of the responsibilities, which as you know, I was fairly young when I started doing my part. Not much older than Devon."

Scott would never be Devon again, but she wasn't even going to discuss *her* son with the madman. She took another route instead. "What? Daddy couldn't handle all the killing on his own, so he had to delegate? How tragic."

"You've grown quite brazen, my dear. You used to not be such a bitch." She heard him shuffle and then felt his breath on her face. A tremor shot through her, but she tried to mask it by shifting again. She didn't want to show any fear. "I don't mind bringing you to heel before killing you."

Lightning pain sliced through her cheek when his fist connected with her face. Her head crashed into the stone floor and she saw stars behind the blindfold. *Don't pass out.* If she did, it'd be over. For good.

He stepped away, and she silently thanked God for the reprieve. She tried to think back, tried to remember the last thing that'd happened to her before she woke up in this hell-hole. She'd been at home with Colonel, wondering what the hell was taking Jack so long to get there so she could be with Scott at the hospital.

Scott. She stifled a sob. If she didn't get out of this—and it wasn't looking good—he'd be on his own, running from his father.

She couldn't dwell on that now. It'd only make her emotional, weak. She needed to stay focused. Subtly twisting her hands behind her back—or at least she hoped she was doing it subtly, she had no idea if people were standing around her—she tested the binding. It barely moved. She wiggled her ankles and felt how constrictive those ties were too. Shit. Okay, she had to keep moving to loosen them. As she worked her hands and feet, she thought back to the house. She'd gone to the restroom, and when she came out, someone had attacked her from behind.

And that was all she remembered.

"I'll kill her if you can't, Collins," a gravelly voice said, and a shiver rocked her. She didn't even try to hide it. It was Colonel's voice. "I've killed other members of your family before."

She gasped.

"Oh, that's right," Colonel said. "That little bit of info I fed Brutus was a lie. He didn't kill your daughter. I did."

Relief, because it hadn't been Brody, swamped her, but it fought with the agony that consumed her. Marco had still ordered Tess' death. And those emotions quickly turned to shame since she'd believed the lie and not trusted in Brody.

"Brutus," Marco growled. "He doesn't deserve to keep breathing."

"Not much longer, sir. Your plan has played out perfectly."

"Ah yes, well, of course it has," Marco scoffed, and Xan heard him walking closer to her, so she braced herself for another strike. "You see," he murmured as he knelt beside her, stroking her hair, "I'd gotten into a little trouble with some street thugs your lover, Brody Jackson, was running with, and he helped me out. I took him in, gave him a job. He'd lived his life on the streets, and I gave him paradise. And what did he do?"

Marco paused, and Xan realized his question wasn't rhetorical. "Grew a conscience?" she offered.

He laughed as if that was the most absurd thing he'd ever heard. "Funny but no. He fell in love with my wife."

What? That was impossible. Marco was trying to rile her up. She'd never met Brody before moving to Mayflower. "No way."

"You think it's impossible for a man to fall in love with a woman from afar as he discreetly watches over her? Or that I'm ignorant enough to let you around my employees? Oh no, I knew your loyalty was lost long ago. The only people you had contact with were family members and security. Brutus might've been my friend for many years, but he was also an employee. Therefore, off-limits to you. But he was around. Every day."

Her head was swimming. Brody had been that close to her all those years ago. And he was in love with her then? She still couldn't wrap her head around that.

"After I had Coleman here take care of that abomination you gave birth to, Brutus changed. Oh, it wasn't right away, but I noticed him becoming distant. And when he planted that flash drive in my office and had the nanny send you in to retrieve some bauble, I knew his loyalty had strayed." Marco leaned down, brushing his lips along her ear, making her gag. "He was too stupid to notice the cameras in my office." Mercifully, he leaned away from her. "I sat back and watched everything unfold. So you see, *tesoro*, day one. And I would have killed you before you fled if Brutus hadn't shot at me before I'd entered my study that night."

She remembered hearing those gunshots, signaling Marco's arrival, and then all hell had broken loose. Wow, it had been Brody.

"Brutus is a traitor, which is why I've named him that. He betrayed his one true friend in this world, and I do not tolerate betrayal. So that night, Coleman took Brody, beat him to within an inch of his life, and dumped his body."

Xan heard footsteps and then Colonel's voice. "Two days later, I went back and the son of a bitch wasn't dead. I reported this to Marco. He took it as a sign that Brutus was meant for greater things, so I admitted him into the hospital."

"Coleman has been with me a long time. This is what trust is supposed to be like."

"Thank you, sir." He looked at Xan. "I even tried creating a unique, interagency team for special operations. It'd been my hope the group would go rogue when they saw how much money could be made, making them a huge asset to the crime family. We codenamed it Orion. The first major assignment involved taking out Devon's nanny. Of course, Orion believed they were smoking out The Shadow. We couldn't tell them they were watching a witness so she could be eliminated.

"Fools," Marco said with a smile, not that she understood whatever they were talking about. She remembered Bryn, though. They woman helped save her life and more importantly, Scott's.

"Orion never gained the traction I'd hoped and was dismantled shortly after. I stayed with the FBI a few more years, handing off your case to other agents, making sure it was handled the way I needed it to be. Since you knew me as Cole, and had only spoken to me on the phone, I had papers drawn up before I left, changing my identity and hiding that fact. Then I had surgery to permanently damage my voice."

Ah, that was why she hadn't been able to identify him before now as her former agent. "While Brutus went through all his surgeries and physical therapy, I retired and bought the garage. The old fucker didn't *want* to sell, but I could be persuasive."

Oh, she could image just how persuasive Colonel could be.

"Orion was a failure, but you learned from your mistakes when you created The Bang Shift. We needed misfits, Coleman, not law-abiding agents."

"Yes, sir."

"Brutus' amnesia was another gift," Marco said, looking at her again. "Because he didn't know who he was, I let Coleman feed him some bits of truths with the lies. That way, if he ever did anything to investigate his past on his own, he wouldn't have any reason to question what he'd been told."

This was a lot to take in, and she was glad they were doing a lot more talking and a lot less beating, but neither one had yet to say why Brutus was used like this, what the real plan was. "Why?"

Marco laughed bitterly. "You, *tesoro*. Coleman stayed

with the FBI long enough for me to get more plants in there, so I've orchestrated your every move. It wasn't a group working together like we'd originally wanted, but these individual agents have no idea there are others like them working for me. In that sense, it was better." He laughed "And before you ask, no, Jack Parsons isn't one of my men. I couldn't risk having someone that close to you. If he didn't roll, then I was fucked. I couldn't take that kind of chance.

"As for Brutus, the betrayal of a friend is the darkest sin one can commit, and he had to pay for his sin against me. You'd think murder would be worse, but it's not. In this business, loyalty means everything, so I punished him by giving him what he wanted. You. Coleman let the guys at the garage believe watching you was an official FBI assignment, when in fact, I'd ordered the official watch. I wanted to give him what he coveted, so I could hurt him. As soon as the sap fell for you all over again, I struck. Outing him as Tess' killer was one way I caused him pain. Letting him live life without you after I kill you, is the other. I get my revenge against you, against him, and I get my son back. Perfect," he purred.

Marco was beyond insane. Xan worked her hands and feet frantically. It didn't matter if they knew she was trying to get away because she was as good as dead anyway.

"Enough talking."

The blow was so fast Xan didn't have time to prepare. The second one introduced her to darkness.

———

BRODY PACED FRANTICALLY as Gauge and Jack Parsons orchestrated the search and rescue of Xan with the twenty or so FBI agents crowded at the shop. They'd gotten a lead there was movement in an abandoned farm down highway 365. It was a vague lead, but he'd take what he could get.

"You wanna cigarette?" Blade asked. Brody was glad his closest buddy was here. He hated leaving Scott alone with Roc, but he felt better giving him a babysitting duty than having him cover his back. If things went to shit, Brody knew Blade and Bear would be there for him. There'd been too much animosity between Brody and Roc for him to let that asshole loose with a gun. He wouldn't put it past the prick to nail him with a round just for shits and giggles.

"I thought you quit those fuckin' things."

"Naw. I try, but I don't last very long. Any word on Colonel?"

He shook his head and started pacing again. Hell no, there hadn't been word. What Gauge had told him he'd found out had left Brody stunned. And he wasn't the only one. Bear looked devastated. He'd been closer to Colonel than anybody else.

And the guys were all shocked to learn about Gauge too. But in a good way. It seemed learning he was an undercover FBI agent propelled his status within the group from newbie to official member—but he wasn't even really a mechanic, and he'd be leaving once this was over. Funny how things worked out like that. As Brody kept pacing, he saw Gauge stepping away from the horde of agents, so he walked over.

"What's up? I've gotta do something, man." Brody was itching to get out of this damn place. He'd tear apart the whole state of Arkansas to find Xan if he had to.

"Adams confirmed the barn was a meeting place for him and Colonel. The feds cut him a deal, so he's spilling his guts. Satellite imagery shows she was carried in, and heat sensors suggest three people in the barn. We're going in."

"Let's go." Brody started to step away and Gauge grabbed his arm.

"I can't let you come. This is an official raid."

Brody got right in his face. "Don't fuck with me, Gauge. I'm. Coming."

Gauge sighed. "Look, Brutus, I like you. If you tag along, you could do something reckless, end up behind bars."

"I'll take my chances," he growled. "Either I'm coming with you, or I'm going without you."

Gauge glared at him for several seconds, narrowed his eyes, and then nodded. "Behave."

Yeah, he'd behave. Right after he sliced Colonel's throat for letting that crazy-ass ex-husband of hers get a hold of her, but not before he put a bullet through that crazy-ass man's chest for daring to harm what was Brody's.

Not waiting for any signal, Brody dashed for his truck with Blade and Bear on his heels.

"Damn you, Brutus!" Gauge called out as the other agents hustled into their vehicles.

"Don't worry, man. We'll get her," Bear said as he grabbed the oh-shit handle, white-knuckling it as Brody peeled out of the parking lot and onto the two-lane country highway. He sped, hitting ninety miles per hour within seconds. He passed a mailman and a tractor several minutes later, not slowing down.

Within fifteen minutes, they'd arrived at the old farm. Brody slammed the truck into park, jumped out, and ran toward the barn as the sounds of the agents' vehicles neared.

"Brody," Bear hissed, but ducked and ran behind him. Brody knew Blade would follow too. Brody ran around back, hearing what sounded like someone beating on flesh, and his blood froze. Gun drawn, he crept to the door, peering through the cracks.

Jesus Christ! Collins was beating the shit out of Xan. He couldn't wait for the cavalry. All he had were his two buddies. They'd do. "I'm going in first. There's a stall door on the east side. Blade, you take that entrance. Bear, you go back around front. You've got fifteen seconds to get there. I ain't waiting any longer," Brody barely whispered.

The guys nodded and left quickly, quietly.

And as Brody watched Marco strike Xan again and again, that was the longest damn fifteen seconds of his life.

After he counted down those heart-wrenching seconds, he trained his gun on Marco, but couldn't get a shot at his chest like he'd envisioned earlier. No problem. His head would work just as well, so he took aim as he burst through the back door. Two shots and Marco keeled over.

The barn erupted in gunfire as Colonel turned on Brody, gun raised, but Gauge popped Colonel before he could get a shot off.

As quickly as the gunfire started, it'd ended, but Brody didn't care. He ran straight to Xan, feeling as if he'd never reach her, hearing muffled shouting all around over the ringing in his ears. He fell to his knees before her and gently turned her. She was covered in blood, cuts, bruises. Oh God, this was bad. "Call an ambulance!"

If he lost her, he'd never forgive himself for not protecting her like he should have.

"I love you, baby," he breathed into her hair as he rocked her blood-soaked body. "Please hold on."

CHAPTER TWENTY-TWO

THE LAST TIME Xan woke up from a foggy stupor, every-thing hurt. This time, she felt as if she was literally dying. And if she wasn't dead yet, she'd love for someone to finish her off.

She groaned as she tried to move, hearing the annoying little beats of a heart monitor and other hospital equipment she was all too familiar with considering her line of work, and suddenly, hands were on her. "Mom?"

Oh crap. She was pretty sure she looked as bad as she felt, so she didn't want Scott to see her like this. But then again, the last thing she remembered about Scott was that he was in the hospital. If he was in her room, then at least he'd been released. Or well enough to ditch his doctors. "Hi, honey," she breathed.

"You scared us all there for a while." He squeezed her. She could feel him shaking a little.

"Us?" Okay, he probably meant the proverbial "us," but she couldn't help hoping it included a certain Viking she'd missed.

"Yeah, the doctors have been in here talking a lot about

stuff I don't understand, but Brody and the other guys have been here to help explain it to me. You've been in surgery getting your broken head fixed, and you punctured a lung and broke a leg, ribs, two fingers, nose—"

"I'll be fine." She had to cut him off because he started to sound a little hysterical. "What happened to Marco?" She didn't refer to him as his father.

"Brody killed him." The anger in his voice was much more preferable to the panic that was building a couple of seconds ago. "That Colonel guy was killed too."

Cole. Once upon a time, she'd thought he was her savior, but he'd never cared about her protection, so she couldn't bring herself to care that he hadn't made it out alive. Now there was one less minion after her and her son.

"How long have I been here? Where have you been staying?"

"Coupla weeks. And I've been staying here as much as Chad's mom would let me, but she's been dragging me out to feed me and making sure I got to school and got some sleep."

She was going to cry. Xan had never had a best friend, someone she could trust with the safety of her son, and now she couldn't have asked for a better girlfriend.

"Brody's been keeping me company up here, helping me with my homework and been trying to get me to play video games. Even bought me *Bloodbath Five* when it hit the stores last week."

Now she did tear up. First Roxie and now Brody. They both had stepped in and taken Scott under their wings when she'd been incapacitated.

"You okay, Mom? What's wrong?" Scott asked frantically.

She sniffled. "No, no. I'm fine. Well, I hurt like crazy, but I'm fine."

He reached for something beside her, and she knew exactly what it was. A morphine drip. Within seconds, her eyes got heavy, and yeah, that was much, much better. Before her eyes completely shut, she heard her door open and saw Brody walk in with a couple of bags of takeout. Their eyes locked and he gasped, walking over to her quickly and dropping the bags on the small bedside table.

"How are you feeling?" he asked as he stroked her hair.

"Sleepy."

He leaned down and kissed her temple. "Then sleep. Everything is okay. No one will ever hurt you or Scott again. I lo—"

He kept talking, but she drifted into sweet oblivion.

———

BRODY SAT in his truck and opened another vanilla-scented air fresher. God, he missed Xan like crazy. These ridiculous pine trees didn't smell a damn bit like her. But that hadn't stopped him from trying. This was his third one this week.

It'd been a month since Collins had kidnapped Xan and a week since she'd been released from the hospital. When Brody had visited her before she was released, they'd talked. Well, as much as they could—she'd been pretty loopy most of the time. But he'd told her about Colonel, and he'd learned about his connection to her and the truth about Tess' murder. What a revelation that'd been. Brody had hoped finding out the truth meant he and Xan would have a fresh start.

He'd been wrong.

As soon as she was out of the hospital, she'd become distant. When he'd tried to have the relationship talk, she'd very subtly shut that topic down. He figured he'd just give her time to adjust to what Marco had done to her and the fact she wouldn't have to run anymore, but he'd been wrong about that too.

So very wrong.

Apparently, the FBI felt she was still in danger. Gauge had explained to him that Collins' father would see Xan as the reason his son was killed and would retaliate. Not to mention Scott was his grandchild. The man was ailing and there'd be a changing of the guard soon, but for now, she and Scott were still under FBI protection and would be moving again, severing all ties with everyone she knew.

Including him.

He'd been pissed because he'd learned through someone else besides Xan that she was leaving. Then he'd fallen in love with her a little more because she was trying to spare his feelings. And really, he couldn't stay mad at her when he knew his time with her was limited. When he'd tried talking to her about it, she acted as if she hadn't wanted to go, but didn't really protest the idea. Scott, though, that kid was fuming mad. He hated his father's side of the family even more. The boy liked his life here. He had new friends and had a little girlfriend. Brody was going to miss him like hell. And Xan...

He sighed, shaking his head and leaning toward the swinging air freshener. Why didn't these damn vanilla-scented pine trees smell like her? He figured he should be happy about that because the guys would rip him a new one if they walked in his house and found these things hanging all over the place.

Hmm, maybe those automatic air freshener sprayer things would do the trick. He'd have to check into that.

Yeah, he was losing it. He was grasping at whatever he could so he wouldn't lose the memory of her. Not that he thought that'd actually happen, but he wanted everything about her to stay sharp in his mind. The feel of her skin, the softness of her hair, the taste of her lips on his, and her scent. God, he didn't know how he was going to live without her.

But he had to learn because her safety was the most important thing. If she had to cut him loose to ensure she'd live, then he'd do it. He'd sacrifice anything for her, including his own happiness.

He drove by her house again. Yeah, he'd done it about a million times over the past week, but he didn't care. It wasn't as if he was stalking her. He had to make sure she was safe. And they'd still spent time together, but not only was she keeping her distance, she was still medicated too. So Brody hadn't crowded her, but God, it was hard not fawning all over her every second of every day, knowing those days were numbered.

He slowed as he neared her house. Then his heart slammed in his chest, the beat double-timing it. She was sitting on the porch stairs, looking up at the sky. The sight of her would've taken his breath away if he wasn't immediately worried about her. Why the hell was she sitting outside? It was after midnight.

He pulled into her driveway, figuring it was best not to pretend he hadn't been driving by. As he shut off the engine, their eyes locked, and he flashed a smile at her before looking away to climb out. He walked around his truck, heading toward her, hoping his damn heart would slow down anytime now.

"Busted," he acknowledged with a casual shrug.

"You've been doing that a lot."

Oh shit. Maybe he should've saved the drive-bys for well after midnight. "Just making sure you're safe," he said as he sat beside her. He let his hand fall to her knee and gave it a gentle squeeze before leaning in and kissing her quickly on the mouth. Even though that was as far as they'd gone in the physical department since her ordeal, Brody still loved the feel of her lips on his, no matter how brief it was. "Whatcha doin' out here?"

"Thinking. Scott's PO'd that we have to move. Jack says they should have a house ready for us next week."

"And new identities." He didn't ask. He just said what it seemed she couldn't.

"Yeah," she breathed.

He tried to keep everything light, but God, he'd missed being alone with her. Almost every other time he'd been around her, Scott was near. "I'm going to miss you like crazy, baby," he whispered, leaning down and nuzzling her hair, her ear. *Vanilla.*

Her breath caught and she turned into him. He didn't know how much longer she'd allow him this intimacy because, if her recent track record was any indication, she'd be pulling away any second now. Oh, he could tell she wanted him. That had never stopped, but she was trying to save them both the heartache that was inevitable. He knew this little vixen better than she knew herself.

"I'm going to miss you too."

He sighed when she eased a little closer, her hand rubbing the length of his arm. Without thinking, he let his lips trace down her cheek to find her mouth again. This time, he nudged her lips once, twice, and licked the plump seam. He wanted to shout when she opened for him. His tongue dove into the warm cavern as his hands fisted in her hair. Oh, how he missed the taste of her.

He devoured her, leaving no crevice of her mouth untouched. His cock was throbbing against the zipper of his jeans, begging to be released. If he wasn't careful, he'd pull her down on this porch and fuck her right here. *Shit.* She was still recovering and he was practically attacking her like some horny animal. He broke away, panting. "I-I'm sorry. How are you feeling, baby?" That should've been the first damn thing he asked her when he walked up. He was such a selfish jerk.

"I *was* feeling just fine, but now I'm feeling deserted." She pouted playfully and his guilt vanished. She'd wanted him too. Probably ached for him as he had for her.

He leaned toward her again, brushing his lips against her neck. "We can't have that now, can we?"

Her head fell back on a gasp. "Uh-uh."

He kissed and nipped his way up her slim neck to her ear. "Is Scott home?" he asked as he nibbled on her lobe.

"No. Ditched me to stay at Chad's."

"Remind me to thank him later." Then Brody abruptly stood and lifted Xan into his arms.

"B-Brody. This doesn't mean—"

"Shh." He swooped in and kissed her lightly as he carried her into the house. "All I want to think about is tonight. Not tomorrow. Not next week. Tonight." He kept walking down the hall and into her bedroom.

"Tonight," she whispered, and threw her arms around his neck, pulling him down for a kiss.

He greedily obliged, sealing his lips with hers. He hungered for her like a man starved, and he knew he'd never feel this way about another woman ever again. Xan was his one and only true love. He'd had a hard time swallowing all the stories Colonel had told him about his past over the years, and the one Xan had told him—about how he'd been in love with her all those years ago—had felt right. He wished he could remember being in love with her before, but loving her now made believing easy.

He gently lowered her to her feet beside the bed, kissing the side of her neck, licking along her collarbone He traced a path from one shoulder to the other, trying to memorize the tantalizing skin exposed from her low-cut shirt. Kissing his way down her chest, he stopped once he reached the cloth barrier, and hastily grabbed the hem, pulling it free from her body.

If he didn't slow down, he'd rush right through this, not relishing what may very well be their last time together. His heart dropped at that thought, so he stepped back, taking her in. God, she was beautiful.

"So beautiful," he breathed, stroking her cheek with the back of his hand.

"Brody." Her voice trembled, but she reached for him, caressing his chest through his worn gray t-shirt. His belly jumped at her touch as her hand lowered, and his cock strained against its denim cage. She pulled his shirt out from his jeans and pushed it up, leaving it gathered under his arms. Then she leaned in and kissed his bellybutton, and oh shit, that felt good. He groaned, swaying toward her, clutching her arms in case his knees buckled.

When she reached for his belt buckle, Brody yanked his shirt completely off. Then slid his hands down her back to unclasp the black lacy bra she had on. When her breasts fell free, he cupped them, feeling their heavy weight, tugging on her taut nipples. She moaned, and her hands briefly hesitated on his zipper. So he rolled her nipples again, loving the way her back arched as she pushed her breasts harder into his hands.

Once she got his zipper down, he reached for her pants, quickly removing them and her soaked panties before stepping out of his own jeans.

He stood before her bare—emotionally and physically. This little hellion stepped into his life and claimed it, claimed him, and he wouldn't have it any other way.

He reached for her, knowing his eyes were raw with his feelings, pulled her down onto the cool sheets, and kissed her. Everywhere. From her temple to her toes, he left no inch untouched, but he saved her pussy for last.

When he hovered over that sweet spot, he breathed in the musky vanilla scent of her and moaned.

"Please, Brody," she begged as her hips writhed beneath him, so he clasped her thighs, spreading her wider. Then he finally licked her tentatively along the seam. She gasped, trying to get closer, her honey dripping from her core. God, he was trying to savor her, but all he wanted to do was dive in and devour her in such a way that her taste would be branded on him. When she whimpered, the decision was made. He leaned in and licked her from her ass to her clit. And then he did devour her, licking, nipping, kissing her, as he stabbed two fingers inside her, reveling in how tight she was.

She was moaning, panting as she tugged on his hair, guiding him to that sweet little clit, and he greedily followed, sucking it into his mouth as he batted it with his tongue and fucked her with his fingers. She screamed, her back arching off the bed, and he continued his ministrations, wringing every last spasm out of her. When she finally collapsed, boneless, he crawled up her body, kissing her tummy, her breasts, lingering a little while before continuing up to her mouth. He lifted her knee, hooking it on his hip, and thrust into her with one powerful move. He groaned. She trembled, reaching for him and pulling him to her.

He made love to her like that, holding her knee as he plunged into her, murmuring against her lips. He wasn't sure what he was saying or if it even made any sense. All he could think was *don't leave me*.

"I love you," he breathed, then took her mouth in a searing kiss. He didn't give her an opportunity to say those words back to him because he didn't want to be disappointed when she didn't. Xan was leaving, and she was distancing herself from him. If that was what she needed to do to help her through this, then he'd allow that. But nothing would ever change how he felt about her.

He grabbed her hips, angling her so he could take her deeper, harder. Fuck, he was close. He could feel his balls getting tighter as he pounded into her, her cries cheering him on.

Then she pushed against his shoulders, startling him. "Xan?" he panted.

She didn't answer, only pushed him over and straddled him. "Fuck, baby." She started riding him hard and he was in heaven.

He grabbed her hips, bent his knees, and thrust up into her each time she came down. Her breasts shook, calling him, so he answered. He sat up and drew one nipple into his mouth, leaving his hands on her hips to help guide her as she led them both to ecstasy. She cried out, her pussy milking him, and his mouth tore away from her breast on a roar as he came with her.

When they both drifted back down from the euphoria of their love-making, he'd realized that he'd wrapped his arms around her, holding her tightly to him, and she'd done the same, her head buried in the crook of his neck. A slight hitch in her breathing gave away the fact she was trying not to cry, and that crushed him.

She didn't want to leave just like he didn't want her to. But they didn't have a choice. Sometimes, life was just fucked-up.

He spent the night in her arms, wondering how he'd go back to the life he had before she'd driven into this town. Well, technically, he'd towed her into this town, but the effect was the same. He loved her, would always love and worry for her. As she lay in his arms, breathing softly in her sleep, he thought about the first day they'd met, and he knew he wanted to do something special for her before she left. Just a little something to show how much he loved her and cared about her safety.

Because all he really wanted to do was keep her.

And he'd have to let her go.

CHAPTER TWENTY-THREE

Xan was miserable. She'd been packing the last several days so she'd be ready when Jack came calling to tear this life away from her. And she hadn't gotten much help out of Scott either. Oh, he'd packed a little. Very little. He dragged his feet around as if he was waiting to be put on death row or something. He knew the drill.

Maybe that was his problem. She knew the drill, too. Knew that this would be a never-ending cycle for them. So she hadn't bitched at him to hurry up. His days were numbered here, and he wanted to spend them hanging out with Chad and Malorie. And she totally understood that because she'd love nothing more than to spend every waking and sleeping moment molded to Brody.

She was in love with him, and she couldn't even tell him. She'd had so many opportunities, but she'd hoped if she didn't spill her feelings, maybe Brody would move on after she was gone. She knew *she* would never move on, but she realized that loving someone meant you wanted what was best for them. And she didn't want Brody pining away for her. So she'd kept him at arm's length from her. Just far enough away to build up walls, but just close enough to pull him back every now and then. She wasn't trying to toy with him. She really wasn't, but letting someone go was tough. And she was hurting.

Groaning at the reality of her life, she grabbed more packing tape and stood from where she'd been sitting on the floor, going through a few knickknacks, and headed to the kitchen for some water. She heard a car pulling into her driveway and what sounded like a couple of trucks. "What the hell?" she muttered. She put the packing tape on the counter, walked into the living room, then peeked through the blinds. She saw Brody, and her heart did a little flip-flop. God, she loved it when he left his hair down.

She nervously smoothed her own hair and blew into her hand, testing her breath, before opening the door and walking out. She frowned when she saw Bear's truck parked behind Brody's truck and noticed someone else parked on the other side of his truck. Bear waved as he climbed into the passenger seat and noticed Blade sitting on the passenger side. He wiggled his fingers and winked at her as Bear backed out and drove off.

"Where're they going?" Xan asked as she walked over to Brody.

"Blade drove my truck over here." He took her hand and tugged, pulling her along with him. "I have something for you."

When they rounded the front end of Brody's truck, Xan gasped as she stared at the brand new Honda Accord. "What's this?" she asked, knowing how stupid the question sounded, but not knowing what else to say.

"Your new Bertha."

She looked up at him, too shocked to speak.

"You once told me that if you could have any car you wanted, you'd pick an Accord. Well, I hate the idea of you driving around in that piece of shit." He took a deep breath, briefly shutting his eyes. "And if I'm not going to be around to fix it for you, I want you to have something dependable."

This was the nicest, most generous thing anybody had ever done for her. Ever. And she felt her throat tightening, her eyes itching, as she looked up at him. "Brody." Her voice cracked, so she covered her mouth, trying to stifle the sob that was building. "I-I can't accept this."

"Shh." He stepped up to her, rubbing her back. "Don't cry, baby. I've been teetering on my own feelings these last couple of weeks." He chuckled, making light of his words, but he squeezed her tighter to him, betraying his true feelings. "You need a new car. I'm not taking it back. Besides, I got it on sale, so I can't take it back even if I wanted to."

She tried to control the hitching in her breath. She really did. But as she tried swallowing back her tears, the sobs built and rushed from her. She broke down, holding on to him, crying her broken heart out.

"I don't want to go. I don't want to leave you. I-I love you, Brody. I love you so much, and I can't stand the idea of never seeing you again."

"Oh, baby," he breathed, holding her, rocking her. "I love you too."

"Maybe, maybe, we can work something out?" She didn't care if she sounded as needy as she felt.

He pulled away from her, gently rubbing his thumbs along her cheeks, wiping away her tears. "You don't know how happy I am to hear that."

"What I want doesn't matter, though. I have to leave."

He brushed her hair off her cheek. "I talked to Gauge yesterday, and after he made a bunch of calls, he was finally able to do just that. Now the big dogs over there aren't happy about this alternative and will strongly suggest you not go along with it, but the only people here who know he was undercover are the guys at the shop. The feds have *reluctantly* agreed to keep him here if you insist on staying. Once he convinced them that it was a genuine possibility and they bitched about how fucking dangerous this is for you, they really didn't have any other choice but to keep Gauge here, especially since I'm the one who actually pulled the trigger, and Collins' father might come sniffing around. Gauge will be working with Jack Parsons to coordinate your safety."

Oh my God, oh my God, oh my God. "I-I don't know what to say." She shook her head trying to process this.

"Now listen, baby. They said it'll be really dangerous if you decide to do this because you'd have to move to another location and pretend as if you weren't under their protection anymore. All other agents who worked the case would also be under that impression. Gauge will go deep cover. Everyone except those I mentioned already and a select few will think he's decided to quit."

"You mean I, Scott, we get to stay here?"

He smiled crookedly at her, leaning down to brush his lips against her. "Well, not here." He pointed to her house. "You'll have to move in with me. You know, for protection and all."

Move in with Brody? Oh, she could definitely do that. "Why didn't you just come right out and tell me I could stay?" She tried to sound irritated, but failed miserably. She was too damn excited.

"I didn't want to presume anything." He shook his head as if he hated thinking that way. "Come look at your new car, baby." He pulled her behind him, acting like a kid on Christmas.

"If I'm staying, I don't need the car," she said jokingly.

He looked back at her, frowning. "I bought it before talking to Gauge, and I told you, I'm not taking it back."

She felt light, free, excited about this wonderful turn of events, and she practically bounced behind him as he opened the driver side door for her. She slid into her new car, grinning wildly, and took a deep breath to inhale the new-car smell that had evaded her for too many years.

Her nose wrinkled. "What's that... Is that *vanilla?*"

Brody shrugged innocently before swooping down and kissing her hard.

No more moving? Getting to live her life with the man she loved? Yeah, her life was definitely looking up.

HUNTER'S little sister gets caught up with the wrong people while away at college, but it's her best friend that's going to need his help...and tempt him beyond all reason in **Hunter**, the next book in The Bang Shift Series!

HEY, y'all!

Thank you for reading my book. :) If you enjoyed it, I'd be very grateful for a review. If you didn't like it, then share that, too... as long as your review is honest, that's all that matters.

And ice cream. Ice cream matters, too.

Want the latest scoop? Be sure to sign up for my Newsletter! I mean, it's not as yummy as ice cream, but nothing ever is.

XOXO,
Mandy

ALSO BY MANDY HARBIN

The Bang Shift Series

Brody

Hunter

Blade

Shelby

Axle

Roc

Tender Tarts Series

Super Hot Supervisor

California Crush

Hardheaded Hubby

Long Distance Lover

Momma's Boy

Part-Time Player

Billionaire Beefcake

Paranormal Romance

Surrounded by Woods

Surrounded by Pleasure

Surrounded by Temptation

Surrounded by Secrets

Young Adult written as M.W. Muse

Goddess Legacy

Goddess Secret

Goddess Sacrifice

Goddess Revenge

Goddess Bared

Goddess Bound

ABOUT THE AUTHOR

Mandy Harbin is a *USA Today* Bestselling author who loves creating stories that explore the complexities of everyday relationships...with some kissing thrown in. She is a Superstar Award recipient, Reader's Crown and Passionate Plume finalist, and has achieved Night Owl Reviews Top Pick distinction many times. She also writes young adult romance as M.W. Muse because teens like kissing, too.

After graduating college and working many years in technology, she threw caution to the wind and began studying writing at the University of Arkansas. Years of trashed manuscripts and rejections eventually led to contracts and representation. With over thirty books published, she now serves on the board of her local writing chapter.

Mandy lives in a small, Arkansas town with her husband and their bossy dog, enjoying her own happily ever after...with some kissing thrown in.

mandyharbin.com/newsletter
facebook.com/Author.MandyHarbin
instagram.com/mandy_harbin
bookbub.com/authors/mandy-harbin